MORE THAN PASSION

by

JOMARIE DEGIOIA

Lachesis
Publishing
www.lachesispublishing.com

Published Internationally by Lachesis Publishing
RR # 1, Rockland, Ontario
Canada K4K 0E3

First published as Raven's Flight in 2001 by
Denlinger's Publishers Ltd., Edgewater, Florida in a print edition.
2012 editions (e-book and trade paper) by
Lachesis Publishing, Rockland, Canada.
Newly revised and edited for 2012 publication.

A catalogue record for the print format of this title is available from the National Library of Canada

ISBN 13: 978-1-897562-96-3

A catalogue record for the Ebook is available
from the National Library of Canada
Ebooks are available for purchase from
www.lachesispublishing.com

ISBN 13: 978-1-897562-95-6

Dedication

To my fabulous agent, Michelle Grajkowski, for her unfailing encouragement. To my amazing editor, Joanna D'Angelo, whose help was invaluable in reshaping this story. To my dedicated readers, who so often requested Geoffrey and Becca's story. And finally to my husband, Jay, and our family for their support and encouragement for lo these many years since I began this writer's journey. I love you guys!

Also Available

in The Dashing Nobles Series

Pride and Fire

PAUL TALBOT, Viscount Leed, is set on avoiding the marriage trap. Though his family has money troubles he won't marry an heiress and dance on her leading strings.

LADY MICHELLE THOMAS is a spirited heiress, piqued with the rules of Society which dictate that a woman must be seen and not heard. And if she has opinions on politics or finance? Well, she had best keep them to herself. Sparks fly when she meets Paul—she believes she's found a man interested in more than her face, form and finances.

They wed, but when Paul refuses her generous dowry she'll do anything to see her money settled on him, even if it means going to his rival and putting more than his career in jeopardy.

Reviews

Highly Recommended *[More than Passion]* is a passionate historical romance with secrets and danger. The story moves at a steady pace, keeping the reader's interest. The love scenes are well done and beautiful.... Ms. DeGioia pens a sweet romance... well-created characters, exciting storyline and a bit of intrigue. For an enjoyable read to cozy up on the couch with, try *[More than Passion]* today. **Five Roses!!**
—Robin Peek, *Under the Covers Book Reviews*

JoMarie DeGioia is a promising newcomer to historical novel writing. She tells a good tale about a likable pair of lovers and a nasty villain or two. ...someone looking for a story with danger and suspense encountered by two very lusty lovers will be pleased with *[More than Passion]*.
—Jane Bowers, *Romance Reviews Today*

Author JoMarie DeGioia spins an absorbing tale of intrigue... Romantic and VERY sensuous story...JoMarie DeGioia brings a smooth, deft style to her gift for absorbing storytelling. Devotees of deep, abiding romantic love stories won't be able to put this one down.
—Bestselling author Maggie Davis, AKA Katherine Deauville

MORE THAN PASSION

Chapter 1

England, 1822

Geoffrey Michael Kane, the seventh Earl of Kanewood, was hot, dusty, and tired. At twenty-eight he was still adjusting to the duties thrust upon him with the death of his father two years earlier, making frequent trips to London to meet with his solicitors. Returning from one such meeting, his carriage hit a dip in the road and skidded to a halt.

"Where are we?" Geoffrey called to his driver.

"Rutlandshire, my lord. Not far from Oakham."

Geoffrey climbed out of the leaning carriage. "Grab the wheel then, Fields. You and I are visiting Oakham today."

After securing Geoffrey's travel bag behind one of the saddles, they rode into Oakham. It was late June and the weather was hot and muggy. The ride was rough and with every new bump and stumble, Geoffrey swore under his breath. For the last hour, he dismounted and led his horse into town. He wore no hat, which was the norm for him, and the sun beat down on his head. He squinted and looked at his surroundings.

The town was quite small—a village, really—but picturesque. His sharp eyes noticed a dry goods establishment, a market, a pub, and even a doctor's office. The shingle on the side of a two-story brick building proclaimed the medical man's residence and place of business. Just past the outskirts of the town, Geoffrey spotted the only business he was interested in today. The wheelwright's shop. The wheelwright shared his space with the blacksmith, and both businesses appeared to do well. Geoffrey snorted. No surprise, given the rutted cobblestone road that led through town.

He brushed off his clothes. There was nothing for it. His tan breeches were stained with wheel grease and his white shirt was crumpled and smudged. He retrieved his brown jacket from behind the saddle and saw it was in a sorry shape, as well. “I don’t much resemble the Earl of Kanewood, do I, Fields?”

Fields reddened before realizing no answer was expected. Geoffrey led his horse in front of the wheelwright’s shop as Fields dismounted and rolled the offending wheel to him.

Geoffrey spied a beefy man standing in the large doorway. “Are you the proprietor?”

“Aye. William Bennett, wheelwright. What can I do for ya?”

Standing there, with an obviously-broken wheel at his feet, Geoffrey bit back a sarcastic reply. “I need a wheel fixed. This wheel.”

Bennett fingered the splintered spokes. “Aye. It’s broken.”

Geoffrey kept his exasperation in check. “Can you fix it?” he asked deliberately.

“Aye. Nothin’ to it. Fix it right as rain.”

“Good.” Geoffrey breathed.

“Goin’ ta take a few days, though.”

“A few days? Why?”

Bennett held up his right hand, wrapped in a cloth bandage. “Got me hand a bit crushed fixin’ the doc’s trap. He told me not to use it till he says it’s okay.”

Geoffrey stared at the man incredulously. “There is no one else who could fix this?”

“Nay,” the man answered. “Not around here.”

Geoffrey’s irritation began to grow to anger, but with one look at the guileless face of the wheelwright, it swiftly faded. “Well, do you have someone to get my carriage out of the road? It’s about a twenty-minute’s ride back.”

“Aye, me boy and I’ll go get it. You be wantin’ it brought here?”

“Yes, thank you. Is there a place to keep my horses?”

“Blacksmith’s got a couple stalls. Wouldn’t put these fine animals there, though. You be stayin’ here till this be fixed?”

Geoffrey thought for a moment. Perhaps a few days away from London, as well as Kanewood, would help him ponder the disquieting news he'd received from his solicitors.

"Is there an inn close by?" he asked.

"Aye. Raven's Inn, just outside of town. Stables to let in back, fine dinin' room." The wheelwright scratched his chubby chin. "Can't attest to the rooms, but I can tell ya the ale is mighty fine."

"Thank you." Geoffrey motioned to his driver. "Let's head over to this Raven's Inn, Fields. It seems we may be here awhile."

They mounted and set off for the inn.

* * * *

The Raven's Inn was surprisingly elegant. The brick structure was trimmed with dark green, its long windows sparkling in the late afternoon sun. Rebecca Kingsley was straightening the beautifully-appointed parlor of the inn. Her father, Thomas, insisted that all the rooms look fine. His father had been a baronet, but all that was left of the family fortune, as it were, was the inn. As a younger man, he'd traveled in the social circles of the ton and claimed to know what the gentry and lesser folk alike looked for in food and lodging. Many travelers stopped at the inn, and they expected service and accommodations as fine as any in London, or so Rebecca's father insisted.

At twenty years old, Rebecca had been working at the inn all of her life. Her mother died when Rebecca was just two, leaving no real memories. Thomas refused to speak of her and Rebecca had long since given up asking. The only thing he'd say was that she took after her mother in looks. This he always said in a gruff, affectionate manner that never failed to surprise her. She supposed she inherited her fair skin from her mother, that and her thick raven-black hair. She could never see anything of herself in Thomas.

He never really gave her much notice. She worked as hard as the servants at the inn, keeping her own room as well as half of the rest abovestairs. Mary, the chambermaid, took care of the other rooms as well as seeing to the guests' personal needs.

Rebecca served the morning and evening meals in the dining room, as well, along with Emmy. Emmy was funny and kind and a shameless flirt. She never hesitated to share her experiences with Rebecca, who couldn't help but blush. She listened, though. Closely.

Rebecca was usually free to go about her own business after finishing her chores abovestairs. But this afternoon, she polished the candlesticks and dusted the furniture in the parlor. As usual, she wore her hair plaited in one long braid coiled at the back of her head. Her simple muslin gown was a few seasons old and well-suited to her task. She paused to gaze longingly out the window toward the stables out back. Beyond them, she could see the gently rolling hills over which she so loved to ride. If she didn't have to see to the parlor today, she'd surely be out riding her black filly.

From her vantage point, Rebecca could see two figures walking out of the stable's wide doors. One man was slight of stature and fell in step behind the other. The man in the lead was tall with broad shoulders and dressed in a brown coat and tan breeches. He walked with a long, easy stride. Sun glinted off hair she fancied the color of honey. He had a strong profile, and Rebecca couldn't tear her gaze away from him. What color were his eyes?

"Fool," she chided herself. She turned back to her work, flicking her dusting cloth in frustration.

* * * *

After leaving the stables, Geoffrey located the innkeeper in an office off the foyer. Thomas Kingsley was a big man, well-dressed but thick through the middle. Gray hair curled over his wide forehead, nearly obscuring his brown eyes.

He smiled at Geoffrey as he greeted him, motioning him to sit. "Thomas Kingsley, proprietor of the Raven's Inn."

"Geoffrey Kane," Geoffrey returned, omitting his title. He didn't much feel like a peer at the moment.

"What can I do for you, Kane?"

"Well, sir, I need a room for a few days, and stables for my two horses. I've left them with your groom down at the stables. I hope I'm not being presumptuous."

Thomas shook his head. "Not at all. I trust you found them satisfactory?"

"Yes, quite. As fine as any stables I've seen."

Thomas's chest swelled at the praise. "I hope you won't find me immodest, but my two-legged patrons are treated to at least the same quality of lodgings."

Geoffrey nodded. "I'll take a room then, and my driver should have accomodations, as well."

When that business was concluded, Geoffrey took his satchel up the narrow staircase and located his room. The upstairs hallway was narrow, with rooms located on either side. At the top of the stairs, Geoffrey turned left and strode down the hall. He found his room elegantly furnished, with a large bed taking up one side. The other was fashioned into a sitting area of sorts, with a plumply upholstered armchair and padded footrest. A mirrored washstand stood across from the bed and a privacy screen stood folded nearby. A small wardrobe completed the furnishings, standing open to receive his clothes.

He hung up his few jackets and shirts, and placed his spare boots on the bottom. "Meager wardrobe, Kane. Good thing your valet is at Kanewood."

His stomach growled, reminding him he'd missed the nooning meal. He glanced at the clock on the bedstand, surprised to see it was nearly six o'clock. Thomas had told him that dinner service began at six, so he washed his face and carelessly ran a comb through his hair. He glanced in the mirror and saw that a light stubble darkened his cheeks and his blue eyes looked tired. "You just shaved this morning, fop," he told his reflection. "I'm hungry."

He changed his shirt for a clean one and shrugged back into his jacket. It was still a bit crumpled but would have to suffice. Who knew how long he'd be stranded here? Somewhat satisfied with his appearance, he took himself downstairs to the dining room.

Geoffrey entered, finding it furnished in the same simple elegance as was his room. The polished floor shone. The round tables were covered with fine white cloth. The place was nearly filled and two or three patrons sat at each occupied table. According to Thomas Kingsley, only half of the diners would be staying in the rooms abovestairs. It seemed the cook was famous in the nearby town and many an unattached man took his evening meal at the inn. Geoffrey located an empty table and sat.

The meal was simple, but it smelled glorious. Apparently, tonight he could look forward to a hearty meal of roast beef with potatoes. He could almost taste the thick gravy covering each helping.

A buxom serving girl bearing a loaded platter sashayed over to his table, her red ringlets bouncing with each step. She stopped in front of him, favoring him with a smile that showed a dimple in her cheek. “I’m Emmy.”

Geoffrey let his gaze fall to her bosom, which was very nearly in his face. “Emmy.”

She set the platter down and placed a hand on her hip, regarding him closely. “Will ya be wantin’ anythin’ else?”

He brought his gaze back up to her face, blinking at the invitation in her brown eyes. He smiled at her and shook his head. She turned away and he watched her bottom as she bent over a nearby table. Perhaps he’d try out the fine bed upstairs with the wench. He soon saw that she favored all of the male customers with the same familiarity. Laughing to himself, he picked up his fork to start on the appetizing meal before him. He nearly dropped it when he spotted the dark-haired girl coming from the kitchen.

She moved with an easy grace through the dining room, her glossy black hair catching the light given off by the candles. Curls framed the perfect oval of her face and teased the back of her neck. Her simple gown hugged her lush figure, the skirt swaying over her hips as she walked. She carried a pitcher of ale, and Geoffrey couldn’t take his eyes off her as she moved from table to table.

A man’s voice broke through his reverie. “Fetchin’, ain’t she?”

“What …?” He hadn’t even noticed the gray-haired man

who joined him at his table. "Yes."

"Peter Jenkins is the name," the slight man offered. "How do you do?"

Geoffrey shook the man's hand. "Kane. Geoffrey Kane," he answered. "Very well, thank you."

The older man gave a flick of his head in the girl's direction. "She's Kingsley's daughter."

Geoffrey raised an eyebrow at that. This beautiful creature was related to the florid-faced innkeeper? Impossible.

Just then, the girl approached the two men. Her mouth curved into a smile for the older man before she turned her attention to Geoffrey. Her rose-colored lips parted as she stared into his eyes for a long moment. "Blue."

Geoffrey blinked. "What?"

She shook her head. "N-nothing."

Geoffrey could only stare at the girl, dumbstruck. Her eyes were the color of emeralds, and sparkled as prettily. His gaze fell on her lips as she flicked her tongue over them. Desire shot through him, want like he'd never felt before. Once again, Peter's voice broke in.

"Rebecca, this is Geoffrey Kane. Kane, meet Rebecca Kingsley."

The girl, Rebecca, curtsied in greeting after a brief hesitation. She seemed as off-kilter as he felt, to his amazement. After a moment, Geoffrey stood and bowed slightly. "Miss Kingsley."

"I'm pleased to meet you," Rebecca said.

Her voice suited her. It was soft and a bit husky. And damn sensual.

"Likewise."

"Will you be staying with us long?"

If I can help it. "A few days, actually," he said, smiling.

She gasped softly, the sound no more than a whisper. "Well, do enjoy your stay," she said, shyly returning his smile.

She stared up at him for a moment longer. Finally, she filled his tankard. With a nod of her dark head, she continued on through the dining room. Geoffrey sank back down into his seat, his gaze glued to her form.

"Rebecca," he breathed. "Becca."

Peter chuckled at Geoffrey's obvious befuddlement. Geoffrey ignored him and turned his attention back to his meal. But because he stopped every so often to stare after the enchanting girl, Becca, his meal was cold by the time he finished.

Chapter 2

The next morning, after seeing to the morning meal, Rebecca was upstairs putting her assigned rooms to rights. She was disappointed that Mr. Kane, Geoffrey, hadn't joined the other lodgers for breakfast. Perhaps he had business to attend to and needed an early start. She grinned to herself. And perhaps Emmy would need help serving the nooning meal.

With an armful of clean towels, she moved from room to room. She paused in front of Geoffrey's door. She knew this was so, for she'd been in her father's office the night before. She smiled. While straightening his desk, she just happened to see the registry.

She placed a hand on the door, trailing a finger over the wood. He'd affected her last night like no man ever had before. His beautiful eyes, his dazzling smile, had made her heart beat faster. The stubble on his finely chiseled cheeks only added to his appeal. Lord, he was handsome. Letting out a sigh, she entered the room.

The chamber was dark as the draperies were still drawn. She placed the towels on the washstand and crossed to the window. She pulled aside the drapes and turned, stunned at the sight before her. There on the bed, Geoffrey lay sleeping. The covers were down around his waist and he wore no night shirt. His broad chest and strong arms were dark against the white sheets. She let her gaze wander over him, noting the thick lock of honey-colored hair that fell across his brow. She quietly crossed to him. She looked down at his face, striking even in repose. She gently brushed the lock of hair back from his forehead. So soft. Would the hair covering his chest feel just as soft? She gently brushed her fingers over his chest.

Suddenly, his hand gripped hers and her gaze flew to

Geoffrey's face. She found him staring at her, his brilliant blue eyes boring into hers. She gasped, a soft sound in the silence of the room.

"Geoffrey …."

"Becca?"

He lifted his head off the pillow, a question in his eyes. Her gaze fell to the firm, masculine curve of his mouth. She bent her head to meet him halfway.

"Becca," he whispered again, his mouth a breath away.

Their lips brushed ever so lightly, the fleeting kiss firing her senses. He began to apply more pressure and she pulled back, shocked by her actions. She fled the room, her cheeks flaming and her lips on fire.

Out in the hall once more, Rebecca leaned against the wall and tried to collect herself. Her heart beat furiously and her breath came fast. She brought her fingers up to her mouth and lightly touched her lips, still tingling from Geoffrey's kiss. Breathing in deeply, she tried to slow her racing pulse. She hurried to the safety of her room, not wanting to run into him. She paused at her door, glancing down the hall toward his room. She was safe. From him or from herself, she wouldn't ponder.

She straightened her shoulders and entered her room, closing the door softly behind her. Almost before she was aware, it was time for the nooning meal.

"Girl!" her father bellowed from belowstairs in his usual manner.

She came out of her room to stand at the top of the stairs. "Yes, Father?"

"Get down here. We got a full dining room."

She nodded, sighing to herself. Only that morning she'd thought to help Emmy, hoping to catch a glimpse of Geoffrey. Now after shaming herself in his room, she knew she'd simply perish if she saw him. She slowly descended the stairs and entered the dining room.

Emmy was busy carrying out the platters of food. The fare was light: cold chicken, crusty bread, slabs of hard cheese. She spied Rebecca and motioned for her to bring the bread baskets to the tables. Rebecca stacked a few full baskets in her arms and moved among the tables. Halfway through her task, she spotted Geoffrey sitting alone. Their eyes met briefly and she looked away. He watched her with a smile teasing his lips, apparently amused at the flush she was certain covered her cheeks. He motioned to her, requesting some bread. She walked toward him resolutely and stopped in front of his table.

"Good afternoon, Mr. Kane," she said stiffly.

"'Mr. Kane'?" he teased. "Why so formal? I'd think that after this morning …."

Her gasp blessedly stilled him. She bent down and placed the basket of bread in front of him.

"Thank you, Becca," he whispered in her ear, his breath warm on her skin.

Rebecca blushed again, hotly this time. She looked at him and read the amusement in his eyes. She straightened and quickly walked away from the table.

Geoffrey broke off a piece of bread, smiling to himself. That morning, when she'd surprised him in his room then left so suddenly, made him wonder if she'd truly been there or if she was part of the wonderful dream he'd had before waking. Her lips had been so soft, her touch magical. She seemed to be having none of it this afternoon.

After finishing his meal, Geoffrey left the dining room, bound for the parlor. The sound of voices stopped him just outside the doorway.

"So what did Kane say to ya that turned ya all red?" he heard the other serving girl, Emmy, ask Rebecca.

"Nothing, really."

Emmy snorted. "Ah, come on, love. He's a handsome devil, and obviously taken with ya."

Geoffrey blinked. Taken with her? Hell, he wanted her, plain and simple.

"What makes you say that?" Rebecca asked.

"The way he looks at ya, silly."

"I like the way he says my name," she said softly. "He calls me Becca.'"

"Does he, now? Ain't that cozy?"

"No. I just like it, that's all."

"Okay, love. I won't tease ya about it, then."

The voices faded, and Geoffrey surmised that the women had left the room. He entered to find that he was right. He lowered himself onto a damask-covered settee. Rebecca had been as affected as he had. He'd felt it in his room. But why the shy blushes? Surely she couldn't be completely innocent, not living in an inn as busy as this one. Not with all the men as taken with her charms as he was. That thought soured his mood. He didn't like the idea of any other man touching her. He was surprised by that sudden wave of possessiveness.

"Easy, Kane," he told himself. "She's just a pretty girl and it's been a while since you've had a tumble."

He turned his attention to the stack of books left on the table. Choosing one, he opened it and put thoughts of Rebecca Kingsley out of his mind.

That evening, Geoffrey entered the dining room. He sat at an empty table and smiled as Emmy placed a platter of hearty beef stew in front of him.

"And how are ya this evenin', Kane?" she asked, running her gaze over him.

"Just fine, Emmy." He smiled.

Although he tried, he couldn't stop his eyes from searching for Rebecca's slender form. He wasn't disappointed. She stood across the room, talking quietly to her father. As Geoffrey watched, she began to wring her hands, a look of distress marring her exquisite features. Geoffrey frowned, unaware of the telling action.

But Emmy didn't miss it. "So it's like that, is it?"

"What?"

"Nothin'. Anythin' else?"

"Not at the moment."

Emmy nodded and turned away to see to the other diners. "About bloody time."

Geoffrey ignored her parting comment, his eyes on Becca as she floated about the room. He didn't miss the obvious lust in the eyes of the other patrons, however. He wanted to flatten every last one of them.

His food seemed to lose its taste, so he washed it down with more ale.

* * * *

"I'm telling you, Jenkins. I've got to get that girl married off, and right quick."

Peter Jenkins nodded at Thomas, then smiled. "I can see what ya mean. All those young pups droolin' after her. Yer goin' ter have to keep her locked up."

"It's not funny," Thomas growled. "I have no dowry for her. And my rank as the third son of a baronet yields me no bargaining power."

Peter hid his smile, narrowing his eyes thoughtfully. "Ya know, Thomas, the way I see it, this here inn is worth a pretty penny. And as likely as not, whoever she marries is goin' ter get it in due time, right?"

Thomas's curiosity was piqued. "Yes, so? What are you getting at?"

"Wouldn't the inn be enough of a dowry?"

Thomas rubbed his chin, thoughtful. "I suppose so, if the man had money of his own. But what good does that do me now?"

"What are you talkin' about?" Peter asked.

"She's a comely girl. Maybe some rich gentleman will pay to have her."

"Thomas, you can't mean …?"

"No! To have her for his wife, you sot." He nodded. "Yes. This bears thinking on."

Peter stared at Rebecca for a moment, a faraway look in his eyes. "The older she gets, the more she looks like her mother, 'cept for the eyes. Aye, she was pretty, with all that dark hair. I remember the fetchin' picture she made when she rode. Her hair flyin' out free behind her, her blue eyes all sparklin'. You were a lucky man, Thomas."

Thomas stiffened at the mention of Rebecca's mother. "Yes," he said in a low voice. "Lucky."

"Well, my friend," Peter said, "ya better do somethin' soon."

"Don't I know it. I better get her wed while she's still pure." Thomas paused to smile wryly. "A virgin would fetch a high price around these parts."

Peter looked shocked for a moment. "Oh, yer jestin'."

Thomas smiled widely. "Of course."

* * * *

As soon as the diners were fed, Rebecca climbed the stairs to her chamber. She longed for some peace and quiet. Her father had spoken of marriage again. She didn't want to marry anyone he picked out for her. She had no real suitors, but she knew there must be someone out there for her. Geoffrey's face popped into her mind. No. He wasn't the man for her, either. He was just a gentleman with enough coin to secure a room at Raven's for a period of time on his way to some other amusement. She'd been wooed by other gentlemen, titled and not, and her heart remained untouched.

She really knew nothing of Geoffrey but his pleasing face. And teasing smile. And his kiss! She still tingled when she thought of it. She'd retire early. Perhaps in the solitude of her room, she could reason through her odd reaction to that particular man.

"Good evening, Becca," Geoffrey said in her ear.

She started and turned, surprised to find him standing close behind her. "Geoffrey!"

He smiled crookedly at her. "Ah, so it's 'Geoffrey' again."

Rebecca stepped back, pressing herself against the panel of her door. He moved closer, bracing an arm above her head. With his other hand, he caressed her cheek. She gazed into his eyes, lost in their blue depths.

"I wished to speak to you at dinner, but you were much too busy," he said, his eyes staring into hers. "Why do you think that was, Becca?"

"I—uh," she stammered. "That is …."

He ran his thumb slowly over the curve of her lower lip. Oh, his touch!

"I think the truth is that you can't stop thinking about this morning," he said, his voice a caress. "About our kiss."

She drew in a breath, shaking her head.

"Yes," he insisted, gently grasping her chin to tilt her head up. "And neither can I."

The full meaning of his words penetrated her muddled mind. She could only watch as he bent his head to hers, his eyes dark. His lips touched hers fleetingly. He pulled back and ran a hot gaze over her face. His gaze settled on her lips. With a soft groan, he kissed her again, harder this time. His tongue flicked over her lips. She didn't know what he wanted, only that his mouth was so warm, so insistent. She opened her mouth to ask him what to do and his tongue swept inside. She whimpered, more surprised than scared. She reached up to twine her fingers in the soft, thick curls at the nape of his neck, moaning in the back of her throat. The little sound seemed to drive him on. He cupped her face in his hands, slanting his mouth over hers again and again.

Geoffrey finally dragged his mouth from hers. He took her hands and brought them down to rest on his chest. "I'm sorry, Becca. I only meant to …."

Her head lay back against the door, her lips parted as she took short breaths. "To what, Geoffrey?"

"To tease you. To … taste you again."

She opened her eyes to stare up at him. "Geoffrey."

His eyes seemed to smolder. "My God—" He kissed her quickly and stepped back from her. "Good night, Becca," he said, an unknown warning in his tone.

"Good night, Geoffrey," she breathed, gazing into his beautiful eyes.

He started to walk toward his own door when he looked back at her. "I like the way you say my name, too, Becca."

That brought her back to her senses. She eyed him as, laughing softly, he closed his door.

She straightened. "Oh, my."

Chapter 3

After breakfast the next morning, Geoffrey borrowed a trap from the inn and drove into town to learn precisely how long the blasted wheel was going to take. He also wanted to put some distance between himself and Becca. The way she responded to him, so giving and trusting …. When her soft mouth opened up for him, he'd shaken with his need. He was very nearly unable to stop himself. Never before had a woman affected him so.

He was no stranger to the pleasures of the flesh. He'd bedded many a wench, and never left one of them unhappy. But this girl was different. She couldn't still be pure, not the way she'd returned his kisses. Hell, if he'd simply opened the door to her room, she'd have given herself to him fully. So what had stopped him?

Those eyes, clear and innocent one minute, then darkened with passion the next. Becca seemed almost vulnerable. Whatever had she spoken of with her father last evening? Her upset had been clear to him. No matter. If he bedded her, that thought caused him to harden, could he just leave? Or would she worm her way into his heart?

He couldn't let that happen.

After Bennett told him he still hadn't started on the wheel, on doctor's orders apparently, Geoffrey returned to the inn. As he sat in the overstuffed chair in his room, he thought back to the meeting with his solicitors. They'd told him that certain entries in his accounting ledgers just weren't adding up. There were payments made to tradesmen for repairs to Geoffrey's estate, but he was not familiar with the firms seeking payment. It seemed however, over the last few months or so, small amounts of capital were somehow unaccounted for. They were examining their books in this regard, seeking to find any clerical error that might have been made. He had no true reason to doubt his solicitors, as the firm was well-respected and had served the Kane family for generations. He rose and stood by the window.

His room had a clear view of the stables and the rolling hills beyond. Perhaps a ride would clear his head. Suddenly, a flash of color caught his eye. There, riding like the wind, was Becca. She wore a green riding habit, but no hat was on her head. Her glorious hair billowed out behind her, unbound. His breath caught in his throat. She looked so free, so beautiful, as she galloped her black filly over the rich green of the hillside.

Intense longing flared through him. "Ah, hell." He turned from the window and went downstairs to the parlor.

He grabbed up a book he'd started to read the previous afternoon. He sat and read quietly for a while until male voices broke through his concentration.

"I'll get her married, Peter. Soon, and to a man of my choosing."

"Rebecca won't want to marry some old man you pick for her, Thomas. Think of the girl."

"I am thinking of her. Keeping her here at the inn wasn't enough for her mother. Sometimes, I regret .... Ah, never mind."

"Then who do you want her to marry?" Peter asked as their voices began to fade.

Unfortunately, Thomas's answer was lost as the two men entered the office and closed the door.

Why was Kingsley worried about marrying her off? She was a beautiful girl. Certainly she had many suitors. And what had Peter meant by "some old man?" Geoffrey refused to let it bother him.

Stay out of it. He had enough to worry about with his accounts. He'd be leaving in a few days and she'd be out of his sights.

But would she be out of his mind? He shook his head. He wasn't going to lose his head over a lovely face again, not after what happened with Patricia four years ago. He'd come upon her and his younger brother in bed together and apparently Geoffrey's betrothed had been playing him false for months as she was carrying John's baby. After a hasty wedding, John and Patricia were given rooms in one wing of Kanewood, and Geoffrey did his best to avoid them.

Now, he took what was offered to him and made no promises, Rebecca Kingsley notwithstanding. She roused a protective streak in him that he vowed to keep dormant.

The next morning, Geoffrey again set out in the borrowed trap. He'd written a letter to his mother to let her know he'd been delayed. He posted the letter in town and climbed back into the trap and started back toward the inn. When Rebecca walked out of a shop not far from where he sat, he changed his mind. She wore a green dress and a straw bonnet with a matching ribbon tied beneath her chin. Her figure was shown to advantage in the laced-trimmed, fitted bodice. How could she manage to be both sweet and sensual?

He alighted the trap to stand in front of her. With her attention focused on the full basket in her arms, she bumped into him. With a murmured beg of pardon, she looked up. Her eyes widened as she saw him.

"Hello, Becca," he said.

She averted her gaze from his. "Hello, Geoffrey," she answered softly.

"No maid accompanies you?"

"No. The inn can't spare it. My father had one of the grooms take me. He'll be back in an hour's time."

"Oh." Odd, but nothing about Rebecca seemed quite the norm. "What is in the basket?" he asked, lifting the cloth tucked over the top.

Inside were some luscious summer fruits, slabs of hard cheese, and fresh bread from the bakery.

"I had to purchase some items at the market."

"Looks like the makings of a picnic to me," he hinted.

She shook her head. "Oh, no. This is for the inn."

She resumed her pace and Geoffrey walked in step beside her. "Well," he began, "it appears that I'll miss the nooning meal. Perhaps I could purchase something from you to sustain me?"

She stopped and quirked a pretty smile at him. "You

certainly don't look as if you're starving."

"Oh, but I am," he insisted. "Please have mercy on me, dear Becca?"

She laughed then, a sweet sound. "All right. You may purchase something."

Geoffrey made a show of perusing the contents of the basket. He scratched his chin. "I don't know. What I really want isn't in this basket."

"And what is that?" she asked innocently.

He looked at her then and felt the pull of her. He forced a smile of his own. "You. Won't you share my meal?"

"I shouldn't."

"I'll replace anything we eat." He pressed a hand to his chest. "You have my word as a gentleman."

She gazed up at him and he must have managed to play down his baser desires and only let one hunger show on his face, for she gave a small nod.

"All right. I'd like that very much."

He relieved her of the basket and turned back to the trap. After locating a blanket from under the seat, he grasped her elbow and led her to the common.

The common was covered with thick green grass and dotted with several large shade trees. He chose a picnic spot at the edge of the common, away from the crowded main road, and handed the basket to Rebecca. With a flourish, he spread the blanket and laid it on the grass. He bowed gallantly to her, and bade her to sit. She smiled and knelt, tucking her feet beneath her.

He watched her as she removed her bonnet and grinned.

"What is it?" she asked as she ran her fingers over that glorious black hair.

"Why were you wearing that silly bonnet?"

She clicked her tongue. "To keep the sun off my face. I don't want to get freckles."

He blinked. She already had freckles, very appealing ones, dotting the bridge of her perfect little nose. He hid his smile and stretched out on the blanket.

They shared some of the hard cheese and she broke off a

piece of bread for him. They ate in silence as Rebecca kept her eyes downcast. Even so, Geoffrey couldn't take his eyes off her. Her hair was pulled back, a few curls escaping to brush her smooth cheeks. They appeared soft as silk. Her voice broke his trance.

"Would you like some more cheese?" she asked.

"No, thank you," he answered. "What else do you have in there?"

When she reached into the basket and offered him an apple, he arched a brow at her. "Like Eve you would tempt me, Becca?"

Geoffrey took the apple from her hand, his fingers brushing hers. She gasped and he felt it like a caress. She chose a red, ripe strawberry for herself and she nibbled at it. He watched her mouth, her lips darkened by the succulent fruit, and lust swirled through him. He had to taste those lips.

"Becca?" he asked softly.

Rebecca turned in answer, her lips parted to respond. He bent his head to hers, brushing her lips with his own. This kiss was gentle but as delicious as the one they'd shared in the hallway. He pulled back and raked his fingers through his hair.

Geoffrey tried to slow his racing pulse. Her lips were so soft, so sweet. If he'd deepened the kiss, he wouldn't have been able to stop.

He turned his attention to the square, watching the people come and go without much interest. After a few minutes passed, he regained his control. He stole a glance at Becca and was struck by her vulnerability once more.

"Becca …."

She looked up at him, her eyes large and shiny with unshed tears. He chose to take another tact.

"Your hair is so beautiful, love." He reached out to finger one thick curl near her temple. It felt incredible to him, as soft and silky as he'd imagined. He let one finger trail over her smooth ivory cheek, and she closed her eyes.

She licked her lips nervously and the action drew his eyes to her full lips. He felt as drawn to her as he had since that first night at the inn. He cupped her face in his hands, coming around to face her fully. His lips captured hers in a searing kiss. He thought to pull away, but Rebecca's hands stole up to the nape of his neck, urging him to deepen the kiss. With a low growl, he obliged her.

She answered his questing tongue with her own, rubbing it gently. He ran his hands down her back, molding her sweet body to him. She whimpered softly and he dragged his mouth away from hers.

"Ah, Becca …" he groaned against her ear.

"Geoffrey," she whispered.

Geoffrey took her hands from around his neck as he had that night in the hallway.

She gazed up at him. "Is something wrong?"

"Not here, love," he answered, stroking her cheek again.

She looked about as if suddenly remembering where they were. "Oh! What must you think of me?"

"I think you're a warm, giving, passionate girl. You have nothing to be ashamed of. I'm the one to blame."

She shook her head, a frown on her lovely face. "No. I wanted you to kiss me." She looked down again. "I still do."

He breathed in sharply at that admission. He had to get her back to the safety of the inn, and quickly. He placed a chaste kiss on her brow and turned to gather up the blanket. Rebecca picked up the basket and stood, her head bowed. He escorted her to the trap, and they rode back to the inn in silence.

* * * *

Geoffrey wasn't surprised Becca wouldn't meet his gaze in the dining room that evening. He longed to apologize for his behavior on the common, but it was obvious she wanted nothing to do with him.

"Girl!" Thomas Kingsley bellowed.

As Geoffrey watched, Becca stiffened, then bowed her head and walked over to where her father sat with Peter Jenkins. He couldn't hear what was said, but whatever it was obviously upset her. She nodded shakily, a frown creasing her brow, and returned to her duties in the dining room. What was her father up to? He thought about asking Jenkins but knew that the old man wouldn't betray the confidence of a long-time friend. Geoffrey pushed away from the table and went up to his room.

That night, Geoffrey awoke with a start. He glanced about the room. What had awakened him? Then he heard it. Someone was rapping on his door, the sound soft yet insistent. He got up, pulled on his breeches, and was at the door just as the knocking came again. As he turned the knob, the door exploded inward, nearly knocking him off balance.

A small figure crashed into him, wrapping her arms tightly around his bare waist. In a flash, he recognized the supple curves pressed tightly against him. She shook in his arms and he could feel the wetness of tears on his chest.

"Becca?"

Chapter 4

Geoffrey closed the door. "What is it?" he whispered.

"Oh, Geoffrey," she sobbed. "Please don't let him do it. Please …."

Now he was worried. And angry. Who was trying to hurt her? He'd kill him! He held her at arm's length, checking her over from head to foot for any injuries. She hung her head, still crying, her hair hiding her face from him. A dark thought flitted through his mind. He tilted her chin to look into her eyes, almost afraid to put a voice to what he was thinking.

"Becca, did someone touch you?"

She seemed confused, then shook her head vigorously. "No, no. He can't make me …."

He hugged her to him and she began to keen softly.

He stroked her back, trying to calm her. "Shh, love. No one is going to hurt you. Shh …."

After a few moments, her crying ceased. She sniffled and rubbed her cheek against his chest. He pulled back and brushed her tears off her cheeks.

"There." He offered her a small smile. "That's better. Can you tell me what's wrong?"

She nodded. "My father wants me to marry him. He wants me to marry Dr. Simon."

Geoffrey shook his head, certain he'd heard wrong. He'd seen the man in town. He was older than her father.

"That can't be. Perhaps—"

"It's true," she insisted. "He told me this evening."

She walked over to the window and pushed the drapery aside. "My father said Dr. Simon has agreed to marry me."

"Agreed? What do you mean?"

She continued to stare out the window, standing perfectly

still. The moon was full and flooded the room with silver light. She wore a nightgown of thin lawn and the light streaming through the window outlined her figure. His mouth went dry—she was exquisite. He caught a bit of what she was saying.

"... five thousand pounds."

He shook his head. "What?"

"Dr. Simon will pay my father five thousand pounds to have me for a wife."

Her last words were mere whispers. The full impact of what she said hit him then. He strode over to where she stood and turned her toward him.

She looked up at him. "I don't know what I'm going to do."

She dissolved into tears once more. He gathered her into his arms. He wanted to tell her what she wanted to hear, but he knew better. Kingsley could do anything he wanted with her and she had no choice but to go along with his decision.

He led her over to the chair and sat, pulling her down on his lap. She rested her head against his shoulder, her tears flowing freely. He held her there for a long while, whispering soothing words and stroking her back.

Finally, Becca looked up at him. "I don't want to marry him. I don't like the way he looks at me."

"How does he look at you?"

She looked down, as if to hide from his gaze. "Like he wants to do things to me."

Geoffrey swallowed his disgust of the image of the doctor's bony hands on her flawless skin.

"Shh," he soothed. "It'll be all right. I won't let him touch you."

She relaxed and leaned against him, rubbing her cheek against his chest once more. He stroked her back for a while as he tried to think of a way to get her out of this mess.

Becca breathed in deeply and he felt as if he was being drawn into her lungs. What was she about?

"You smell heavenly," she whispered.

When she ran the tip of her tongue over his skin, a shiver coursed through him. He breathed in sharply and looked down at her.

She met his gaze, her eyes dark. “You taste just as good.” She began trailing hot kisses on his skin.

He grasped the back of her head and urged her face up to his. He captured her lips with his own. How could desire flare so quickly? Her tongue eased into his mouth and he groaned. He quickly took control of the kiss, cupping her face in his hands.

Her hands were driving him to distraction. She ran her fingers slowly over his chest as he kissed her, trailing her fingertips down over his belly to pause at the waistband of his breeches. He held his breath. God, yes. He wouldn’t force her, but he wanted those nimble fingers on him. When she finally traced the outline of his manhood through the fabric, he grew harder.

“I want you, Becca,” he rasped. “Like I’ve never wanted any other woman.”

He grabbed her hand and brought it up behind his neck. Her other hand followed as she pressed herself against his chest. He kissed the smooth skin of her neck and a soft moan escaped her lips.

“Geoffrey ….” She breathed, leaning her head back.

He unfastened the tiny buttons on the front of her nightgown, kissing the smooth skin he revealed. His hand cupped one breast, his thumb brushing across the nipple. She gasped at the intimate contact.

He looked at her, his expression serious. “I don’t care who you’ve been with. I want you.”

Becca raised her head in confusion. “But I haven’t—” His mouth closed over her hardened nipple and she lost all thought. Pleasure blazed through her. She shifted in his lap, straddling that intriguing bulge in his breeches. His hands cupped her bottom, pressing her to him as he groaned. He cursed softly and stood, carrying her toward the bed.

She slid down the length of him to stand on unsteady legs. He ran his gaze over her face, his expression blatantly carnal. She’d caught men in the pub looking at her like that before, but the desire in Geoffrey’s eyes didn’t disgust her like those unwanted gazes. No. Her breath quickened at the look in his eyes. He gently tugged at and removed her nightgown and she shyly stood there as his gaze roamed from her toes to her breasts. Her skin flushed and her nipples tightened.

He finally settled on her face. "You are so beautiful," he said huskily.

He scooped her up and laid her on the bed. She watched him, liking the way the moonlight made his skin glisten. He quickly removed his breeches and joined her, his body nearly crushing hers.

She gasped as his hair-roughened chest pressed against her breasts. He nibbled on her lips, his tongue thrusting in and out of her mouth. His mouth left hers to claim her breast again as her fingers tunneled through his hair, holding him tight. His hand slid down to the curls that shielded her womanhood. She opened her legs to him, instinctively needing his touch. He caressed the folds of her, finding a sensitive spot she hadn't known she had.

"Oh, my!" She gasped.

Geoffrey knelt between her legs and she felt the tip of his arousal near the heat of her. He began to enter her, then froze.

She squeezed her eyes shut, moving against him to ease the burning he'd started. "Geoffrey, please …."

With one smooth thrust, he entered her fully. She cried out, her eyes snapping open. The pain!

"Easy, love." He captured her lips in a deep kiss. "I can't keep still. God, you're so …." He moved inside of her and the pain was eclipsed by the shaft of pleasure the movement caused. "Hold on to me, Becca," he ground out.

She clutched at him, scoring his back with her nails. He moved again, slowly at first. Soon, he was driving into her, harder and deeper. She tightened around him and her heart began to pound.

"Geoffrey?"

"It's all right," he said hoarsely. "I've got you."

His words freed her. Waves of pleasure washed over her as she cried out his name. He moved a few more times, then shuddered, holding tight as she felt his release deep inside of her.

They lay there for a long time, his body on top of hers. Finally, he leaned up on his elbows and dropped a kiss on her brow.

She found her voice. "That was …."

"Incredible?" he finished for her, an arrogant grin on his face.

"Yes. No wonder Emmy is always doing this."

He laughed softly. "It isn't always this way."

She blinked at him. "It would be with you."

His eyes flashed his satisfaction at that. He rolled off her onto his back, and she cuddled next to him.

She thought of something then, something he'd said earlier. "I've never been with a man before."

"I know that now, love," he answered, a smile in his voice.

"How?"

He opened his mouth, then brushed her hair away from her face as he looked down at her. "I'm sorry I hurt you."

She glanced up at him. "The pain wasn't so terrible. I suppose I could grow accustomed to it."

He laughed again, the sound coming from deep in his chest.

"What do you find so funny?" she asked.

"It only hurts the first time, Becca."

Pity she wouldn't ever be with a man again. That thought caused her throat to tighten. It was better this way. He would leave and she would go back to her life at the inn. But what about her father?

"What am I going to do?" she wondered aloud.

"I'll speak to your father if you wish."

"No, I couldn't ask you to."

"You didn't. Let me speak to him."

She chewed on her thumb. "All right. Will you tell him I can't marry that awful man?"

"I'll do my best."

She relaxed and curled her fingers in the hairs on his chest. Soft and springy at the same time. His chest was strong and his belly flat. And his—

Geoffrey placed his hand on hers. "Don't."

"I like touching you," she said, moving her fingers again.

"Your body is so different."

Geoffrey stiffened. "Different from whose?"

Her fingers moved again. "From mine."

With a soft groan, he grabbed her hand and brought it to his lips. "If you keep touching me like that, I'll want you again."

Again. Would that be so terrible? One last time?

"Good." She smiled.

"Becca," he said in warning.

She propped herself up on her elbows, resting her chin on her hands. "You said that it only hurts the first time."

He gave her a small smile, stroking her cheek. "But it's too soon, love. You're too tender."

She was still quite sore, but it seemed so strange speaking of it. "Oh," she whispered, turning red.

"Blushing?" He tilted her chin up. "After what we just shared?"

She returned his smile, shrugging her shoulders. His gaze wandered over her and she watched as his eyes darkened. She felt him harden against her belly.

"You'd better get back to your room," he said.

She nodded, climbing off the bed to retrieve her nightgown. She put it on and buttoned it up as Geoffrey pulled on his breeches. She stood behind him as he peeked out into the hall.

He turned from the door, hugging her to him. "Good night, Becca," he whispered against her hair.

"Good night, Geoffrey," she answered, standing up on tiptoe to place a kiss on his lips.

He opened the door for her and urged her to hurry. She crept out into the hall and turned once, waving to him as she opened the door to her room.

She fell into bed but couldn't seem to fall asleep. The memory of what Geoffrey did to her, what she'd begged him to do, still thrilled her. The memory of this night would be enough to sustain her through her lonely life at the inn. Geoffrey said he'd talk to her father, get him to listen to reason. She prayed her father would have the sense to listen. She wouldn't marry Dr. Simon. She'd rather die than live with him. Imagining the doctor doing to her what Geoffrey had, she shuddered.

"Never." Her mind was determined if her life wasn't. At least now she could find sleep.

* * * *

The next morning, she was slow to awaken. She sat up to swing her legs over the side of the bed and groaned as she stood. Lord, she was tender. Geoffrey hadn't been wrong, then. She rushed through her toilette and dressed with care. Her pulse quickened. She couldn't wait to see him—how could she face him after last night?

She chose a blue walking dress for today. As with all of her dresses, it was a bit snug through the bodice, but that couldn't be helped. She'd left off wearing stays last season. It took her a long while to brush all of the tangles out of her hair, then with her dress straightened and her braid done and coiled, she finally headed downstairs.

Geoffrey was sitting at his usual table when Becca walked into the dining room. He caught her eye, his blue eyes sparkling, and grinned broadly. Her pulse tripped as she looked away. She hurried to join Emmy to oversee and help with the morning meal and saw that her friend hadn't missed the exchange.

"So, ya dallied with the devil, did ya?"

Becca flushed hot, nodding.

Emmy leaned closer to whisper, "Well? How was it?"

"It was wonderful!" Becca whispered. "He's wonderful."

Emmy nodded and crossed her arms. "So it's like that, is it?"

"Like what?"

"You're in love with him," Emmy whispered in triumph.

Becca was stunned speechless. In love with Geoffrey?

"Well, are ya?" Emmy pressed.

"I … I don't know."

Emmy put a hand on Becca's arm. "Be careful, girl. Love can be awful messy."

She wasn't in love. She couldn't be. Geoffrey would leave for wherever he was headed when he'd landed in her midst, and probably very soon. No. She couldn't be in love.

She picked up the teapot and began to walk toward his table, unable to keep a small smile from her lips. Maybe not love, but it was something. She'd keep the memory of it close in the long, lonely years ahead.

Chapter 5

As Becca poured him a cup of tea, Geoffrey watched her. Her hand shook and he flattered himself to think it was due to their close proximity. Apparently, she wasn't the only one affected. He picked up the cup and drank, regarding her over the rim. The blue dress she wore made her eyes a deep green. Lovely.

He set his cup down. "I have to go into town this morning, Becca. Would you care to join me?"

She shook her head. "I'm afraid I can't. I have to do an inventory of our supplies and I have the rooms to straighten abovestairs."

"Yes." He grinned wickedly. "Mine is in awful disarray. I can't imagine what happened in there."

"Hush, not here." A pretty blush lightly stained her cheeks, but he didn't miss her smile. She shook her head at him and continued on through the dining room. He watched her, noting her walk was a little stiff. He smiled to himself, knowing full well just what had caused her discomfort. Hell, he couldn't stop thinking about their … tryst didn't seem quite adequate a word to describe it. He'd never felt that kind of passion before. And the way Becca responded to him, she fired him like no other woman.

But what was he going to do with her? He'd promised her he'd talk to her father. Bloody bastard. Selling her to the doctor? Kingsley obviously didn't care about Becca if five thousand pounds could buy her from him.

He finished his breakfast and left the inn but not before looking his fill at the beautiful girl he couldn't get out of his mind.

A short while later, he finally had some good news from the wheelwright. It seemed that the esteemed Dr. Simon, filthy rotter, had finally given Bennett permission to use his hand again. Geoffrey had felt a flash of anger at the doctor's name, knowing the lecher planned to buy Becca.

With Bennett's assurance that the wheel would be ready in no more than two days' time, Geoffrey strolled the thoroughfare, thinking to walk off his anger. As he passed the good doctor's office, the door opened. Out walked the man himself. Geoffrey stiffened, raking his gaze over the bastard. Simon was a thin man, his narrow shoulders stooped. His hair was straight and gray, his eyes small and nearly black.

Geoffrey forced a smile of greeting on his face. "Good morning, Dr. Simon."

"Good morning … Kane, isn't it?"

Geoffrey nodded.

"Staying at Raven's, aren't you?"

"Yes."

"Then perhaps I'll see you there. I plan to dine there this evening."

"Oh, really?"

The old man's lips curled as a spark lit in those dark eyes. "Yes. Thomas and I have some unfinished business to conclude."

Geoffrey wouldn't have been surprised if the good doctor started rubbing his hands together. His own hands itched to be around the man's neck.

"Good day," he said, managing to sound uninterested. Years of society functions had given him that ability if no true enjoyment.

"Good day," the doctor fairly crowed.

With a curt nod, Geoffrey walked deliberately away from Simon. He hopped back into the trap and set off for the inn. He'd have to talk to Becca's father. Perhaps if he offered him the money himself, her father would take it. He was a business man, after all.

He'd make the man swear not to try it again, though. If he ever learned that Kingsley forced another marriage on her, he'd come back to Oakham before the words were out of his informant's mouth. He'd have to employ a local, then. His connections in London would be of no use here in the wilds of Rutlandshire.

At least Becca wouldn't have to worry about marrying some lecher. And when she met someone she wished to marry, she'd be free to do so. His stomach tightened at that thought. When he pictured her with another man, a man who would exercise his husbandly rights, his stomach churned. That unknown gentleman might have her hand, but Geoffrey had her virginity.

"Kane, you're a rake," he told himself.

Pushing aside the thought of Becca's future husband and his acute wedding-night disappointment, he set off to find Kingsley. The door to the man's office was ajar and he could hear the sound of Kingsley's voice bellowing from inside.

"Girl, you will do as I say!"

"But, Father, I don't like Dr. Simon."

"You don't have to like him. Just marry him."

Don't give in. Geoffrey waited for Becca's answer.

"I won't marry someone I don't love!"

Good girl!

Thomas snorted. "Love? What does love have to do with it? This is business."

Geoffrey heard Becca mutter something.

"You think to defy me, girl? Just as the money is nearly in my hands—"

"This is about money?"

"Don't think to tell me my business. You're just like your mother."

"But, Father ...."

Geoffrey heard Thomas's footfalls as he stomped around the office.

"You will marry Simon. That's final."

Geoffrey heard the unspoken threat even if Becca didn't. He pushed the door open.

"You will do as I say!" Thomas slammed his hand down on the desk, and Becca jumped at the show of violence.

"That's enough," Geoffrey said.

Becca and her father turned to the doorway. Becca's eyes widened, but Thomas was the first to find his voice.

"Get out of here, Kane. This isn't your concern."

Geoffrey nodded. "I'm making it my concern."

"Geoffrey, don't," Becca implored. "Please."

He looked at her and saw the fear in her eyes. God, she thought he was going to tell her father about their night together. He gave a quick shake of his head and faced her father. "You can't force your daughter into marriage, Kingsley."

"And what do you know of it?"

"Enough to know she shouldn't have to marry someone just because he pays you," he ground out.

"Look at her!" Thomas sneered. "She has no dowry. Nothing to recommend her but her looks. Who else will marry her?"

"I will," Geoffrey stated.

The two Kingsleys wore matching looks of surprise. Geoffrey didn't know why he'd said it, but it made sense. He'd marry her. She was beautiful, sweet, and giving. She was nothing like Patricia. Yes, he'd marry her.

"You?" Thomas scoffed. "Who are you?"

He nearly gave Thomas his full title, but Becca hadn't lost her look of bemusement. He couldn't reveal that he'd kept something so important from her now. Not in front of her opportunistic father.

"Someone who will treat her with the respect she deserves," Geoffrey said.

Thomas snorted again. "I have a deal with Simon and I'm a man of my word. Now get out!"

"Ask Rebecca," Geoffrey dared. "Ask Rebecca if she'll marry me."

Becca gasped and he looked at her in alarm. She'd gone white, her eyes huge in her pale face. He made a move toward her, but Thomas grabbed his arm to stop him.

"Well?" Thomas asked Becca. "Will you marry him, girl?"

Her gaze darted between the two men, her breath coming fast. "No," she whispered.

Thomas barked out a laugh. Geoffrey could only stare as she ran from the room.

* * * *

Becca flew up the stairs and shut herself in her room. She couldn't believe what had just happened. Marry Geoffrey? Never. He'd simply offered marriage to put an end to her father's plan or, worse, to make up for the guilt of taking her virtue last night. With no dowry, she'd be a burden to him and he'd grow to resent her. Wasn't that how her father saw her?

The way she felt about Geoffrey—was it love? She didn't know. She couldn't bear it if he grew to despise her. She fell on her bed and cried until her throat was sore.

* * * *

In the dining room that evening, Becca wouldn't meet Geoffrey's gaze. After a few attempts to get her attention, he stopped trying. She'd rejected his offer, leaving him free of any obligation. He should be grateful. He drank more deeply of his ale and tried to content himself with watching her. She moved with her usual grace through the room, her skirt swaying. The memory of their lovemaking in his room, of her sweetly begging him to do what he'd been wild for, sent desire coursing through his veins. He wanted her, plain and simple. But with her refusal of his offer, he'd never have her again.

When Dr. Simon walked into the dining room, Geoffrey didn't miss the gleam in his eye as he watched Rebecca. Once more, he longed to feel his hands around the man's neck.

As he emptied his tankard, a small sound caught his attention. His gaze sought its source and found Becca. One of the diners, a man of Geoffrey's age, held her by the wrist. As he held her captive, he reached up and stroked the hair at the nape of her neck. Geoffrey's hands clenched.

"Soft, just like a kitten," the man said. "Come now, little pussy. Purr for me." He pulled her down on his lap and Becca cried out.

Geoffrey bounded to his feet and grabbed her up off the man's lap. "Get your hands off her!"

He smashed his fist into the man's face. The man reeled,

then came to his senses. Geoffrey braced his legs apart, his hands in fists at his sides. The man stood and faced Geoffrey's challenge.

As Becca stood behind Geoffrey, the man lunged at him and landed a punch in his middle. Geoffrey recovered quickly and swung his arm, knocking the man to the floor.

Thomas stood between them, his arms spread wide. "That's enough!" He fixed his gaze on Geoffrey. "Kane, I won't tolerate this kind of behavior here. Sit down or I'll throw you out."

Geoffrey slowly went back to his table and sat down. He saw that Becca was no longer in the dining room.

"You!" Thomas dragged the other man off the floor. "That's my daughter you were pawing. Get out, and don't ever come back."

With a dark scowl in Geoffrey's direction, the man grabbed his hat and stalked out of the room.

Thomas motioned for Emmy to clean up the mess and walked back over to where Simon was standing.

The doctor shook his head. "The deal is off, Thomas."

"What?" Thomas sputtered. "Why?"

"I don't wish to worry about men pawing my wife or fighting over her. She's too young and pretty for my sanity. Good night, Thomas."

With a tip of his hat, he took his leave. Peter walked over to his friend, smiling and shaking his head. Thomas gave him a glare of warning, and Peter held his tongue. With a sigh, Thomas sat down.

"What am I going to do, Jenkins?" he asked. "The way these young bucks are after her, she's bound to get poked. And who will marry her then?"

Geoffrey had the grace to redden at her father's words. He nodded to the two men and left the dining room.

He stopped in front of Becca's door and knocked softly. "Becca?" he whispered. "Are you all right?"

At last she opened the door a crack and peered out at him. He made a move to enter, then checked himself. She opened the door a bit wider, and he took in her appearance. Her face was still pale and she was visibly trembling.

"Are you all right, love?"

She shakily nodded. "Yes. I'm fine."

He didn't believe her for a moment. "Let me—"

She straightned her shoulders. "I'm fine, Geoffrey. I don't need you."

Her words would have cut him if he believed them.

"Well. Good night, then."

* * * *

The next morning, Geoffrey sought Becca out. He strode into the dining room and Becca froze when she met his gaze. As he watched, a look of cool composure settled on her features. He didn't miss the way her hands shook, though. She wanted to appear strong? Fine. He'd dance to her tune. For now.

"Becca," he said.

"Good morning," she said stiffly.

She sounded strange to him, stilted.

"How are you this morning?" he asked.

"Quite well, thank you," she said in that same flat voice.

She looked as she always did: exquisite. Yet something wasn't right. His eyes never leaving her, he sat. She poured him a cup of tea, her stance still rigid.

He took a sip and set the cup down. "Becca, I wanted to talk to you about—"

"I'm very busy today, Geoffrey. I have to go into town this morning."

Trapped! He smiled. "Then save the groom's time. I'll drive you. I have need to go into town myself."

Her composure faltered, then she nodded. "Thank you."

She left him then, seeing to the other diners in the room. He watched her go, knowing that she'd never be able to keep up her cool detachment on the drive into town. He smiled to himself and finished his breakfast.

By the time they reached the village, he was ready to throttle her. She remained aloof, speaking to him only when spoken to. While she went to the market, he strode over to Bennett's.

The big man grinned broadly when Geoffrey approached, wiping his hands with a rag. “All fixed, sir. Right as rain.”

“Wonderful,” Geoffrey answered gruffly.

“The carriage will be ready by this afternoon. Figured you’d be wantin’ to be on your way.”

Geoffrey looked at him sharply. He didn’t know what he wanted anymore. “My driver will be by tomorrow morning if that suits.”

“Fine, fine,” Bennett answered.

“Very well, then.” Geoffrey left the shop and headed for the trap.

Tomorrow morning. He could leave tomorrow morning. But he’d talk to Becca first. And if she gave him another cold answer, he would throttle her.

Chapter 6

Becca was waiting for him when he reached the trap. She placed her basket in the back and climbed in, not waiting for his assistance. He sat next to her and urged the horse on. They rode in silence, Becca ramrod stiff at his side.

After twenty minutes, he pulled the trap to the side of the road and stopped. "All right, that's quite enough!"

Becca jumped and turned to him. "What's quite enough?"

"So, you're talking to me now?"

She looked away from him. "I was talking to you."

"No." He alighted the trap. "You were acting as if I was some kind of stranger."

She blinked at that. He shrugged out of his coat and threw it in the back. He grabbed the blanket from beneath the seat and walked around to her side.

"Come," he said, holding his hand out to her. "We're going to talk, Becca. Now."

After a brief hesitation, she put her hand in his. He helped her down and led her over to a large shade tree. He spread the blanket on the ground and sat. With a sigh, she sank to her knees on the blanket.

"Why wouldn't you talk to me last night?"

She said nothing.

"Were you angry with me? About the fighting?"

Her eyes opened wide. "No, not at all. I could never be angry with you."

Relief flooded him. "Then what was it?" He needed to know.

She took a breath and began. "I was embarrassed by what had happened in my father's office. I didn't want you to concern yourself. And then, when that man …."

He took her hands in his. “Shh, love. It’s all right.”

She looked up at him, her calm facade a memory. “I was so frightened! And when you started fighting—”

“I shouldn’t have done that in front of you. But when he touched you, when I saw him grab you, I went a bit mad.”

Geoffrey gathered her in his arms, gently stroking her back. Becca rubbed her cheek against him, snuggling closer. He dropped little kisses on her hair, feeling its softness with his lips. He rested his chin on her head and sighed, content for the first time that morning. She felt so right in his arms.

“I didn’t want him to touch me,” Becca said in a small voice.

He nodded silently, knowing she had to speak of it.

“I only want you to touch me, Geoffrey,” she said. “Only you.”

He breathed in sharply, looking down at her. She stared at him with such innocence, such trust.

“Becca,” he said hoarsely, both a warning and a plea.

She turned in his arms and placed her hands behind his neck, leaning against him. She brushed her lips against his.

“Only you,” she whispered.

With a soft growl, he crushed his mouth down on hers. The kiss was hot, wild. Her tongue rubbed against his, setting him on fire. He fumbled with the hooks in the back of her dress, needing to touch her. She opened his shirt, her hands stealing inside to stroke his chest. He pushed her sleeves off her shoulders, tugging the bodice down.

“My God, love,” he breathed against her ear.

He laid her down on the blanket, trailing kisses on her throat, her breasts. His mouth closed over her nipple and she arched against him. His hand stole under her skirts, searching for the very center of her. He could feel her heat through her thin drawers and pulled them down, finding her wet and ready for him.

Becca writhed beneath him, whispering his name. He pulled back just long enough to unbutton his breeches and, in one smooth thrust, he entered her.

She cried out in pleasure, her nails raking his back. He

drove into her, again and again. The pressure became almost too much to bear. With one final thrust, he climaxed. He shook with the power of his orgasm, bringing her release.

Geoffrey rained kisses on her face, waiting for his breathing to slow. Her eyes were closed, her breath coming in little puffs.

She opened her eyes and stared up at him. "Oh, my," she breathed.

He laughed a bit shakily, leaning up on his elbows. "You make me forget myself, love." He dropped a kiss on her parted lips. "I didn't even remove my boots."

She smiled and hugged him tight.

After a while, he helped her up and they straightened their clothes and climbed back into the trap.

He turned to her, taking her hand in his. "Will you marry me?"

She blinked, then a sweet smile curved her lips. "No."

What? His mind must be addled from his orgasm. But no. There she sat, shaking her pretty head.

"But …. Why not?"

She placed her hand on his cheek. "I can't permit you to marry me."

"Permit me?"

"I have no dowry, and I won't be a burden to a man of such simple means."

He nearly choked. Simple means? He was an earl, for God's sake! Wealthy and titled, but he couldn't tell her. Not now. If he did, he'd never know if she only married him for his money. He wouldn't be able to stand for that, not after Patricia's machinations.

"There could be a child."

That got him a reaction. Her lovely mouth fell open. "No."

"Yes. Twice we made love and twice I came inside you."

"If there's a child …." She shook her head. "There won't be a child."

"My God! You're the child if you think you can wish it away." With a flick of the reins, he set off once again for the inn. They rode back in the same manner as earlier. In silence.

* * * *

That evening, Becca was pleasant enough to him, but she didn't dally at his table. He watched her walk among the other diners, a scowl on his face. He'd have to watch her for more than her father's plans now. If she began to increase, he'd have to know. What a bloody mess.

Long after his meal was finished, he called Emmy over to his table. "More ale, Emmy," he grumbled.

She cocked her head to the side, regarding him closely. She filled his tankard and stood in front of him.

He took a long sip, watching her over the rim. He slammed the tankard down. "What?"

"That's not goin' to help ya."

"What are you talking about?"

"The ale. It's not what ya really want."

Geoffrey spied Becca as she escaped into the kitchen. He turned back to Emmy with a wicked smile. "And just what is it that I really want?"

Emmy gave an easy laugh. "Don't think ta use me that way, Kane. It's Rebecca yer wantin'."

He blew out a breath. "Ah, Emmy, you're right. But she doesn't want me."

"What are ya, blind? The girl's mad for ya."

Geoffrey shook his head. "No. I asked her to marry me and she turned me down flat. Twice."

Emmy arched an eyebrow at that. "Did she, now? Well, if I know Rebecca, she thinks she's doin' what's best for ya."

Geoffrey looked at her, puzzled. "Why?"

"The girl never thinks of herself," she added.

She left him then, clearing the remaining tables.

Geoffrey sat drinking his ale, his mind on Becca. Her rejection stung. She'd told him she didn't wish to be a burden. A burden? He'd never met anyone as giving. She gave of herself completely, body and soul. He thought back to her argument with her father. She'd said she'd never marry someone she didn't love. That galled him. She didn't love him? Well, she damned well better learn to love him!

He shook his head and drained his tankard. He motioned for Emmy. He hadn't seen Becca for a while and assumed she'd gone upstairs to bed. Emmy poured him another ale, clicking her tongue at him as she shook her head. He glared at her, warning her to keep silent. With a shrug of her shoulders, she left him blessedly alone.

* * * *

Becca tossed and turned in her bed, unable to sleep. She couldn't stop thinking about Geoffrey and his proposal. She wished that she could have said yes. She cared very much for him. But she didn't want to be a burden to him. So she'd have to let him leave, let him go back to the life he had in London or wherever.

She could have loved him. She stroked her belly. There won't be a child, no matter what Geoffrey said. God wouldn't be so cruel as to make her bear a constant reminder of her shame. Or her weakness.

She began to drift off to sleep when a strange sound woke her. She sat up in her bed, cocking her head to the side. It came again, a faint thump from out in the hall.

"Becca?" came a hoarse whisper.

It's him! She scrambled out of bed and opened her door a crack. He stood, or rather leaned, in the hallway. He thumped on the door to the room next to hers. Thank God that room was unoccupied tonight.

She opened her door. "Geoffrey, what are you doing?" she whispered.

He turned then, a crooked smile on his face. "Becca."

She took in his appearance. His clothes were rumpled, his face red. She could smell the ale on his breath and wrinkled her nose. "You're sotted!"

"Just had me a bit of ale," he said, still smiling.

"Go to bed," she said, her hands on her hips.

His gaze wandered over her form, and she felt naked despite the nightgown she wore. "All right, love," he drawled, making a move to step into her room.

She placed her hand on his chest, halting his progress. “Your bed, Geoffrey.”

His smile faded then, a look of pain on his features. He leaned against the wall and closed his eyes.

“What is it?”

He groaned, a mournful sound. “I need you, Becca. Please.”

She couldn’t refuse him her help. She managed to get him into his room and sat him on the edge of his bed. His eyes were open now and he regarded her solemnly. She removed his coat and folded it neatly over the chair. She walked back to him and stood between his outstretched legs. She unbuttoned his shirt and had just removed it when he grabbed her by the waist. She sucked in a breath, surprised he could move so quickly. He pulled her to him and closed his mouth over one nipple. His mouth was hot and moist through the thin cloth and her body clenched. With a ragged breath, she pulled out of his grasp.

She turned away from him and straddled his leg. She held his booted heel and pulled to no avail. He ran his hands over her bottom, gently kneading her flesh.

She fought the feelings he aroused. “You know, I could use your assistance.”

He removed his magic hands and braced them on the bed. He placed his other foot on her backside and, with one shove, sent Becca and the boot halfway across the room. She recovered herself and favored him with a scowl. Much to her dismay he was grinning broadly at her. She flipped her hair back from her face and straddled the other leg. She’d just removed the second boot when he grabbed her waist again.

He pulled her down on his lap, nuzzling the back of her neck. “So many ways, Becca,” he murmured, his breath hot on her skin. “So many ways for a man and woman to make love.”

Her mind began to float in a sensual haze …. Could he take her from behind as Emmy had said men loved to do? Ease his shaft high inside her as she bent over and let him ...? She gave a shiver. Surely that would be impossible and scandalous!

She quickly turned and pushed him back on the bed. He didn’t resist, all of his energy seemingly spent. He simply lay there, his long legs dangling off the side of the bed. She grabbed his legs and hauled them up on the bed, grunting from the strain.

She looked down and saw he was nearly asleep. Gone was the sensual cast to his face, the teasing touch of his hands. She dropped a chaste kiss on his brow and turned to go. He grabbed her by the wrist as he had that first morning.

His eyes flew open. "Don't go. I need you."

She couldn't leave him, not with him beseeching her with those beautiful eyes. Not with such tenderness in his voice. With a sigh of resignation, she stretched out beside him. He wrapped his arms around her and fell fast asleep. His loud snores told her he was dead to the world.

She pulled up the covers and snuggled against him. She'd just rest for a while. She yawned.

Just for a little while.

Chapter 7

The sunlight woke Geoffrey. He looked down at the sweet bundle cuddled up beside him. Becca. What happened last night? He brushed her hair away from her face, trailing a finger on her cheek. She let out a little sigh, and he couldn't care less how she happened to be in his bed.

He had to get her back to her room, though. "Becca, you—"

The rattle of the doorknob stilled him. Before Geoffrey could say anything, the door swung open. In walked Mary, the upstairs maid. She set a stack of linens on the washstand and faced the bed.

"Oh!" She knocked over the washstand. It fell with a loud crash.

"What …?" Becca mumbled, sitting up and clutching the sheets to her bosom. She saw Mary. "Mary!"

Mary fled the room.

"No, Mary, don't!" Becca buried her face in her hands. She turned to Geoffrey, who couldn't hide his smile. "This isn't funny!"

He managed to wipe the smile from his face. "You're right, love," he said in a serious tone.

She turned from him in exasperation. "Now, what am I going to do?"

"Marry me."

She stiffened and looked at him again. She started crying then, big loud sobs.

"Not precisely the response I was anticipating," he said.

She sniffed at him, wiping her eyes. "You don't have to marry me."

He grabbed her arm and pulled her down to rest on his chest. He lifted her chin and looked deeply into her eyes.

"Listen to me. I want to marry you."

She started to shake her head, but he held her still.

"Yes, I do," he insisted. "Not because you were found in my bed. Not because of your father's plans for you. Not because I might leave you with a child. But because I want to."

"But—"

He smiled then, stroking her cheek. "I want you. You're sweet and kind and beautiful. You're caring and loving."

She still looked undecided.

"And I … I care for you very much."

And then she smiled. A bright, beautiful smile, and Geoffrey felt his heart clench. "Will you marry me?"

Becca took a deep breath, and then finally nodded.

"Yes." She hugged him. "Yes, I'll marry you!"

He let out a breath and returned her embrace. He tilted her head up and brushed her lips with his own. He pulled back and stared at her, his bride. He made a move to kiss her again.

"Girl!" Thomas bellowed from belowstairs.

Becca found her voice. "Yes, Father?" she squeaked.

"I want to see you in my study in ten minutes, girl," Geoffrey heard him shout. "And bring that rotter Kane with you!"

Becca shot him a questioning look and Geoffrey nodded.

"Right away, Father," she called.

After sharing a tender kiss, she left him to go dress while he saw to his own toilette.

Ten minutes later, they were in Thomas's study. Becca sat on the chair facing her father's desk, her back straight and hands clasped in her lap. Geoffrey stood behind her, his hand resting on the back of her chair. Thomas paced behind his desk, muttering to himself, his face beet-red. Finally, he spoke.

"How could you do this, girl?"

Becca opened her mouth to answer, but Geoffrey was faster.

"None of this is Rebecca's fault, Kingsley. I'm the one to blame."

Thomas swung his gaze to Geoffrey. "You couldn't keep your hands off her, could you? And now what?"

"Father, I …."

Geoffrey touched her shoulder, signaling her to remain silent. "I want to marry her, Kingsley. I hope you'll give us your blessing."

Thomas sank down into his chair and rubbed his hand over his face. "Why the hell not?" he grumbled. "You've ruined her. No one else will have her."

Becca sucked in a breath at her father's low opinion of her.

Geoffrey laughed without humor. "Yes. And I'm looking forward to becoming a member of your family, as well."

Thomas stiffened in his seat. "Never mind that. When will it be done?"

Geoffrey thought for a moment. Special license, proper clothes …. "I have some matters to attend to. Will three days be soon enough?"

"No banns." Thomas snorted. "No time. I suppose I'll have to pay for the license."

"No."

Thomas's eyes narrowed. He nodded, dismissing them. Geoffrey took Becca's hand and pulled her from the room. When they were out of her father's sight, he held her in a tight embrace and kissed her.

Becca stared up at him. "Three days?"

He nodded. "Yes, love. And don't fret. I'll take care of everything."

She blinked in confusion.

He laughed and kissed her again. He pulled back to look searchingly in her eyes. "We will be happy, Becca. You'll see."

Becca thought of something. "Where will we live? I never asked you where you make your home."

Geoffrey shook his head at her. She'd had too much upheaval in the past few days. He wouldn't reveal the truth of Kanewood and his earldom this morning. "In Northumberland, love. A long carriage ride, I fear."

"I see." She still wore a look of confusion.

He smiled. "All in good time, sweetheart. You shall know everything in three days' time."

* * * *

When Becca awoke the next morning, she was full of determination. While Geoffrey had assured her that he'd see to matters, which she took to mean seeing to the license and the like, there was still the matter of her wedding gown. The dresses she possessed were serviceable for the work she did at the inn, but she lacked even the simplest dancing gown. Perhaps she'd find something in the attic.

She was free from all of her duties at the inn from this day forward. Her father had told her the previous evening that she shouldn't work at the inn any longer. She was to be a married woman, he'd said, and her husband's responsibility. Becca thought she'd seen a tear in the man's eye as he'd dismissed her. He'd never been one to show emotion, not in the whole of her memory. Her heart twisted as she recalled every attempt she'd made to get close to him when she'd been growing up. Did he even love her? He'd thought to marry her off to Dr. Simon, for goodness sakes! Would he have regretted that? Although the answer was most likely no, she held on to the possibility that he did care for her. He was her father, after all.

She dressed and soon found herself in the attic of the inn, dust motes floating lazily around her in the sunlight streaming in through the small windows.

After sorting through quite a bit of accumulated frippery, she unearthed what looked like an ancient trunk. She tugged on it, dragging it farther into the light. It was leather-bound and of a good size. Becca squinted at the brass plate set close to the latch. Using a corner of her skirt, she rubbed the dust and grime from the plate. She brushed her loose curls back from her face, leaving more than a few smudges there, and peered at the plate. To her astonishment, it was engraved with one word: Raven. Confounded, she worked the latch free and lifted the lid. A bright smile lit her face as she spied the clothing within. Surely these were her mother's things!

After dismissing much of the trunk's contents, she found what she sought at the bottom, a gown of lace that she guessed had once been white. She gingerly lifted the garment free of the trunk and held it out in front of her. It was yellowed with age and the lace hung in tatters from the long sleeves. Nonetheless, she held the dress against herself and closed her eyes, reveling in the closeness she felt toward her mother in that moment. What had her mother thought before her own wedding? Had she been as nervous as Becca was? True, she didn't need her mother's advice about the marriage bed. A smile teased her lips. Geoffrey had taken care of any such maidenly ignorance on her part. Still, what would it be like to have a mother to confide in? To come to with dreams and hopes and promises? She took in a breath, drawing the scent of dust and neglect deep into her lungs. It was of no consequence. Her mother was dead and nothing could bring her back. Sighing, she set the dress aside and closed the trunk, pushing it back into the shadows where she'd found it.

Becca enlisted Mary's help and saw to the cleaning of the delicate gown. After soaking the lace for as long as they deemed safe, they carefully spread it on Becca's bed.

"It's of no use, Mary," Becca said sadly. "The yellow stains remain. And the lace …," she added, delicately fingering one sleeve. "It's all but a memory."

"Rebecca," Mary answered, "perhaps if we mend it, we …."

Becca shook her head, silencing the girl. "I'll have to wed Geoffrey in one of my muslin dresses. Perhaps we can find some lace and ribbons to adorn it?"

* * * *

Fields, Geoffrey's driver, returned from London two days later with the items Geoffrey had requested. That morning, Geoffrey himself had obtained a special license, so all was set in his mind. All but one thing. He went in search of his betrothed.

He found her down at the stables, handing the reins of her filly to the groom.

She turned to find Geoffrey standing behind her. "Geoffrey!"

"Becca!" he mimicked, hugging her tight.

He eased his hold and she quirked a smile at him. "What are you about?"

"I have a surprise for you, love. At the inn."

She studied him for a moment. With a shrug of her shoulders, she acquiesced. He grabbed her hand and all but dragged her from the stables and toward the inn, her hair flying out behind her. Without giving her a chance to catch her breath, he led her upstairs and opened her door, pushing her ahead of him. She spun to face him, her hands on her hips.

"Geoffrey," she said, arching an eyebrow. "Just where is this surprise?"

He led her over to a large wooden wardrobe. With a flourish, he pulled open one of the doors. Becca gasped, precisely the response he was hoping for. There, inside the wardrobe, were six new dresses. Below them sat shoes to match each one. He'd told Fields what colors to choose and the man did quite well. The dresses were in jewel tones: violet, emerald, bronze, gold, blue and rose, and well-suited to Becca's fair skin and dark hair.

She looked at Geoffrey, a question in her green eyes.

"They are yours, Becca," he said. "All yours."

"How did you …?"

He crossed his arms over his chest. "I have my ways."

She stared at him, her brow furrowed. He finally took pity on her.

"I had a bit of help," he explained. "Emmy appropriated one of your dresses and a pair of your shoes. My driver took them to London and found these for you. I hope they are to your liking."

"Oh, yes!" She came into his arms. "I love them. Thank you!"

He set her from him and gestured toward the chair near the window. On it sat a large box.

"And in that box you will find petticoats and undergarments. I daresay my driver must have been in quite a state having to pick them out."

"This is too much."

"Not for my bride." He turned her again to the wardrobe. "There's more, love."

"More?"

He nodded and pulled the other door wide open. There, filling the remaining space in the wardrobe, hung a creamy-white gown, trimmed with pearls, beads, and tiny satin bows. Matching slippers sat beneath it.

She let out a happy squeal. He barely had time to open his arms before she was hugging him again. “It’s so beautiful!”

“It’s your wedding gown, love,” he informed her. “I hope it will serve.”

She bowed her head. “You’ve noticed how ill-suited my dresses are, then.”

“I did.” He trailed his finger over the tight bodice of her day dress. “I daresay they don’t render you any less fetching.” He stroked her nipple through the muslin and she drew in a breath.

“What are you up to now?” She sighed at his sensual touch.

He walked to the door and shut it tight.

“You shouldn’t be in my room with the door closed. It isn’t proper.” She couldn’t help smiling at the roguish look on his face.

He pushed off the door, removed his coat, and tossed it on the chair near the window. “Ah, Becca. When I’m with you, being ‘proper’ is the last thing on my mind.”

He stopped in front of her, bringing his hands up to caress her shoulders. She stared up at him, her eyes dark, and he brushed her lips with his.

He pulled back and regarded her closely. “No,” he went on. “I don’t want to be ‘proper’ at all.”

“Really?” She breathed.

He began unbuttoning his shirt. “Really …. And, Becca?”

“Yes?”

“Neither do you.”

She went to him and proceeded to prove him right.

Chapter 8

"Rebecca," Mary said breathlessly. "You look like a princess."

Becca regarded herself in the mirror. The dress Geoffrey gave her was the prettiest thing she'd ever beheld and in it she truly felt like a bride. Geoffrey's bride. Her nerves, in a tangle since waking this morning, settled as she took a deep breath.

"I hardly recognize myself," she agreed.

A knock sounded at her door.

"Yes?" Becca called.

"Girl," Thomas boomed, "are you ready?"

"Yes, Father." She crossed to the door and pulled it open.

Thomas stood there, his mouth agape. "Rebecca," he said, using her name for the first time in years. "You look beautiful. Just like your mother."

Becca didn't know what to say to that. Moved by his words and the strange yet tender expression on his face, she stood on tiptoe and gave him a quick kiss on his cheek. "Thank you."

Thomas cleared his throat and took a halting step back. "Well, let's get going. Kane isn't going to wait forever."

He crooked his arm, Becca placed her hand on his elbow, and he led her to the top of the stairs. They descended slowly, coming to a stop at the entrance to the elegant little parlor.

Geoffrey was standing there, so dashing in his black formal wear and white cravat. Her father led her to Geoffrey's side and put her hand in his. He left her to stand beside Peter Jenkins. He and Emmy were the only guests present for the ceremony, but well-wishers would come afterward to join them for the celebration to be held in the inn's dining room.

Geoffrey bent his head to Becca's. "You look incredible, love," he whispered.

She drank him in with her eyes. "You look so handsome," she answered softly.

He flashed her a dazzling smile and turned her to face the minister. Reverend Grey began the ceremony. When he recited Geoffrey's full title during the exchange of vows, Becca went still. It couldn't be! The minister had to repeat the words to elicit a response from her.

"Rebecca Kingsley, do you take Lord Geoffrey Michael Kane, the Earl of Kanewood, Viscount Darlington …."

Geoffrey was an earl? She stared at him, taking in his ordinary clothes and open countenance. No. There was nothing ordinary about Geoffrey. He was clever, and handsome, and he made her laugh. He made her dream.

"Becca?" Geoffrey asked, his voice soft yet holding a note of worry.

She looked at him and saw that certainty once again. She nodded and whispered her vows. The rest of the ceremony was a blur. Geoffrey accepted her, promised to honor and cherish her, and turned to her expectantly. She blinked up at him, confused. He smiled then and bent his head to hers. He kissed her tenderly, sealing their union. Peter and Emmy clapped enthusiastically.

Thomas stood perfectly still, shock clear on his flushed face. "An earl?"

A short while later, Geoffrey and Becca stood together, greeting the wedding guests. Word of Geoffrey's title spread quickly.

"Congratulations, Lord Kanewood," those gathered said. "Lady Kanewood."

Becca blinked as people she'd known her entire life used her new title. Geoffrey was an earl? He never should have married her. She'd do something to embarrass him and make him regret their hasty marriage. Her heart twisted at that thought.

Geoffrey leaned toward her. "Whatever is the matter, Becca?"

"Nothing, Geoff … my lord … I'm sorry, I don't know what to call you."

He smiled down at her. “Geoffrey, love. Just call me Geoffrey.”

She relaxed then, seeing once more the Geoffrey she’d known before learning of his title.

Her lips curved in a small smile. “Geoffrey.” She breathed.

The feast the cook had spent the last two days preparing was served in the dining room. Becca and Geoffrey, however, planned to take their wedding supper in the privacy of his room. With expressions of gratitude to the wedding guests, they ascended the stairs.

A small table had been set up in the room. It was beautifully set, with the candle glow reflecting off the fine china. Geoffrey pulled Becca’s chair out for her and she sat. He took the chair opposite her and reached for her hand. She felt his fingers grasp hers and kept her eyes downcast.

“What is it?”

She looked at him then, her eyes stinging. “You never should have married me. You’re an earl and I’m—”

“You’re the woman I wanted to marry. That hasn’t changed.” He stared at her for a long moment. “Don’t you believe me?”

She looked deeply into his eyes again and saw his sincerity. He’d been so sure, even as she’d wavered. From the beginning, he’d been set on making her his wife. She would borrow a bit of his confidence and believe him. Believe in herself. She smiled then, and nodded. His eyes bright, he brought her hand to his lips. They set about their wedding supper, pausing every now and then to touch or kiss.

With their meal only half-finished, Geoffrey stood. He pulled Becca up from her seat, a wicked smile on his face, and Becca’s heart raced. He wrapped her in his arms, bending his head to capture her lips. She opened up for him, welcoming his probing tongue. He groaned softly, running his fingers through her hair. Pins scattered everywhere, her thick locks loose and free.

He pulled back, running his gaze over her face. “My God, Becca,” he said in a low voice. “You’re so beautiful. And you’re mine.”

Her breath caught at the possessive gleam in his blue eyes. He kissed her again, running his hands over her back. She reached up, twining her fingers in the thick waves at the nape of his neck. He couldn't manage to unfasten the hooks of her gown. He gave a playful growl, nibbling on her ear.

"Let us ready for bed, wife," he said, his breath hot on her skin.

She nodded, leaving the circle of his arms to step behind the privacy screen. There she found a beautiful nightgown of lawn with delicate flowers embroidered around the scooped neck. She managed to unhook the back of her gown and carefully set it aside. The unfamiliar stays were a bit of a challenge, but she persevered. She slipped the filmy nightgown over her head, smoothing it down. Her breath caught as her fingers brushed over her breasts. She could hardly wait for Geoffrey to touch her. She ran the brush quickly through her hair and stepped out from behind the screen.

Geoffrey had already undressed. He sat waiting for her in the bed, the sheets down around his waist. He crooked a finger at her. "Come here, wife."

She climbed into the bed and into his outstretched arms. He kissed her deeply, caressing her through the thin fabric. She rubbed against him, a soft moan escaping her lips. She pulled away from him to kneel on the bed. He looked at her, confused. She smiled and pulled her nightgown up over her head. Geoffrey swore softly and rose to his knees, embracing her.

He ran his lips over her face, her throat. He cupped her breasts, his thumbs brushing across her nipples. She leaned back, reveling in the sensation. He lowered her to the bed, his mouth taking over for his hands. She arched as he teethed a taut nipple, moaning his name. He trailed hot kisses down the front of her, pausing to flick his tongue in her navel. She breathed in sharply.

She opened her legs to him. His fingers caressed her, making her wet. His head went lower, kissing the very center of her.

"Geoffrey!" She gasped, shocked. "You can't!"

He paused, dropping a kiss on her belly. "I can."

His mouth claimed her again. Passion blazed through her and she fell back, wanting more. His tongue drove her mad. Her climax startled her and she shuddered, crying his name. He came up to kiss her and before she stopped trembling, he entered her. He thrust into her deeply, again and again, until she tightened around him. She clung to him and found her second release. With one final thrust, he climaxed.

He stayed inside her, cupping her face in his hands as he waited for his breathing to slow. "Did you like that, sweetheart?" he asked softly.

Her eyes fluttered open. "Oh, yes."

He smiled and rolled off her, bringing her with him to lay against his side. "There are so many ways to make love, Becca."

"I know."

He froze. "How do you know?" he asked sharply, a fierce frown on his face.

She picked up her head to look at him. "You told me."

"I did? When?"

"The night I helped you into bed," she said. "The night before Mary found me in your room."

He smiled. "And did I show you that night?"

"No," she said, laughing. "You fell asleep."

He placed a hand over his eyes and groaned. "I'm never drinking ale again."

He removed his hand from his face and flashed a dazzling smile at her. His eyes sparkled merrily.

She gazed at him, her heart fluttering. "I love you."

His smile left his face. "What did you say?"

Becca hadn't planned on saying it, but it was true. There was no taking it back. "I love you."

He sat up, startling her. He held her at arm's length and studied her face. She couldn't begin to guess what he was looking for, but the look in his eyes was intense.

"Do you mean it, Becca?"

"Yes."

He pulled her to him and kissed her soundly. He didn't say the words back to her but when he began to make love to her again, she knew her declaration had been important to him.

* * * *

Geoffrey was the first to awaken and set about readying for their departure. After dressing, he called to Becca before he left the chamber. “Do you think Mary would like to be your lady’s maid? It would be nice for you to have someone familiar at Kanewood.”

Becca peeped around the screen. “That would be wonderful! I could use her help with these stays, at the very least.”

“Consider it done, then. I’ll speak to Mary and your father.”

The maid was eager to follow her friend, now her mistress, to Kanewood and went to pack her things and help Becca as Geoffrey sought out Thomas in his office.

The older man stood as he entered the room. “My dear Lord Kanewood!” he said in a booming voice. “Good morning, my lord.”

Geoffrey arched an eyebrow. “Good morning, Kingsley.” He lowered himself into the chair facing the man’s desk. “I wanted to inform you that Mary will be joining us at Kanewood in a few days. She’s to be Rebecca’s lady’s maid.”

Thomas nodded vigorously and took his own chair. “Fine, fine. Anything for my daughter.” His eyes narrowed. “She’s well worth it, wouldn’t you say?”

Geoffrey leaned forward with narrowed eyes. “What are you getting at?”

Thomas stood again and folded his hands across his wide middle, a smug look on his face. “As you know, Dr. Simon was prepared to pay to wed Rebecca.”

“Yes,” Geoffrey answered in a low voice.

“It seems to me your being an earl and all, that you would be able to pay a bit more.”

Geoffrey stood. “You won’t sell your daughter to me, Kingsley. I married Rebecca because I wished to. The very same reason she married me.”

Thomas gave an ugly laugh. “She married you because you took her to your bed.”

Geoffrey's hands were fisted at his sides. "Don't speak of my wife in that manner."

Thomas went on. "Because of you the girl was ruined, along with my plans for her. I think I should be compensated."

"I can't believe your gall and lack of regard for your daughter. I won't dignify your suggestion with a reply. Rebecca is worth more than any man could ever pay. It's a shame you will never see that."

He turned to leave when Thomas's voice stopped him cold.

"You'd better keep her close, Kane. Otherwise, the girl might turn out like her mother."

Geoffrey turned slowly to face him. "I don't understand."

Thomas curled his lip. "Her mother was nothing more than a common trollop."

"What?"

"I cared for Rebecca as best I could. Did my best to keep the men from sniffing around her skirts, too. You're welcome to the trouble now. Take her. Take her and mark my words!"

Geoffrey smashed his fist in Thomas's face, sending the man sprawling. Without another word, he turned and left.

How could a man place so little value on his own daughter? Just like her mother, the man had said. Would Becca prove to be unfaithful? He'd never give her the chance to stray as Patricia had.

And if any man dared to touch her, he'd kill him.

He'd calmed by the time he reached Becca's old room. The servants carried her few trunks down to Geoffrey's waiting carriage, leaving them alone in her room.

He held her close, brushing his lips against her hair. "Ah, Becca."

"What is it?"

He shook his head, pulled back, and took her hand. "Let's be on our way, love."

As they reached the drive in front of the inn, they found Thomas standing there rubbing his jaw.

"Father, what happened to your face?" Becca asked, her eyes round.

Thomas fixed a dark scowl at Geoffrey and turned to Becca.

"It's nothing, girl. Just slipped. I trust I'll see you sometime?"

He directed that particular question to Geoffrey, who nodded curtly. "We'll stop at the inn on our way to London in a few weeks' time." He assisted Becca into his carriage and turned to Thomas before boarding. "Never mention what transpired in your office, Kingsley."

He boarded and signaled for the driver, closing the door on Becca's father and her past at the Raven's Inn.

Chapter 9

Although the interior of the carriage was spacious, Geoffrey sat close to Becca, his long legs stretched toward the opposite seat. He looked so noble in his fine clothes. His elevated status struck her square in the face.

"Geoffrey, what will your family think of me?"

He smiled at her. "You are my countess, Becca. They'll accept you."

"I'll try to be what you need in a wife."

His eyes sparkled. "You are precisely what I need in a wife."

She flushed and ran her hands over the skirt of her dress. She'd chosen the violet one with Mary's assistance. "At least I look the part. Thank you again for the dresses."

"It's nothing, love." He studied her for a moment. "When did you know that you loved me?"

She was struck by the vulnerability in his eyes. "I don't know precisely. But I thought I might that morning in your room."

"Ah .... When Mary found us?"

She shook her head. "No. The morning I came to your room when you were sleeping."

Remembrance dawned on him, a sweet recollection of that first morning when she'd stolen into his room and stood hesitantly over his bed. He'd been afraid to breathe, certain she would vanish once he fully awoke. She hadn't. No, she'd leaned over. She'd come closer.

"When you kissed me ...," he now leaned closer to her, "like this?"

He brushed her lips lightly, then crushed his mouth down on hers. He pressed her to him, moving his mouth to the side of her neck. He caressed her breasts through her dress and she arched toward him, straining for his touch.

"Husband?" she asked softly.

"Yes, love?" he answered, his breath hot on her skin.

"Forget yourself," she whispered.

"What?"

"Don't remove your boots. I can't bear to wait."

Grinning broadly, he happily honored his wife's request.

* * * *

The carriage rolled on as they collected themselves and again sat on the cushioned seat. She brushed at the skirt of her new dress. "Look at these wrinkles! What will your family think?"

Geoffrey smiled. "Don't worry. After a long trip in a carriage, wrinkles are to be expected."

"They are?" she sounded skeptical.

"Speaking of dresses," he added, changing the subject, "we shall have the dressmaker ready some gowns for you."

"Gowns?"

"Yes, love. We'll be expected to throw a ball celebrating our marriage."

A ball? How would she host such an event? "I've never been to a ball, much less hosted one."

"Surely Raven's Inn hosted parties now and again," he said.

"Yes," she admitted, embarrassed once again by the menial role she'd played at the inn. Her father never allowed her to attend, let alone preside over such gatherings. He always told her it was for her own protection. To keep her safe from unwanted advances. But it made her feel as though he were ashamed of her.

"Don't fret. My mother possesses vast experience at throwing the most wonderful bashes. I'm most certain she'd be very pleased to take over the task, tutoring you in the process."

"Do you think so? I so want your mother to like me."

He took her hands in his. "How could anyone not like you?"

She felt a flush creep over her cheeks and dipped her head. "Tell me about your mother."

Geoffrey leaned back, still holding her hand. "Well, my father passed away two years ago, so her mourning period is over. Lady Margaret loved him dearly, but she's enjoying getting out again," he said. "You'll like her, Becca. You're a lot like her. You both have hearts as big as the ocean." He paused, a half-smile on his lips. "I daresay she dotes on me shamelessly."

Becca stroked his cheek. "Who could blame her?"

He kissed her hand and settled back against the seat.

"What of the rest of your family?" she asked.

"My brother, John, and his wife live at Kanewood, as well. John is one year younger than me, twenty-seven. They have a little girl, Ann. She's three years old. John and Patricia are constantly out and about, at one function or another. They rarely see her." He was quiet for a moment.

Becca could feel the tension in Geoffrey when he spoke of his brother and sister-in-law. She wondered what was behind it. "Will they be at Kanewood now?"

Geoffrey shook his head. "No. They're in London for the Season. The child remains at Kanewood."

"Well, I am definitely looking forward to meeting your mother and little Ann." She beamed at him.

He turned to her and couldn't help but return her smile. "They're going to love you, just like I …."

"Just like you … what, Geoffrey?" she asked hesitantly.

"Just like I know they will." He cleared his throat, uncomfortable with the direction of the conversation.

She sensed his unease. For a moment, she thought he was going to tell her he loved her. After all, she had already declared her love for him. Perhaps it was too soon. She would be patient. For now.

"Will we join your brother and his wife in London, then?" she inquired, changing the subject.

"I doubt we'll see them. But I'm looking forward to showing off my beautiful wife to the rest of the ton. The dressmaker had better get busy if you're to have gowns befitting your beauty."

Becca blushed at his ridiculous statement, but it served to

turn the attention from the discussion of his brother and sister-in-law. If Geoffrey's demeanor toward them was any indication, she was very pleased she wouldn't have to make their acquaintence any time soon.

They stopped at an inn to rest and arrived at Kanewood the next afternoon. Becca stared out the window in awe as they approached the great house. It sat on the rise of a crest, overlooking lushly verdant grounds and neat little cottages. A long winding road led up to the wide cobblestone drive, directly in front of the estate. It was an impressive structure, of gray stone with a slate roof. The roof was peaked, and many gables protruded from the central structure. Becca couldn't count all of the windows peeking out of the stone face of the building.

Geoffrey turned to her. "Welcome home, Becca."

"My goodness." She breathed. "It's magnificent."

He smiled at her and kissed her lightly. The carriage rolled to a stop and Geoffrey alighted. He assisted Becca down and escorted her to the wide carved door at the front entrance. He rapped sharply on the door and, as it was being opened, he swept Becca up into his arms.

"Geoffrey!" A gasp of laughter escaped her as she clutched his shoulders.

He carried her through the door and into the marble-tiled foyer, his deep laughter echoing through the cavernous space. His mother—Lady Margaret, Becca recalled—came out of the front parlor just as he set Becca on her feet.

"Geoffrey, I didn't expect you today." Lady Margaret eyed Becca with interest. "And whom do we have here?"

Geoffrey kissed his mother on the cheek and turned to take Becca's hand. "Mother, this is Rebecca. My wife."

Lady Margaret blinked in surprise but said nothing.

Becca curtsied to her in greeting. "I'm very pleased to meet you, Lady Margaret."

Lady Margaret returned the greeting with a nod, a small smile on her face. Becca noticed a marked resemblance between Geoffrey and his mother, and felt drawn to the woman. Her eyes were the same brilliant blue as her son's, and her hair was the same tawny shade, albeit streaked with gray. She had an elegant bearing, and Becca so wished to earn the woman's favor. Without Mary to assist her, she'd chosen to wear her violet gown from yesterday's travel and felt decidedly rumpled.

"And when did all this take place?" Lady Margaret asked.

"Yesterday afternoon, Mother. Reverend Grey performed the ceremony."

Lady Margaret nodded at that news. "Rebecca, why don't you go upstairs and refresh yourself? The butler will show you to Geoffrey's rooms."

Relief threatened to swamp Becca. "That would be lovely, Lady Margaret. Thank you."

Geoffrey kissed Becca's cheek and told her that he'd see her personal effects sent up. Becca nodded to the two of them and started up the sweeping staircase.

"Was it a rough journey, dear?"

"Not particularly, Mother," Becca heard him reply. "Why do you ask?"

"Your wife's dress seems quite wrinkled."

Becca froze, turning to fix a glare at her husband.

He returned her stare with a crooked smile. "Well, Mother. I suppose you could say the trip wasn't without incident."

Becca gasped and hurried up the stairs. His laughter followed her.

* * * *

"Geoffrey, do join me in the parlor?" his mother asked.

He nodded and waved her ahead of him into the elegant room just off the foyer. Geoffrey closed the paneled doors and crossed to one of two settees upholstered in gold damask. He took a seat opposite his mother and looked at her expectantly. "Isn't Rebecca wonderful?"

Lady Margaret smiled. "Yes, she's lovely. Though I am surprised at your announcement, to say the least."

"It was quite unexpected, I'll admit."

"Who is she? Where is she from?"

"I trust you received my letter regarding my mishap enroute from London?"

At her nod, he continued, "Well, I met Rebecca at an inn nearby."

"An inn?"

"It isn't what you think, Mother. Rebecca's father owns the Raven's Inn, and it's quite an elegant establishment."

"But, Geoffrey, an innkeeper's daughter?"

Geoffrey met her gaze evenly. "Rebecca's grandfather was a baronet if that remote title pleases you. You'll remember that the girl with whom I was last involved was from an excellent family with impeccable lineage. You undoubtedly recall how nasty that turned out."

"I admit Patricia isn't a favorite of mine." She furrowed her brow. "But you've known this girl for such a short time."

"And everything I know about her, I admire. Her father …." He shook his head. It wouldn't do for his mother to learn how Becca's sire had treated her. His own father had been kind and loving, and there was no doubt she would find it appalling. "Becca is more than an innkeeper's daughter to me."

She smiled and leaned forward. "Tell me about your Rebecca, then."

"Oh, Mother, she's everything one could ever want in a wife. She's beautiful, as you can plainly see. But she's so much more than that. She's sweet, and kind, and …."

"And what?"

"She loves me."

"And do you love her?"

He frowned over her question. "I care for her. More than I have ever cared for anyone," he said. "Love? I thought I had loved Patricia and recall how that turned out."

"Well, I can't remember the last time you wore such a smile. If Rebecca put it there, I already love her for that."

* * * *

That evening, Becca readied herself for bed. She'd unpacked her few belongings herself, hanging her treasured dresses in a wardrobe the servants had moved into a small room adjacent to Geoffrey's sleeping chamber. Geoffrey had instructed them to move a mirror-topped vanity into the chamber and Becca now sat before it. The beautiful room she was to share with her new husband was reflected in the mirror's oval surface.

The room was decorated in masculine colors—brown, green and burgundy. The furniture was heavy and large in proportion. A huge four-poster bed dominated the chamber, its thick draperies tied back. A large fireplace took up the wall opposite, flanked by two wing chairs. A dressing room separate from Becca's held Geoffrey's wardrobe. He walked out of this room and into the sleeping chamber, clad in only his breeches.

Becca slowly ran the brush through her curls. She wore a nightgown much like the one from London, with a matching wrapper. The thin material hugged her curves and she watched as his eyes darkened.

"Geoffrey."

He crossed to her and bent his head to hers. "Come to bed, wife."

"Wife," she marveled aloud. She laid her brush on the vanity and turned to him. "Yes, husband. I'm quite tired."

"How I love to hear you call me that." He pulled her to her feet, cupping her face in his hands. "You're not too tired, I hope?"

"Never."

He placed his lips on hers, rubbing gently. Her fingers stole up behind his neck as he untied her wrapper and nudged it off her shoulders. She felt the heat of him through her thin gown and her nipples hardened. She rubbed against him and he moaned.

"Take me to bed, husband." She breathed.

The softly spoken request spurred him on. He swept her up into his arms and carried her to the big four-poster. He laid her in the middle of the bed and she felt she could get lost in it. He peeled off his breeches and climbed in beside her. He closed his mouth over her nipple through her gown as he'd done that night she'd helped him into bed.

"Oh, that makes me feel so—"

He lifted his head and grinned. "So—what, my darling?" He found her other nipple and nibbled at it.

"So—good!" She gasped as she felt him cup both her breasts, squeezing them gently.

He relieved her of the garment and bent his head once more. He teased her, running his open mouth over her breasts until she cried out for him to cease tormenting her.

With a sensual laugh, he came up and kissed her. He rolled over on the bed, taking her with him. She lay halfway across his chest and suddenly became the aggressor. She moved to place wet kisses on his throat, his chest.

Becca wanted to kiss him everywhere, as he'd kissed her. Her fingers moved down his belly to gently grasp his manhood. He groaned, telling her he liked what she was doing. Emboldened, she took him in her mouth and he nearly came off the bed.

"God, Becca!"

She licked him gently and felt him quiver. She closed her mouth over the tip, liking the salty taste of him. With a loud growl, he pulled her up and held her tightly.

"You don't like that?" she asked.

He breathed out raggedly. "I like it too much."

"Why, then?"

"If you went on, love, it would have been all over."

She brought her lips to his and he kissed her with all the passion she'd aroused. She lay fully on him and rubbed against his arousal. He nudged her legs apart and his fingers moved between their bodies. He stroked her and she arched against him, craving more. She felt the tip of his arousal near her center.

"What are you—"

"Take me inside, love," he gently instructed.

"I don't know …."

He lifted her gently. "Lean back."

She did, and felt him enter her fully. She gasped. It felt wonderful!

He held on to her hips and thrust up into her. She threw her head back and rode him. The pressure was almost too much to bear. She climaxed, crying his name, as he found his release, shouting hers.

She collapsed against his chest and he gently stroked her

back. “Tell me, Becca.”

She lifted her head and saw the need in his eyes, need that went beyond the one they’d just satisfied. “I love you, Geoffrey.”

He hugged her tight and they soon fell asleep wrapped in each other’s arms.

Chapter 10

The next day, Lady Margaret took charge. She summoned the dressmaker to Kanewood and by late morning Becca stood perched on a stool in her and Geoffrey's chamber. She wore her chemise, stays, and petticoat and held her arms straight out. As the dressmaker measured and pinched and pinned, draping fabric after fabric over her, Becca sighed and endured it until Lady Margaret finally waved the woman out of the room.

"I admit I was surprised to learn of your marriage," the woman said.

Becca stiffened. What had Geoffrey told her? That she'd given herself to him before the wedding? Of the horrid plans her father had for her future before Geoffrey intervened?

"Geoffrey was persistent," she said softly.

Lady Margaret tilted her head to the side. "He swept you off your feet," she stated.

Becca nodded. "Yes. I didn't know about his title, otherwise I would have insisted he reconsider."

"Reconsider?" Lady Margaret smiled then. "I know my son, dear. He wanted to make you his wife and there would be no argument on the matter. I daresay he can be very convincing."

Becca flushed as she recalled all the many ways he convinced her of his intent and passion. "Yes."

She studied Becca for a long moment. What did she see? Could she tell Becca was in love with her very determined son?

A warmth stole into the lady's eyes, and Becca felt it like an embrace. "He is very much like his father, you know."

Becca knew then that his mother had loved the late earl very much. Her throat tight, she simply nodded at the disclosure.

"Well," Lady Margaret said with a sharp nod. "You'll need quite an extensive wardrobe, Rebecca, if you're to attend the important gatherings in London."

She didn't begrudge the lady her generosity or her guidance. She saw another spark in her blue eyes, one of maternal concern, and her heart swelled. "Yes, Lady Margaret. I appreciate your assistance. I'm woefully unaware of the latest fashions, I fear."

The older woman smiled. "You'll look lovely in any gown, regardless of fashion."

Becca blushed at the praise.

"I agree," Geoffrey said from the doorway, startling them both. "You look perfect in what you're wearing right now."

"Geoffrey!" Becca exclaimed, covering herself with her arms.

He rounded his eyes in mock-innocence. "Am I intruding?"

To her credit, Lady Margaret held her composure until she left the room, but Becca had seen the hint of a smile on her face.

Geoffrey placed his hands on her waist and helped her down. "I have to ride the estate this afternoon, love."

"May I accompany you?" she asked.

"I'm afraid not. There are a few repairs I need to see to. You would be terribly bored."

"I could never be bored with you."

He hugged her to him, kissing her lightly. "You would distract me from my duties, wife. I'll be back much more quickly if I go alone. We'll ride together soon so I can introduce the tenants to the new countess."

Countess. Again the reality of her new role struck her. "I'll gladly wait."

He rubbed her shoulders, then her arms. "Why don't you get dressed and we'll go down to the dining room?"

"I can't get dressed if you keep untying my stays." She grabbed his hands to still them.

"Hmm?" he mumbled against her throat.

"Geoffrey!"

With an exaggerated sigh, he left her to get dressed.

* * * *

That afternoon, while Geoffrey attended to business on the estate, Becca and Lady Margaret shared tea in the parlor.

"Rebecca," she asked when they were nearly finished, "would you like to see more of the house?"

"I would indeed, but would you accompany me? I'm afraid I might get hopelessly lost."

The older woman laughed. "My son would never forgive me if I lost his wife."

Becca smiled at Lady Margaret and followed her through the main floor of the house. They toured the salon, the sitting rooms, and the grand ballroom.

"When the Season is over, we'll host a ball to celebrate your nuptials," Lady Margaret said.

"Will you help me? Geoffrey said how gifted you are with such arrangements."

The lady's eyes sparkled. "Certainly. I can't think of anything more pleasurable." She waved Becca ahead of her out of the ballroom. "Let's go abovestairs."

As they ascended the grand staircase, Lady Margaret informed Becca of the history of some of the past residents of the house. Her eyes misted a bit as she spoke of her late husband and Becca's affection for the woman grew.

When they reached the top of the staircase, Lady Margaret waved in the direction of the main hallway. "The guest rooms are here."

Becca glanced farther down the hallway toward her and Geoffrey's chambers. She'd explored that part of the house, finding Geoffrey's study, a small reading room and a sitting room. "I'm a bit familiar with Geoffrey's rooms."

"They are your rooms too, dear." Lady Margaret led her in the opposite direction. "John and Patricia's rooms are at the far end of this hallway. The nursery is set abovestairs. Would you like to meet my granddaughter?"

"I would love to."

The nursery abovestairs was bright and airy. The child's nanny was present when they arrived, a gray-haired woman with warm brown eyes and a kind expression.

She greeted Lady Margaret and Becca with a curtsy. "Good

afternoon, my lady. Lady Kanewood."

"Good afternoon, Mrs. Riley," Lady Margaret said. "Is Ann awake?"

"Yes, my lady. She awoke from her nap just a short while ago. She's in the playroom."

They proceeded to the playroom and found the little blond-haired girl amid a pile of blocks. She didn't notice them when they first walked in, so intent on the tiny tower she was trying to construct. She placed a block on top of her creation, which stood five blocks tall, and clapped her hands with glee.

She turned then and noticed Lady Margaret. "Grandmother!" she squealed, a big grin on her face.

Lady Margaret held her arms out to the little girl and Ann flew into them. She soon noticed Becca and stared at her with wide gray eyes.

Becca crouched down to her level. "Hello."

"Ann, this is your Aunt Rebecca. She's married to your Uncle Geoffrey."

Ann nodded solemnly, her gaze not leaving Becca's face. Suddenly, her hand shot out, lightly stroking a curl near Becca's cheek. "Pretty."

"Thank you," Becca said.

Ann grabbed Becca's hand. "Come see my blocks."

Becca nodded and let the little girl lead her to the chaos on the floor.

"I trust you can find your way back down, Rebecca?" Lady Margaret asked.

"I'll persevere." She laughed. "Thank you for the tour."

"You're quite welcome, dear. I'll see you downstairs, then."

Becca passed a pleasant hour or so with the little girl, finally taking her own leave to ready herself for dinner. Ann made Becca promise to return to play another day. It was a promise Becca was happy to make. How she longed to remember something of her own mother, of her time at the inn before her death. Had they played and cuddled as she had with Ann?

A memory teased her as she walked back to her room, as dusty and tattered as her mother's wedding dress—her mother holding her close in the dark, whispering sweet words in her ear. For some reason, the recollection filled her with a chill. It was as if the words felt like a sad farewell.

* * * *

A few days passed and Becca's fondness for both Kanewood and her mother-in-law grew. She made frequent visits to Ann in the nursery abovestairs. She so enjoyed playing with the little girl. It was a pity the child's mother wasn't at Kanewood. She knew what it was like to miss her own mother at that age. Once again, she felt the loss keenly. No child should have to experience such a thing. Being with Ann also spoke to a part of her she'd never dared dream about. A longing for her mother, yes. But also the yearning for a child of her own.

What kind of father would Geoffrey be? Would he be like his own father—loving and caring, or like her father—distant and aloof? She wanted him to love their children as much as she would. But he hadn't told her he loved her yet. Would this bode ill for building a family together?

Geoffrey was very busy, and told her he wished to make up for time lost while he was waylaid at Raven's. His occupation suited Becca on this particular day, as she had yet another fitting for her new wardrobe.

She stood on the stool as before. As Lady Margaret looked on, Becca tried on a few of the nearly-complete gowns and dresses. Mary assisted her, having arrived at Kanewood the previous afternoon. She seemed to take to her position, assisting Becca with the dresses, careful of the many pins holding bits and pieces of them in place.

The last fitting of the day was for the gown Becca would wear to their first ball in London. It was blush pink, the color nearly matching Becca's skin tone. At first glance, she appeared to be wearing nothing at all. At second glance, however, one was aware of the daring bodice dipping low to reveal much more of her bosom than Becca was accustomed to. As the dressmaker stood back and admired her creation, Becca glanced in the cheval glass.

"Lady Margaret, this dress is indecent!" She gasped.

Lady Margaret smiled. "Indecent would be one word for it. I prefer 'breathtaking.'"

Becca looked into the mirror again. "What will Geoffrey say?"

"I daresay he won't be able to say a word, dear. I think it's wise to keep my son on his toes, Rebecca. I predict you'll take London by storm."

Becca just nodded. She wasn't sure of that, but it was worth the inconvenience of these fittings to make certain she didn't embarrass her husband or her mother-in-law.

Lady Margaret escorted the dressmaker out of the chamber, leaving Mary to assist Becca out of the gorgeous gown.

"Are you settling in, Mary?" Becca asked.

"Oh, yes, my lady." Mary carefully hung the gown with the others. She returned with a rose-colored dress, one of the gifts from Geoffrey.

Becca stepped into the dress. "How are your quarters?"

"Quite fine. Larger than at the Raven's. And so many servants to talk to! It's so very pleasant."

"I'm glad, Mary. I'm so pleased you're here."

Mary nodded, twitching the curls at the nape of Becca's neck. "Are you in need of anything else, my lady?"

"I think not. I believe I'll find my husband and—"

"And what?" Geoffrey said.

Mary bowed her head to them both and took her leave.

Becca crossed to him. "Geoffrey."

Geoffrey kissed her and cupped her cheek. "Good afternoon, Becca."

"I missed you at lunch."

"I ate at one of the cottages." He took her hands in his. "I have a surprise for you."

She noted the twinkle in his eyes, and smiled up at him. "I fear you will spoil me."

"Never, sweetheart. Come," he urged. "It's down at the stables."

"Stables?"

He hurried her down the stairs, obviously intent on his

surprise. They soon arrived at the stables, her breath coming fast. “Geoffrey,” she gasped, “what is it that we must hurry so?”

“I simply couldn’t wait to see your beautiful face when you saw this.”

He stopped in front of one of the stalls, waving his hand. Her horse from Raven’s stood inside, as content as if born there.

“My filly!” she cried. “How did you do it?”

“I had my driver retrieve the horse when he went back for Mary.”

Becca cooed to the horse, stroking its shining mane.

“I thought we could go riding tomorrow.”

She turned to him. “Could we?”

He gathered her in his arms. “Yes, love. I have the entire day free. I thought we could picnic?”

She hugged him tight. “That would be wonderful.”

Geoffrey tilted her chin and captured her lips with his. She parted them for him, reaching up behind his neck. His tongue swept into her mouth, firing their passion.

“Ah, Becca.” He breathed raggedly.

“Husband, we can’t.”

He remembered himself and dragged his mouth back to her lips. He kissed her once and rested his forehead on hers.

“I very nearly wrinkled another one of your pretty dresses, wife.”

Becca sighed as he freed her from his grasp, brushing her hands over her skirt. Lord, the man could make her forget herself.

He took her hand. “Let’s return to the house.”

* * * *

Meanwhile, Lady Margaret shared tea with her son John and his wife.

“I didn’t expect you back from London so soon, John,” Lady Margaret said.

“We grew tiresome with the company, I fear,” Patricia answered for her husband. The blonde, fashionably pale woman sat on the settee, her cup and saucer in her slender hands. “We trust you are in good health?"

"Yes. We've had some excitement here at Kanewood," Lady Margaret said.

"Oh?" John stood at the window, which afforded a partial view of the stables. He narrowed his eyes at the couple emerging. "Who is that with the esteemed earl, Mother?"

Lady Margaret stood and crossed to the window to stand beside John. "That, John, is the new Countess of Kanewood."

John blinked at her. "What?"

Patricia stood and squeezed close to John to peer through the window. "Hmm."

"Your brother has taken a wife," Lady Margaret said.

John watched Geoffrey and Becca come up the path. Their hands were clasped, his head bent to hers as they strolled. His big brother's smile was clear from where they stood. How interesting.

"A wife?" Patricia asked. A frown marred her face. "Kane?"

John simply stared. "She's gorgeous."

Patricia snorted.

A few moments later, Geoffrey strode into the parlor with Becca in tow. He stopped short at the sight of John and Patricia.

"John." He offered his hand in greeting. "We didn't expect you back so soon."

John came forward and took it, smiling. "So Mother also said. Good to see you, Kane."

John looked at the girl beside him, running his gaze over her. Her hair was tousled, her cheeks flushed. And her figure! She was incredible.

"And who is this lovely creature?" John asked.

Geoffrey placed his arm around her shoulders in a show of possession. Wise man, his big brother. At long last he's learned to keep his woman close.

"This is Rebecca," he stated. "My wife." He turned to Becca. "Becca, let me introduce my brother, John, and his wife, Patricia."

"I'm very pleased to meet you," Becca said, inclining her head.

"Rebecca. Have you been in London this Season?" Patricia asked sharply. "Where did Geoffrey meet you?" She turned to Geoffrey. "Marriage, Kane? I never would have thought it of you."

Geoffrey's eyes narrowed. He nodded curtly and turned back to his wife. "Sweetheart, let us ready for dinner."

With a nod to the company, Geoffrey led Becca from the room.

"A wife." Patricia sniffed.

John went to the doorway of the parlor and watched Becca as she climbed the stairs beside his brother. "Indeed."

* * * *

When they reached their rooms, Becca turned to Geoffrey. "You don't care for them, do you?"

He laughed, apparently at her choice of words. "No, love. Not overmuch."

"Why not?"

A strange expression crossed his face, one of regret and discomfort. "I suppose you have the right to know the whole of it." He obviously didn't want to tell her. Had he been involved with Patricia before she married his brother?

He sat in a chair beside the fireplace, pulling her down onto his lap. He told her all of it, from his engagement to Patricia to John's betrayal. How could his brother do such a thing? And however could Patricia betray the man she'd promised to marry?

"Did you … care for her, then?" She couldn't bear to know that he'd loved her.

"I thought I did." He shot her a look of worry. "We were never intimate, love, if that was what you were wondering."

She had worried about that! To think he had shared his extraordinary passion with the cold Patricia was something she could not bear. She nodded, relief washing over her. She leaned on his shoulder. "I'm sorry they hurt you."

He smiled down at her. "I'm not, sweetheart. For if I had married her, I never would have found you."

She kissed him and settled back against him. Her heart clenched for what she'd almost lost with him.

"Tell me again," he said softly.

"I …."

"I need to hear the words," he insisted, nuzzling her throat.

"I love you," she admitted on a whisper.

He did not say the words back to her. She hadn't expected them, yet she longed for them just the same.

They sat for a while, finally rousing themselves to get ready for dinner.

Chapter 11

Dinner was a tedious affair. Geoffrey barely spoke to his brother, keeping his attention turned to his lovely wife. He guessed Becca could feel the tension, and every so often, he caught Patricia staring at her with disdain. She might be of aristocratic birth, but she wasn't lady enough to share a table with Becca in his opinion.

"Where did Kane find you, Rebecca?" Patricia asked in a false-friendly tone.

Becca began to answer, but Geoffrey was faster. "Rebecca's father owns the inn where I waited out the repairs to my carriage."

"An innkeeper's daughter?" Patricia snorted.

"A serving wench?" John gazed at Becca hungrily. "How diverting."

"Hardly," Geoffrey said angrily.

Becca responded to Patricia's insult. "The Raven's Inn offers the finest dining and lodging from here to London. And my father owns it."

Geoffrey knew she could hold her own against a witch like Patricia. Lady Margaret nodded her approval, a small smile on her face. The remainder of the meal was without incident, or much conversation.

After dinner, Geoffrey stood, excusing himself and his wife from the table. He bade the others goodnight, and led his wife upstairs.

John and Patricia's untimely arrival didn't sit well with him. While he and Patricia hardly ever spoke, he'd always been on good terms with his brother. When the men were alone, they could ride and hunt and share a brandy together after a meal. Even John's seduction of his fiancée, once a sufficient amount of time had passed, hadn't hampered their relationship. He didn't begrudge John his marriage to that grasping witch. She had shown her true colors when she'd hopped into bed with his brother. He realized that what he had felt for her was nothing. It wasn't love. But that was before Becca ... she was working her way deep inside of him.

Becca gave him a sweet kiss and went into her dressing room to ready for bed. Geoffrey stripped off his clothes and climbed into the four-poster to wait for her, picturing her figure behind that door.

He hadn't missed the way his brother ogled her all through dinner. He'd wanted to smash his fist into John's face, wiping away his lustful grin, the heat in his gray eyes. Perhaps he was overreacting. Perhaps he was overprotective where Becca was concerned. No matter. No other man would ever touch what was his and live to tell about it.

And if that other man proved to be his own brother, so be it.

* * * *

As John drank his after-dinner brandy, Patricia's mind worked. Lady Margaret hadn't lingered long after her favorite quit their company. No deficit there. Kane married? To a commoner? Little Rebecca wouldn't hamper her well-laid plans.

Patricia had fully intended to wed Geoffrey four years earlier, but her attraction to John couldn't be denied. While the elder Kane kissed her chastely, his younger brother ignited her passion. They would meet in the stables, at a vacant cottage, anywhere. Even now, watching him sipping his drink, she wanted only him.

When she learned she was pregnant, she wanted to bed Geoffrey and tell him the child was his. John, however, wouldn't stand for it. He'd arranged for Geoffrey to discover them in bed, freeing her to marry John.

John was second in line to the title, and the family was extremely wealthy. She'd have it all. Passion, money, and ultimately Kanewood. And with Geoffrey so set against ever marrying, John's son would ultimately inherit the title. When

Ann was born, Patricia had been disappointed. But they would have a son one day.

With the arrival of Geoffrey's young bride, however, matters could change. If Rebecca gave him an heir, all would be lost. And what if she decided she didn't want the earl's younger brother and his family residing at Kanewood? Patricia would never let anything move her from the estate. She shivered and John glanced over at her. "Cold, darling?" He patted the seat beside him. "Come. I'll warm you."

She rose and crossed to him, letting his fingers trail over her neck, her back, until her tension began to ease.

Yes. Something must be done about the earl's new bride.

* * * *

"Becca?"

Becca stepped out of the dressing room to find Geoffrey sitting up in bed. She smiled sweetly at him. "Good morning, husband."

Tension showed in the tight lines around his mouth. "I thought you'd left."

She blinked. "Where would I go without you?"

He smiled, that odd tension gone. "Do you have a kiss for your husband?"

Becca crossed to him, thinking to kiss him lightly. He grabbed her and pulled her down on his lap. She ran her fingers through his hair, trying in vain to smooth the unruly waves.

"What has you up so early, Becca?"

"My husband is taking me on a picnic today."

He pretended to ponder that statement. "Yes. I think I remember something about that."

She clicked her tongue and stood. She crossed over to the vanity and sat, brushing her hair. He got out of bed and pulled on his breeches, coming to stand behind her.

Their gazes met in the mirror and Becca breathed in sharply at the intent in his. "Geoffrey, we should …."

"Yes, we should," he cut in, nuzzling her neck.

She closed her eyes and sighed before she recalled what it

was she'd started to say. "We should get ready for breakfast."

"Mmm," he murmured. "I have what I want right here."

"Mary will be here in a moment to help me dress," she whispered, turning to him.

He lifted his head and stared at her for a moment. "All right, love." With a sigh of resignation, he released her and stepped back. "I'll meet you downstairs, then."

She nodded and kissed him lightly. He turned and went into his dressing room, closing the door behind him.

Mary came in a short time after. She greeted her mistress warmly and asked what she was about this day.

"Lord Kanewood is taking me riding today, Mary. Is my new riding habit ready?"

"Yes, my lady. And what a picture you will make in it!"

Becca smiled with pleasure. She so wanted to look just right as this was the first time since their coming to Kanewood that she'd have Geoffrey to herself for the entire day. She fidgeted as Mary pinned her hair up on top of her head. While she was pleased with the style, she was uncertain it would suit the day.

"Mary, my hair is much too heavy to stay up when I go riding. Perhaps a braid?"

Mary nodded, once again freeing the thick curls. She fashioned a thick braid and coiled it securely at Becca's crown. Becca nodded, comfortable with the familiar hairstyle.

Mary walked into Becca's dressing room and emerged with the new riding habit. It was a deep burgundy and trimmed with black velvet cording. Becca stepped into the skirt, waiting as Mary fastened the hooks in the back. The skirt was topped by an adorable matching spencer, the jacket stopping at her waist. Becca regarded the outfit in the mirror.

Becca smiled at her. "Thank you. That was just what was called for."

Becca took herself downstairs to the breakfast room. When she entered the room, Geoffrey was already seated.

He rose when she entered, crossing to her. "You look splendid," he told her, kissing her behind her ear.

"Thank you, Geoffrey."

He led her over to the sideboard to start their meal.

Breakfast was very informal, with the diners arriving at different intervals and serving themselves. Becca chose a small amount of eggs along with some fresh rolls while Geoffrey piled his plate with eggs and ham. Becca cast him a sidelong glance.

"I fear I'll need my strength today, love," he said.

She blushed as her own blood warmed. They took their seats at the long table and began their meal.

Lady Margaret soon joined them. "Good morning, dears. And what are you two about this fine day?"

"I'm taking my lovely wife riding, Mother. We thought to picnic on the grounds."

"That sounds like a lark," John intoned from the doorway. "Perhaps Patricia and I will join you."

Geoffrey turned to his brother. "I think not, John. I wish to have my wife all to myself today."

Becca nodded. "Geoffrey cleared his day of work to take me riding."

John turned to Becca and Geoffrey didn't miss his slow perusal. Patricia joined them then. She filled her plate and sat next to Lady Margaret.

"Rebecca," Patricia began, "that outfit is lovely. Is it new?"

"Thank you, yes. Lady Margaret chose the color."

Patricia bristled at that. "Hmm. Lady Margaret must consider you a pet project, then. She doesn't usually show such condescension." When no one gave her comment attention, she turned her attention to Geoffrey. "Kane, you're going riding today?"

"Yes."

"I thought we could join them, Patricia, but my brother wouldn't have it," John stated in jest.

Patricia shot him a look that showed her pique, just as quickly covering it with cool composure. "We have correspondence to see to, John. I had hoped for your assistance."

"Certainly, dove." He kissed her hand. "Anything you need."

Becca finished her meal and looked to Geoffrey, who laid

his napkin on the table and stood. "Well, we're off." He gave his mother a kiss on the cheek.

"I trust you will be back for supper, Geoffrey," Lady Margaret teased.

He winked at Becca. "We shall make every effort."

The couple took their leave and set out for the stables.

* * * *

After Patricia and John finished their meal, they went into the library. John followed his wife into the room and closed the paneled doors leading from the hall. The room was large, with shelves stacked nearly to the ceiling with leather-bound volumes. It was a pleasant room, with large windows to let in the light and comfortable chairs arranged throughout. A writing desk sat at one end of the room, and it was here that Patricia settled herself.

John took one of the chairs facing the desk, stretching his long legs to prop his feet on the desk. "Now what is this about correspondence, my dove?"

Patricia sighed in irritation. "John, we must send notes to the people we saw in London."

"But why now? I thought we were finished for the Season."

"I didn't like leaving when we did, John." Patricia stood and paced slowly. "But if you hadn't spent so much time at White's—"

John sat up quickly. "I told you that was just a bit of bad luck, that's all," he insisted. "We didn't have to leave town so soon."

"Yes, we did. Your 'friends' at White's were beginning to call for you at the Spencers's."

They had stayed at the home of some of Patricia's friends in London. The couple regularly stayed in their own rented townhouse, but John hadn't secured the rental of one this Season, thinking to use Geoffrey's. But with Geoffrey coming and going on business these past few months, they couldn't intrude. Patricia had been quite upset with the arrangement, having planned to use the earl's large townhouse for entertaining.

John looked at her a bit sheepishly, acknowledging the truth in her statements.

She relaxed her stance and faced him. “We must speak of your brother’s wife, John.”

“What of her?”

“I won’t have our position usurped.”

John quirked a smile at her. “And just what is our ‘position’, Patricia?”

“You know precisely what I mean,” she said in exasperation. “She could decide that the earl’s younger brother and his family shouldn’t reside at Kanewood. She may take her position as lady of the manor to heart.”

John shook his head. “I sincerely doubt that. Rebecca seems pleasant enough. Shy as well. I can’t imagine she’d do any such thing.”

“Well, you had better open your eyes. She has already ingratiated herself into your mother’s good graces. There is more to her than what she seems. Mark my words.”

“I think you’re overreacting, my dove.”

“I think not. Kane is quite smitten with her, that much is obvious. She keeps him ‘happy,’ I’d presume.”

John looked off for a moment. “I daresay she keeps him very happy,” he said, a grin on his face.

Patricia looked at him in disgust. “Enough about that,” she spat. “We won’t be thrown out of Kanewood by anyone, least of all that little country mouse.”

John nodded then. “All right. But what of the correspondence?”

“Apparently, Kane and his wife are planning to visit London for the last few weeks of the Season. Lady Margaret wishes to be there, also. It’s obvious she has grown attached to the girl.”

“And I presume we must go back, as well?”

“We’re expected to attend functions with the newly married earl and his bride. We must advise our friends that we’ll return to London soon.”

“At least we can stay in Kane’s townhouse,” John said.

A sharpness came into her cool blue eyes. “Try to keep me out of it.”

Chapter 12

Geoffrey and Becca passed a very pleasant morning riding the estate. As Geoffrey pointed out certain buildings and cottages she marveled at the size of his property, seemingly stretching as far as the eye could see. After a while, they crossed into the more pastoral areas, with virtually no buildings in sight. Her breath caught as she took in the stunning landscape.

"Geoffrey," she said in awe. "Everything is so beautiful. So lush and green."

He smiled and nodded. "Yes, love. We're not far from Scotland, and I suppose that accounts for such greenery."

He reined his chestnut gelding close to her black filly. "The land isn't nearly as beautiful a green as your eyes, Becca."

She smiled at his fanciful compliment. "Thank you."

He pulled back. "Let's find a spot for our picnic."

Becca nodded and they rode on for a while, passing a brook where the clear water danced over the rocky bottom. He informed her that if they followed it upstream, they would come to a lovely clearing.

It was just as he said. Geoffrey reined in his horse and jumped from his saddle, turning to help Becca down. He retrieved a blanket from behind his saddle and carried it over to a spot under a large shade tree. He spread it on the ground, returning to help Becca with the other items.

The kitchen staff had prepared a delightful lunch of light fare: cold roast beef, fresh bread, and cheeses. Some summer fruits and strawberry tarts, Becca's favorite, rounded off their picnic. They carried the filled satchels over to the blanket and settled down on it. They shared their meal, chatting about nothing in particular, pausing every so often to touch or kiss.

When they had consumed the simple fare, Geoffrey sighed

contentedly and stretched out on the blanket, his hands behind his head.

Becca turned to him. She hadn't seen him this relaxed since their picnic on the common in Oakham.

"You certainly look satisfied, husband," she offered.

He looked at her, a crooked grin on his face. "Satisfied, love?" he answered. "Not particularly. But I know what will satisfy me."

Becca saw the flash of lust in his eyes and felt her pulse quicken. She returned the uneaten portion of their meal to the satchels and rose to wash her hands in the brook. As she wiped them on a cloth from the satchel, he hugged her from behind. He nuzzled the nape of her neck.

Becca breathed in sharply, turning in his arms. Her hands came up to rest behind his neck as she kissed him lightly. Geoffrey cupped her face in his hands, running his gaze over her face. His gaze settled on her lips. He captured her lips with his, sweeping his tongue inside her mouth. She caught his passion, stretching up to press herself against him. She could feel his arousal through her many layers of clothing.

Geoffrey placed his hands on her bottom and lifted her, holding her tightly against him. He strode over to the large tree, bracing her against the trunk. He held her still while he ravaged her mouth. She melted against him, loving what he was doing to her. He managed to free her curls from her braid, and twisted her hair gently in his fist. He eased her head back, deepening the kiss. She moaned softly as he moved his lips to her neck.

"Ah, Becca," he breathed in her ear. "I want you so badly."

"Take me," she said breathlessly.

He unbuttoned her jacket, pulled her chemise down. He buried his face in the valley between her breasts, teasing her. She bowed back, begging him without words. He took one straining nipple in his mouth, eliciting a gasp of pleasure from her.

"Oh, what your touch does to me!"

"And how I love to touch you," he rasped.

His hands were everywhere, pulling her skirt up to touch her intimately. Before she was even aware of it, he'd removed her drawers and unbuttoned his breeches. He stretched her arms over her head, wrapping her hands around a stout branch there. He placed his hands on her bottom and lifted her.

"Love, wrap your legs around my waist. That's it. That's ...."

With one smooth thrust, he entered her. She cried out, the feeling intense. He pressed her tightly against the tree, driving into her again and again. She started to tighten around him, close to her release.

"Do you love me, Becca?" he rasped.

"Yes, Geoffrey," she cried. "Yes!"

She shuddered from her climax, arching in pleasure. He drove harder still, seeking his release. His orgasm was explosive, bringing her with him again. She clung to him as he rained kisses on her hair, her face.

When their breathing returned to normal, she looked at him in surprise. "Oh my," she whispered. "I didn't know we could do that."

"Could do what, love?" he whispered back.

"Stand up."

He chuckled softly, dropping a kiss on her brow. A while later, they rearranged themselves and readied to return to the manor.

"Lovely afternoon, wife." He grinned as he swung back into the saddle.

"Lovely picnic, husband," she teased as she followed his horse back to the manor.

While alone with her husband, so relaxed and at ease, she could almost forget that Geoffrey's brother and his cold wife waited at the manor. The memory of John's narrowed gray eyes running over her body until she felt naked, Patricia's pale gaze always on Geoffrey. Yes, she could almost forget.

Almost.

* * * *

They departed Kanewood for London two days later. Becca was nervous about going to town, having been there but once when she was very small. Inside the carriage, Becca sat close to Geoffrey, with Lady Margaret on her other side. On the opposite seat, Patricia and John faced them. Patricia talked incessantly about which balls they simply had to attend and those to avoid. "Everyone will be looking at you, Rebecca," she advised. "You have much to live up to, being an earl's wife."

"Patricia, Rebecca has nothing to worry about," Lady Margaret said. "She and Geoffrey make a stunning couple."

Geoffrey chuckled. "Mother, no one will take notice of me with my lovely wife standing beside me."

"Indeed," John said.

Patricia glared in his direction until he turned to look out the window.

"Lady Margaret, Rebecca has never had a Season," Patricia continued. "It falls on us to see that she doesn't do anything to cause embarrassment."

"That's enough," Geoffrey said. "Rebecca may not have attended the bashes, but that doesn't mean she'd ever embarrass me." He took Becca's hand, bringing it to his lips. His touch warmed the chill from her fingers. "My wife possesses a natural grace and beauty that hundreds of balls could never bestow."

"Thank you, Geoffrey," Becca said softly.

He leaned over and placed a kiss on her ear. She dropped her gaze and Geoffrey settled back against the seat, pulling Becca as close to him as was proper.

It was Patricia's turn to stare out the window, Becca saw. John and Geoffrey conversed for a while, mostly about what some of their mutual friends had been about in London. The ladies talked more about the upcoming functions, and Becca eventually felt at least as much enthusiasm as nervousness.

* * * *

They stopped for the night at the inn they'd frequented on their trip to Kanewood and set off early the next day. As they neared Oakham that afternoon, Geoffrey announced they would be making another stop.

"And where will we be stopping, Geoffrey?" Lady Margaret

asked.

"At the Raven's Inn, Mother."

Becca sharply drew in a breath, clasping her hands together. "You'd said we might stop at Raven's, but when you didn't mention it, I thought you'd changed your mind."

He smiled at her obvious delight. "I wanted to surprise you."

She hugged him in answer and turned to his mother. "Lady Margaret, I know you will enjoy the inn," she promised. "Our cook is the best for miles around."

"I concur," Geoffrey said.

"I doubt I shall be so impressed with a country inn," Patricia said.

John rubbed his hands together. "Well, I'm famished."

"And I'm looking forward to meeting your father, Rebecca," Lady Margaret said.

Geoffrey held his countenance, unwilling to let Becca see his anger and guess something had transpired between him and her father that last morning. Luckily, the carriage soon rolled to a stop and her attention was taken.

"The inn is just lovely, Rebecca," Lady Margaret said.

Becca turned to the woman and smiled. Patricia wore a look of surprise as she stepped down. "I hadn't expected such …." She smiled cooly. "Elegance."

Geoffrey alighted after them, handing first his wife, then his mother, down. They entered the inn and searched out Becca's father.

"Kingsley?" Geoffrey called out in greeting.

"Yes, yes." Thomas came out of his office. "What is it? Rebecca!"

Thomas grabbed Becca by the arms, running his gaze over her face. She seemed surprised by his display. Little wonder that, as Geoffrey had never seen much affection there before.

"Hello, Father," she said softly.

"I wasn't expecting you, girl." He turned to Geoffrey. "Kane, it's good to see you."

"Yes, sir." Geoffrey took the man's outstretched hand. "I'd like you to meet my family, Kingsley."

Thomas nodded in greeting as Geoffrey introduced the others, respectively.

"Will you be staying to dinner, then?" he asked Becca.

"Yes." She smiled at Geoffrey. "I'm afraid I've extolled Cook's talents."

"Capital." Thomas led them into the parlor. "It'll be about an hour." He bowed and left them.

Patricia and John settled themselves on a couch.

"The place is quite pleasant, Rebecca," John said.

Becca favored him with a smile. "Would you like some refreshment, Lady Margaret?"

"Some tea would be lovely, dear," she replied.

"And for you, Patricia?" Becca asked.

"Yes, please," Patricia answered.

Becca nodded and went off to the kitchen to see to it. Geoffrey watched her go, a small smile on his face. It fled when Thomas stepped into view.

"Kane?" he asked.

"Yes," Geoffrey answered coolly.

"I'd like a word with you if I may."

Geoffrey stood. "Of course."

"And if you will excuse me, ladies," John said. "I believe I'll take a look around."

John left and Geoffrey followed Thomas into his office.

In Thomas's study, Geoffrey stood ramrod stiff.

"Please sit, Kane," Thomas said.

Geoffrey did. "What is this about, Kingsley?"

"Kane, I wish to apologize for what I said the day you left."

Geoffrey stared at the man, certain he'd heard him wrong. Thomas sat for a moment, apparently collecting his thoughts. In the silence, Geoffrey heard footsteps in the hall outside the door. He glanced toward the doorway, but Becca's father spoke again.

"I was wrong to ask you to pay for the girl, Kane."

"Damn right you were."

"I can see that she loves you. You make her happy."

Geoffrey nodded.

"You had to marry her, I know," Thomas went on. "But you

have affection for her, yes?"

"Kingsley, what are you getting at?"

"I hope I'm wrong about this, but I don't want you to make the same mistakes I did."

He stood and crossed to the window. Geoffrey watched him, his interest piqued.

"Keep her close, Kane," Thomas continued. "I meant what I said about her mother. Don't let the girl stray."

"What the devil happened to her mother, then?" Frustration bit at him. "You have mentioned her before, and in less than glowing terms."

Thomas shook his head. "I loved her mother. That's all you need to know."

There was something the man wasn't saying. He appeared almost angry where his late wife was concerned, a strange thing as she was dead and gone. Had she betrayed him?

"Kingsley, I can assure you my wife keeps herself to me."

Thomas turned then. "I know you don't love the girl, but I trust you don't want anyone else to have her."

Geoffrey wouldn't discuss what he felt for Becca with him, a man who surely never showed Becca much. "I keep what is mine."

Thomas nodded, satisfied. The two men rose to join the others in the parlor.

John stepped into the room soon after, his eyes narrowed on Geoffrey.

"Where were you, John?" Geoffrey asked.

"Did a bit of exploring, brother." He settled himself beside Patricia. "Lovely inn."

* * * *

The dinner hour arrived and they adjourned to the dining room. Emmy saw them and let out a loud whoop of joy.

Becca smiled and took her hands in hers. "Emmy, how are you?"

"Never mind me, Rebecca. Don't ya look fine!" She leaned closer. "Marriage agrees with ya, I think."

Becca blushed and Emmy turned to the other guests and greeted them.

"Hello, Emmy," Geoffrey said easily.

Patricia turned her nose up at the serving girl and ignored Geoffrey's introductions. Emmy paid her no attention, noting instead the way John eyed her. She favored John with a grin, showing the dimple in her cheek. She faced Becca again. "I got my duties, Rebecca. We'll talk more later."

Becca nodded and sat herself next to her husband.

They enjoyed a simple but excellent meal of lamb, vegetables, and potatoes. Geoffrey sat very close to Becca, picking food off her plate now and then. She swatted his hand away with a smile.

"Really, Kane," Patricia said.

"Country manners, Patricia," Lady Margaret said with a smile. "I for one greatly enjoy seeing my eldest son so relaxed."

Near the meal's end, Becca excused herself to talk to Emmy. "I miss you, Emmy."

"How is everything, Rebecca?"

"Just wonderful."

Emmy looked across the room and found John staring at them. She turned her attention back to Becca. "I'd watch out for Kane's brother. I don't like the way he looks at you."

"What do you mean?"

"He wants ya, 'tis plain to see."

Becca shook her head, but Emmy nodded just as adamantly. "Yea, he does. And if his cold fish of a wife finds out, there'll be trouble for sure."

"That can't be."

"Promise me you'll be careful?"

"I …." Emmy looked so worried, Becca nodded. "All right. I promise."

When she returned to their table, Geoffrey arched an eyebrow at her. "What is it, love?"

Becca shook her head, setting aside Emmy's worries and her own regarding Geoffrey's brother.

Chapter 13

As the carriage rolled into London, Becca bolted upright, gaping out the window. Lady Margaret pointed out the pertinent landmarks, the imposing bridge and looming towers, giving Becca a brief history on them, as well. Geoffrey supposed it was a lot to take in, raised as she had been in the little hamlet of Oakham. He sat back and smiled at the wonder on his wife's beautiful face.

They crossed over into the fashionable West End near Mayfair, where Geoffrey's townhouse was located. The carriage came to a stop in front of the white brick structure and Becca's small gasp drew his attention.

"Geoffrey, your house is so beautiful." She breathed.

"Our house, love," he gently corrected.

They alighted the carriage and he held her elbow as they walked up the short path to the glossy-black front door. A liveried servant opened the door, bowing to Geoffrey. He greeted the servant and turned to Becca who apparently saw the intent in his eye a moment too late. He swept her up in his arms to carry her over the threshold as he'd done at Kanewood, letting loose a big booming laugh as he twirled her around.

"Here we go again!" Becca laughed.

He set her down and hugged her to him.

Patricia snorted at the display and swept past them to head up the stairs. "Come, John."

"Yes, my dove. Kane, I'd enjoy sharing a brandy a bit later."

"Very well, John," Geoffrey said. "Mother, do you want me to show you to your room?"

Lady Margaret shook her head and winked at Becca. "I shall see you in the morning, children." She went upstairs to retire for the evening.

Geoffrey turned to Becca and tilted her head up, running his gaze over her face. "I'm so happy you're here with me."

"I love you. I wouldn't want to be anywhere else."

He nodded, pleased as always to hear it. He kissed her lightly and proceeded to show her the townhouse, happy to finally be sharing the lonely place.

"Why don't you return to our chamber, love? I promise I won't be long with John. And tomorrow we'll ride in Hyde Park."

She nodded absently. "Which dress …?"

Geoffrey watched as she drifted up the stairs, her mind no doubt on the coming day, even as his was on the coming night.

Geoffrey met John in the study. John already had a generous amount of liquor in his glass.

"Attending the bashes, Kane?" John asked. "That's sure to raise some eyebrows."

Geoffrey smiled. "True. I haven't been very sociable the last few years."

"That's putting it a bit mildly, brother."

"Well, now that I have Rebecca, I'm actually looking forward to the stuffy, pretentious, uncomfortable affairs."

John sipped his brandy and smiled crookedly at him. "I predict your lovely young wife will have them jumping through hoops."

Geoffrey arched an eyebrow. He hadn't missed John's interest in Becca. "How so?"

"She's simply magnificent, Kane. If she were my wife, I wouldn't let her out of my sight."

Geoffrey held his composure. "Don't fret, brother. No one will come anywhere near her."

John apparently missed the warning in Geoffrey's tone and smiled in agreement. Geoffrey eyed him over his glass, twirling the amber liquid absently as talk turned to more mundane matters.

* * * *

The next morning dawned bright and as clear as London could be at that time of year. Becca awoke to find Geoffrey fully dressed.

"Are you eager for our ride this morning?" she teased.

He shook his head, regret clear on his face. "No, love. I must meet with my solicitors this morning."

Becca sat up. "But you assured me you wouldn't be attending to business for a few days."

He crossed to the bed. "I know I did, but this couldn't be helped."

Fully awake now, Becca noticed the look of worry on his face. "Geoffrey, what is this about?"

He turned to the cheval mirror and adjusted his cravat. "It isn't anything for you to worry about, Becca."

She was confused by his demeanor. As he pulled on his waistcoat and jacket, she fancied that with each article of clothing, he was becoming more distant from her. She rose from the bed and touched his shoulder lightly.

He turned with a start, his face serious. "I need to see to this matter."

Becca tried to hide her disappointment but failed. He stroked her cheek, his gaze tender, and once again he resembled the Geoffrey she knew and loved.

He kissed her. "I'll return as soon as possible."

She watched him go, bemused. As she sat at the vanity and brushed her hair, her mind worked. He'd seemed so distant to her for those few moments. Not like himself at all. Finally, she rang for Mary and set about her morning toilette.

Downstairs at breakfast, Lady Margaret suggested that she ride with Becca herself. "We'll ride on the Ladies' Mile at Hyde Park, Rebecca," she said. "And perhaps trot down Rotten Row?" Her eyes sparkled. "I want to make sure the ton get's a good look at my new daughter-in-law."

Trepidation filled her limbs. What would the fashionable set think of her, the simple girl who had married so far above her station?

"I don't know if I should go out today," she said softly.

"Nonsense!" Lady Margaret patted her hand. "The ton like

nothing more than gossip, dear. And you are precisely whom they would love to talk about."

Becca's stomach seized. "I'd rather not be gossiped about!" she replied nervously.

"Yes, but not to worry. You're fresh and lovely, and you're married to my remarkable son." She flashed that smile so like Geoffrey's as she said this. "You will outshine all of the debutantes this Season, depend upon it." She waved a hand. "Besides, no one would dare speak ill of my daughter-in-law."

Becca took a deep breath and squared her shoulders, trying to affect a bit of Lady Margaret's bearing. "I shall do my best not to misstep."

"I have no worries on that count. To the park, then?"

Becca smiled at last. "That would be lovely, Lady Margaret."

Becca was surprised to see so many people out riding that morning. It appeared Lady Margaret couldn't have been more pleased, however. A number of matrons asked to call later that day and more than a few gentlemen appeared very solicitous. After stopping to make a few calls themselves to Lady Margaret's oldest and dearest friends, they returned to the house.

Soon after lunch, the callers began to arrive. Lady Margaret and Becca received them in the parlor, Becca was relieved that John and Patricia were out making calls of their own. Her nervousness was nearly nonexistent when her caring and supportive mother-in-law was the only one present.

Many older ladies called, expressing their pleasure over Geoffrey's marriage. They were chagrined, however, to find the earl absent. This wasn't the case for the gentlemen who called later that afternoon. They were more than happy to talk to Becca without Geoffrey in attendance, in Lady Margaret's company, of course. One man, Viscount Roberts, was extremely attentive. He was a man about Geoffrey's age and very good-looking, with black hair and gray eyes.

"Lady Kanewood," Roberts began. "Will you be attending the Winslow bash next week?"

Becca looked to Lady Margaret for an answer.

"Yes, Lord Roberts," the older woman replied. "We received an invitation just this morning."

Roberts turned his attention back to Becca. "Wonderful," he offered, his eyes sparkling.

Finally, the last of the callers departed. Lady Margaret looked at Becca then. "You look quite done in, dear. Why don't you take yourself upstairs and rest a bit? We won't dine before seven."

"Thank you, Lady Margaret. Who would think that sitting and talking would be so tiresome?"

"Society, my dear," Lady Margaret said with a smile.

Becca went to her and Geoffrey's chamber. Mary assisted her out of her tea gown and stays, and removed the pins holding her hair in place. Mary left and Becca stretched out on the bed. She was asleep in less than five minutes.

* * * *

Geoffrey sat in his carriage on the way back from his meetings, his mind working furiously. The news he'd received didn't sit well. Not at all.

He'd thought to simply review the accounts for Kanewood, having discovered some oddities on his recent tour of the estate. It seemed that the repairs he'd ordered hadn't been completed. Several cottages needed their roofs re-thatched and the fencing bordering the properties were in a woeful state. He'd wondered if these conditions were somehow related to the missing funds and that morning his suspicions were confirmed. What the devil was going on?

As the carriage pulled up to the townhouse, he shook his head to clear his thoughts. He alighted and strode into the foyer, surprised to find the salver full. The silver tray now held more calling cards than he'd seen in recent memory. Many of the names were familiar and a small smile lifted the corner of his mouth as he went in search of his very popular wife.

He found Lady Margaret reading in the parlor. "Hello, Mother. Where is Rebecca?"

"I sent the poor dear upstairs, Geoffrey. The social whirl

was quite a bit much for her today."

He nodded. "Yes, I saw that there were many callers. I'm most pleased I was absent."

"Oh, you," his mother said with a shake of her head.

"I'll see you at dinner, Mother."

Geoffrey left the parlor, bound for their chamber. He opened the door and his breath caught at the sight before him.

Becca lay sleeping on the bed, clad in only her chemise and petticoat. Her hair fanned out in delightful disarray, framing her face. Her lashes were dark on her cheeks, which were flushed from sleep. He stared for a long moment, feeling the tension of the day melt away. He closed the door and crossed over to her.

He watched as she slept, her chest rising and falling as she breathed deeply through her parted lips. He shed his clothes and, wearing only his breeches, he stretched out alongside her.

He trailed a finger down her cheek, her neck, causing her to stir. He bent his head to nuzzle her smooth skin, flicking her ear with his tongue. A soft moan escaped her. He untied her chemise, placing feather-light kisses on her breasts.

Her eyes fluttered open and she smiled sleepily. "Geoffrey."

"Yes, Becca." He came up to kiss her. "I'm back."

He proceeded to make love to her, gently and thoroughly. A while later, they lay on the bed.

"What a lovely way to awaken." She sighed.

Geoffrey wrapped her in his arms, her head resting on his chest. "Indeed."

"I missed you today."

He dropped a kiss on her hair. "I know, love. I missed you, too."

She turned to face him, placing her hands on his chest. She appeared to hesitate. "Won't you tell me what had you so troubled this morning?"

He stiffened, used to keeping his own counsel on such matters. But when he looked into her beautiful eyes and saw the concern there, he relented.

"There have been some disturbing entries in my accounts for the last few months. I discovered them on my last trip to town."

At her nod, he continued.

"And today, I learned that repairs I had ordered were not made to the estate, yet the account had been billed. It's very puzzling, to say the least."

She rested her chin on her folded hands. "What do you think is going on?"

"That's precisely what I intend to find out."

"Why didn't you share any of this with me before?"

He stroked her cheek. "I didn't wish to trouble you, love."

She furrowed her brow at that. "I was more troubled that you didn't trust me with your problems."

He smiled then and kissed her frown away. "I took note of the many calling cards, Becca. You passed a busy afternoon, I daresay."

"Yes. You have a great many friends."

"Really?" he asked, smiling crookedly.

"Quite a few gentlemen called today. They were disappointed that you were out."

He chuckled. "I'd wager they weren't."

"What? They were most solicitous. Especially your friend Lord Roberts."

"He is a good friend," Geoffrey said. "I believe when next he calls, I shall receive him, as well."

"Good." She roused herself and ran her fingers through his hair. "Let's ready for dinner?"

He nodded and happily followed his wife's order.

* * * *

The next few days were a whirlwind of activity for Becca. Geoffrey took her riding in Hyde Park and they went calling together.

"Geoffrey?" she asked him as they rode back to the townhouse one afternoon.

"Yes, love?" he answered, taking her hand.

"Why is it we have yet to call on your friends?"

"Which friends, Becca?"

Her mouth quirked in a half-smile. "The gentlemen who

called on your mother and myself."

With a playful growl, he gathered her into his arms. "I refuse to watch my friends drool over my lovely wife."

"Don't be silly. They were merely paying their respects."

He said nothing to that, but she didn't think he believed her.

The night of the Winslow bash arrived. Becca was very nervous to attend her first ball. She very nearly burst into tears when Geoffrey asked her if she'd be ready on time. After dropping a kiss on her brow, he thankfully left her to her own devices while he readied himself for the function.

She sat and fidgeted as Mary tugged on her heavy curls. She turned to dismiss the girl but finally permitted her to work her magic on the glossy mass.

When Mary announced that she'd finished, Becca looked in the mirror and gasped. Long tendrils curled down her back from the nape of her neck, while shorter ones framed her face.

"Mary, it looks wonderful. Even better than it did on my wedding day."

Mary smiled and twitched a ribbon in place. She'd located thin ribbons the exact shade of blush pink as Becca's gown and had twined them through her black curls.

Becca turned her head this way and that, marveling at Mary's handiwork. "You're a treasure, Mary."

"Thank you, my lady." She went into Becca's dressing room to retrieve her mistress's gown.

Geoffrey walked out of his dressing room then, looking extremely striking in his black, formal attire and white shirt and cravat.

Becca turned when she heard him. "Geoffrey, you will drive the ladies mad this evening."

He flashed a dazzling smile, which made her heart skip a beat. He crossed to her. "There is but one lady I wish to drive mad." He kissed her lightly. "You're breathtaking, love."

She blushed at that. She noticed then that he carried a velvet jewelry box. "What is this, Geoffrey?"

"This, darling, is the finishing touch to your attire this evening." He placed the box on the vanity. "You did say your dress was pink, yes?"

She nodded, staring as he opened the box. Inside lay a pearl choker, the pearls as big as a child's marbles. Matching earrings accompanied the necklace.

"Oh, my!"

He took the choker from the box and draped it around her neck, fastening it in the back. He dropped a kiss on her nape, sending a shiver through her.

She glanced in the mirror, her fingers fondling the round pearls. "Thank you. They're beautiful."

"No, Becca," he stated, catching her eye in the mirror. "You're beautiful."

She turned around and he kissed her thoroughly. He straightened then and tugged at his cravat, breathing a sigh. "Are you nearly ready, love?" he asked.

She nodded and he told her he'd wait for her downstairs. Mary returned with the daring gown and Becca stepped into it. She still wasn't very comfortable wearing such a revealing dress, but Lady Margaret assured her that it was stunning and just perfect for her. She stepped into the matching satin slippers and pulled on long gloves of satin in a matching shade of pale pink. Mary brought one of the long curls forward to rest against her breast. Becca giggled at her image. "Well, at least something is covering my bosom, Mary."

"My Lady, you look like a princess, you surely do!" Mary said, her expression solemn.

Becca hugged the girl. "Thank you, Mary."

Mary sniffed. "Now, off you go."

Becca nodded happily and followed her orders.

Geoffrey stood in the foyer with John and Patricia. Lady Margaret joined them just as Becca began her descent. Geoffrey turned with a smile. The expression left his face as his mouth gaped open. She smiled at his reaction.

"My God, Becca. You look …." His eyes narrowed on her daring bodice. "You're not leaving the house in that dress."

Becca started, "But I—"

"Geoffrey," Lady Margaret stated calmly. "I helped Rebecca choose this gown and I believe she looks enchanting."

"Ravishing, more like," John put in. "Well done, Mother."

Patricia glared at him and Becca felt a flush spread upward from her chest to her cheeks.

Geoffrey furrowed his brow in their direction, then let out a breath. He crooked his arm for her to grasp. As they left the house, he bent his head to hers. "When we return, I'll take this dress off you, Becca," he promised in a whisper. "And you will love every moment."

Becca felt her cheeks flame at what he was suggesting, causing him to laugh softly in her ear. The party boarded the carriage, bound for the Winslow ball.

Chapter 14

Many carriages lined the drive in front of the Winslows' large home. Liveried attendants assisted the guests down, directing them into the large foyer. Geoffrey held tightly to Becca's elbow as they made their entrance. They were received by the hostess, a somewhat plain woman with a pleasant smile who looked to be nearly Lady Margaret's age. Geoffrey introduced his wife, and the couple made their way to the ballroom.

When they entered the large room, most of the guests were milling about and chatting. Becca clutched at Geoffrey's arm, nervous once more.

He caught the action and placed his hand over hers. "You have nothing to fear, love."

She nodded, swallowing. They stepped down into the throng and were immediately joined by several of Geoffrey's friends.

"Kane!" a brown-haired man exclaimed. "Where have you been hiding?"

"Yes," another offered, this one blond. "We haven't seen you or your lovely wife since you arrived in town."

Geoffrey smiled crookedly. "I noticed your cards missing from the salver. No doubt Roberts told you I wasn't in to receive?"

They laughed, their gazes shifting to Becca.

"Gentlemen, this is my wife, Rebecca." Geoffrey nodded to her. "Becca, allow me to introduce the Earl of Chester and Viscount Leed."

"Lady Kanewood, it's a pleasure to meet you," Lord Leed, the brown-haired gentleman offered, grasping her hand lightly and bringing it to his lips. His blue eyes were darker than Geoffrey's.

Becca curtsied. "Lord Leed."

"Lady Kanewood, a pleasure." Chester turned to Geoffrey, his brown eyes still on Becca. "Kane, where did you find this ravishing creature?"

"Yes," Leed added. "I hear you found her in the country? Perhaps I should leave town during the Season, as well."

Geoffrey laughed at their jests, and turned to lead Becca from them. "Chester, may I have a word later?"

The blond-haired man arched his brows in mild curiosity. "Certainly."

"What was that about?" Becca asked.

"Chester is a long-time friend, love. I thought to get his opinion on the situation of which we spoke." Geoffrey found a few vacant chairs well away from the orchestra and urged her to sit. "I shall return with some refreshment."

Becca sat and was soon surrounded by gentlemen, several she recognized from their calls at the townhouse. They asked after Geoffrey, who soon returned with a glass of punch in his hand.

"Hello, gentlemen," he said, his tone tight.

They nearly fell over themselves clearing a path for him. He stood beside her chair, a hand placed possessively on her shoulder. Most of the men bade the couple farewell though some of the younger ones stayed. Geoffrey's scowl finally scattered them.

Becca sipped at her punch as she glanced about the room. "What a wonderful party."

"Yes, love." He gazed across the ballroom. "Do you mind if I have a word with Chester? It has to do with the matter we discussed."

"Certainly."

He kissed her lightly and crossed the large room to speak with the blond-haired gentleman.

"Enjoying yourself, Rebecca?" a masculine voice said to her right.

Becca gave a start. Turning, she saw John sitting next to her. "Yes, John. It's a lovely affair."

He nodded, his eyes sparkling. "Would you care to dance, sister?"

She hesitated, then spotted Geoffrey across the way, deeply embroiled in a conversation with two men now. She shrugged and placed her hand in John's.

John guided her out onto the dance floor, keeping a proper distance between them as he led her about the room. He smiled down at her. "You look very beautiful tonight, Rebecca."

"Thank you."

He pulled her a bit closer, his thighs brushing hers through her heavy skirt. The hand he held on her waist began to curve around to the small of her back, pressing her closer still. She stiffened. Surely this wasn't proper. She began to pull away just as the music came to an end and John bowed to her. "Thank you for the dance." He escorted her to her chair. "I believe I'll go in search of my wife."

Becca had just settled back down when a young, red-haired man stood in front of her. She looked up at him and smiled.

He bowed to her. "Forgive me, Lady Kanewood. I know we haven't been introduced."

"I'm sure it's all right."

He nodded and smiled. "I'm Gilly McClair." He had a nice smile and a pleasant burr in his speech.

"I'm pleased to meet you, Mr. McClair."

"Please forgive my forwardness, but I had to speak to you," he added. "May I join you?"

She nodded and he sat. He turned to her, gazing at her strangely, until he smiled at her once more.

"Lady Kanewood, you bear a striking resemblance to Laird McClair's wife. Have you ever been to Scotland?"

"No, I haven't. But I hear it's just lovely."

"Aye, that it is. McClair is my cousin, and lord of our clan. His wife has the same raven-black hair as yours and is very like you in features." He paused. "His lady is also very beautiful."

Becca blushed at the man's compliment. She spotted Geoffrey coming toward them, a puzzled frown on his face. When he reached them, Becca introduced Mr. McClair.

Geoffrey nodded curtly at the gentleman.

"'Twas a pleasure meeting you, Lord Kanewood. Lady Kanewood." Gilly frowned for a moment, then his eyes widened. “I know what was puzzling me!” He grinned. “Lady Charlotte’s eyes are blue, not green. Well, good evening.”

Becca gripped the seat of her chair. It couldn’t be.

“What is it, Becca?” Geoffrey asked, his brow furrowed.

She shook her head, a thin smile on her face. “Nothing, Geoffrey,” she assured him. “I suppose I’m just a bit hungry.”

He led her into the supper room. After making sure she’d eaten a few bites, he kissed her on her temple. “You had me worried, love.”

“I’m fine, really. But when Gilly McClair mentioned Lady Charlotte ….”

Geoffrey had missed her exchange with the Scotsman. She told him what the man had said, about her strong resemblance to Laird McClair’s wife.

“She must be a very beautiful woman,” he said.

She waved away his compliment. “Her name is Charlotte, Geoffrey. That was my late mother’s name. What do you think that means?”

“Was your mother Scottish?”

She blinked. “No.”

He shrugged “Then I imagine it’s simply a coincidence.”

She nodded, placating him. Maybe there was a connection, despite what Geoffrey said. Perhaps she’d find a way to know her mother after all, even if it was through a distant relative. She put this remarkable new information aside for now, however. There was far more to concern her at present. She would do nothing to shame Geoffrey or his mother, or make them regret their faith in her. Her nerves would only allow one concern at a time.

A while later, they returned to the ballroom. Geoffrey led Becca over to where his mother sat and left them to have a word with Lord Chester. A scant five minutes later, a familiar face smiled down at Becca.

“Lady Kanewood.” Viscount Roberts took her gloved hand in his, bringing it up to his lips. “It’s wonderful to see you again.”

Becca smiled up at him. “Hello, Lord Roberts.”

"May I beg Lady Margaret to release you so that we may share a dance?"

Becca looked at her mother-in-law, who nodded her encouragement. "Perhaps my son will realize he shouldn't abandon you all evening."

Becca laughed lightly and put her hand on Roberts's offered arm. In the course of the dance, Roberts placed his hand on her waist. His other hand gripped hers as he danced her across the floor.

"Lady Kanewood," he began. "May I call you Rebecca?"

"If you wish," she answered.

He smiled winningly at her. "Rebecca, may I say that you look exquisite this evening."

"Thank you, Lord Roberts."

"Please. Call me Roberts."

"All right." She smiled. "Roberts."

He leaned closer, brushing his cheek against her hair. The contact was brief, fleeting. He inched his hand upward, until it rested just beneath her breast and turned her a bit faster. The music pounded in Becca's head and the room suddenly felt too hot.

His gray eyes showed concern. "You look flushed. May I suggest some fresh air?"

She nodded weakly and allowed him to lead her out onto the terrace. The cool night air did feel quite wonderful and she breathed in deeply.

"Are you feeling better?"

She turned to answer him, startled to find him standing so close to her. "Yes. I'm feeling much better now."

She licked her lips in her nervousness and his eyes darkened.

"Good." His voice sounded a bit husky. "I was quite worried about you."

Becca blinked at the intensity in his gaze and took a step back from him. "How are you acquainted with my husband?" she asked, thinking to turn his attention.

"Kane and I worked together," he answered. "For the government."

The governement? Geoffrey had never mentioned it. Roberts trailed a finger down her cheek and grasped the thick curl resting on her breast. She opened her mouth to rebuff him when a large figure loomed in the doorway. Geoffrey! She breathed a sigh of relief until she saw the dark scowl on his face.

"What is going on out here?" He kept his voice low, his words, deliberate.

"Kane, there you are." Roberts stepped back from Becca and smiled that damn charming smile at him. "Rebecca was feeling ill, so I thought she could use some fresh air."

Rebecca? He'd seen how closely Roberts had held her on the dance floor, and how she'd reddened when the man touched her.

"Rebecca, I thank you for the dance and the conversation." He sketched a bow. "Kane."

As Roberts returned to the ballroom, Geoffrey studied his wife closely. Had she encouraged the viscount?

She grabbed onto his arm. "I'm so glad to see you."

He held himself stiffly.

She pulled back, confused. "Is something the matter?"

He read the innocence in her beautiful eyes. She didn't appear guilty of anything save naiveté.

He stroked her gloved hand and led her back to the ballroom. "Do you feel up to a dance, love?" he asked as they crossed the floor.

"Only with you, husband."

Damn right. He led her out onto the dance floor, holding her a bit closer than was proper. He glanced down the daring bodice of her gown. He could nearly see her nipples where they grazed the fabric. "My God, Becca," he whispered. "I can see clear down the front of your gown."

She blushed. "I had to leave off my chemise."

He breathed in sharply. "Who else danced with you this evening?"

"Only Lord Roberts," she answered. "And your brother."

Geoffrey frowned at that. Knowing his brother, he must

have taken full advantage of the enticing view. When the dance ended, they returned to Lady Margaret. "Mother, I believe my wife and I have had enough frivolity for one evening."

"Is that so?" Lady Margaret smiled. "Very well."

"I'll send the carriage back for you and John and Patricia."

"Thank you, Geoffrey." Lady Margaret smiled at Becca. "Good night, dear."

"Good night," she returned.

They thanked their host and hostess and took their leave. As Geoffrey handed Becca into the carriage, he paused. "Take the long way home, Fields," he instructed the driver.

"Yes, my lord."

Geoffrey climbed into the carriage and settled himself close to his wife.

She snuggled against him. "I'd have liked to dance a bit more, husband."

"Ah, wife. If we had gone on dancing, I fear I'd have taken you there in the ballroom."

She reached up to caress his cheek. "I daresay I'd have permitted you."

She rubbed her lips on his. She placed little kisses on his throat as she loosened his cravat, running her gloved fingers over his chest. His hands caressed her back as his passion built. She soon had his shirt unbuttoned and ran her lips over his skin. She reached the waistband of his breeches, noting his state of arousal through the black fabric.

She paused for a moment, then unfastened his breeches and grasped him gently. Her satin gloves were cool on his hot skin. He sighed and laid his head back against the cushion as her mouth took over for her hands.

"Ah, Becca."

Her tongue stroked the length of him. When her lips closed over the tip, he nearly came off the seat. With a growl, he grabbed her and kissed her deeply. She climbed on his lap and wrapped her arms around his neck.

She leaned her head back and he pulled her bodice down, freeing her for him to touch, to taste. His mouth closed over a nipple and she strained toward him.

"Oh, I love the feel of your mouth on my skin …."

He shifted in the seat and reached under her layers of clothing to caress her through her drawers. It wasn't enough for him and the fabric gave way with a soft tearing sound. "I need you, love. I need to be inside you."

He placed his hands on her bottom and lifted her. In one smooth motion, he lowered her onto himself, filling her completely. She cried out and clutched at his shoulders. He drove into her again and again as she held on to him. She chanted his name as she neared her fulfillment and Geoffrey threw his head back with a shout as he joined her.

She collapsed against him, her breath coming fast.

"My God," he whispered. "What you do to me."

She smiled up at him lazily. "I love you," she said simply.

He nodded and held her for a while. He managed to arrange his clothing as best he could as she adjusted her gown.

She turned to him in surprise. "Geoffrey, where are my drawers?"

He smiled sheepishly at her and bent to retrieve them from the floor of the carriage. She saw their tattered state and clicked her tongue at him. He shrugged and tucked them into his pocket.

They arrived back at the townhouse a short while later and immediately headed upstairs to their chamber. He proceeded to make good on his earlier promise.

He slowly removed her gown, and she loved every moment.

Chapter 15

Geoffrey was kept very busy over the next few days, meeting with his solicitors and others, so Becca had to content herself with riding in Hyde Park with Lady Margaret and receiving callers at the house. John suggested that she come calling with Patricia and himself, but she declined. Becca knew without a doubt that her sister-in-law greatly disliked her, and the feeling was nearly mutual. The blond-haired woman barely hid her disdain and Becca soon grew tired of placating her.

Late one afternoon, after making quite a few calls with Lady Margaret, Becca climbed the stairs to her and Geoffrey's chamber. She looked forward to a rest before readying for dinner and walked down the dimly lit hallway toward their door. She stopped in front of the door and a pair of strong arms hugged her gently from behind.

"Good afternoon, Becca," a masculine voice whispered in her ear.

She turned with a smile but was soon shocked to see it wasn't Geoffrey holding her so closely. "John!" She backed up against the door.

He raked his gaze over her. "You look very lovely today, sister." He stroked her hair, her cheek.

She leaned away from him. "John, you shouldn't—"

"What has you so flustered, Becca?" he asked smoothly.

She straightened. "That's Geoffrey's name for me, John."

"Ah, but we're brothers." He brushed his lips over her hair. "We share everything."

A small gasp escaped her lips.

"I know everything about you."

"What are you—"

"I know that Kane had to marry you. That he wouldn't pay

your father for you."

"But that's not—"

"Yes, it's the truth." He trailed his finger down her neck. "I also know how passionate you are."

"You don't know anything of the kind."

He traced her lips with his finger. "Kane told me all of the delightfully wicked deeds you do for him with this lovely mouth of yours."

She shook her head. Surely Geoffrey would never divulge such things, not to his brother!

He nodded and braced his arms on either side of her. "He doesn't love you."

She stiffened.

"Oh, he wants you in his bed. Who could blame him? But he'll grow tired of you." He placed his lips against her ear. "And when he does, Becca, you will come to me."

He punctuated his statement by flicking his tongue in her ear. She gasped, at which he laughed softly and strode down the hall to the room he shared with Patricia.

Becca closed her eyes, her mind reeling. Had John spoken the truth? Had Geoffrey shared the intimate details of their life together? She refused to believe that, despite John's assertions. Yet how did he know about …? No! Should Geoffrey ever tire of her, and she could not give that painful possibility more than passing consideration, she would never go to his brother. Or any other man.

Her hands shook, but she managed to open the door and stumble into their room. She removed her tea gown and carelessly draped it over the chair. Sinking into the chair before the vanity, she stared at her reflection. Geoffrey refused to pay her father? Had her father begged money from him? John said he'd had to marry her. It couldn't be true. Oh, had Geoffrey told his brother about Dr. Simon, as well? Was there nothing in her past that didn't have the potential to shame her husband?

She thought Geoffrey loved her. True, he'd never told her. Not even once. But she had assumed he loved her as she loved him because of the way he treated her—both in bed and out. She knew that he felt affection for her …. But what of love?

Perhaps he only wanted her in his bed, as John insisted. If that were true, than she was the worst kind of fool. She was in love with a man who only wanted her body, not her heart.

She buried her face in her hands and wept.

Geoffrey found her there, nearly an hour later. He closed the door and crossed to her, placing his hands on her shoulders.

She started and met his gaze in the mirror. "Hello, Geoffrey," she said, her tone flat.

He smiled crookedly at her. "Is that how you greet your husband?"

He bent his head to nuzzle her neck and she stiffened, pulling away from him.

"Becca," he began. "Is something wrong?"

She shook her head. She couldn't speak of it. If he were to admit to any of it, she'd simply perish.

"Nothing is wrong." She came to her feet. "I must ready for dinner."

She walked into the dressing room and closed the door behind her.

Geoffrey didn't know what to make of her behavior. He stared at the closed door for a moment, frowning. He readied himself for dinner and sat in a chair, waiting for her to emerge.

Becca opened the door and walked out, wearing a gown of dark bronze. It was a somber color but stunning on her. He noted that she still wore that strange look on her face. She was a bit pale, her eyes vacant.

They went down to dinner where Geoffrey tried to draw her into the conversation at the table. He failed miserably. Lady Margaret barely managed to get two words out of Becca. Patricia dominated the conversation, oblivious to the tension at the table as John paid copious attention to every word she uttered.

When the meal was nearly at an end, Becca excused herself and rose from the table.

Geoffrey looked at the others. "Has Rebecca been ill?"

Lady Margaret shook her head. "No, Geoffrey. She looked tired earlier, but she seemed fine."

"No doubt the girl is overwhelmed, poor thing," Patricia said.

"Pardon?" Geoffrey asked.

"This city can be a bit … much for one such as Rebecca," she explained, an expression of superiority on her face. "Surely it is far from her life in Oakham."

Geoffrey glared at Patricia but didn't respond to her barb. Instead, he went upstairs to get to the bottom of the matter. He opened the door and was surprised to find the room in shadows. No candles had been lit. He crossed to the bed and found Becca laying there, wearing one of her thin cotton nightgowns. She stared at the ceiling. Something wasn't right.

"Becca?"

Becca turned and stared at him, expressionless. His breath caught. She looked as beautiful as always, but her eyes …. Their beautiful green fire was missing. He'd bring it back.

He readied for bed and stretched out beside her. "What is it, love?"

She whimpered at the endearment. He kissed her gently, surprised when she didn't return his kisses. He held her close and stroked her hair, her back, and she suddenly clung to him. He cupped her face in his hands, staring down at her. "Tell me, Becca," he gently ordered. "Tell me you love me."

Becca turned her head, her eyes closed tight. He sat upright, stunned. She rolled away from him and curled herself into a ball.

Her soft sobs reached his ears and he touched her shoulder. "What is it?"

"You don't love me."

The softly-spoken statement struck him. "What do you mean?"

"You want me, but you don't love me. This is passion, nothing more." Her voice cracked on the last words. She took in a shuddering breath. "I don't know if I can do it, Geoffrey, but I'll try very hard not to love you."

He pulled back from her, speechless. He stretched out, his turn to stare at the ceiling. Was what she said true? He wanted her, yes. What man wouldn't? He cared for her. He wanted to make her happy. And when he held her, he felt deep contentment like he never had before. A happiness he'd not felt in years. She was all fire and warmth and love.

Love ….

The truth hit him. He did love her!

He looked over at her, her slight shoulders shaking with her quiet sobs. He couldn't tell her now. Not tonight. She'd never believe him. He'd find a way to show her. He'd bring the smile back to her lovely face, the spark back to her beautiful eyes.

He curled up next to her and held her gently, stroking her hair. "Shh, love," he soothed. "Shh …."

He knew when she drifted off to sleep by her soft, even breathing. It took longer for him to fall asleep, however.

The next morning, Geoffrey awoke before her. He studied her face, exquisite in repose. He felt the love he had for her surge through him. She would have no doubt of his feelings after today. He rose and dressed in his riding clothes. He wouldn't waste another day shut away with his solicitors or on any other matters save his wife.

When he met with Chester the previous afternoon, the man promised to investigate the matter of Geoffrey's disappearing funds. Knowing how connected Chester was in parliament and behind the scenes, Geoffrey felt confident he could get to the bottom of this.

He stepped out of the dressing room to find Becca sitting up in bed, the sheets clutched to her bosom.

He smiled at her and dropped a kiss on her tousled hair. "Good morning, wife."

She stared up at him, still half-asleep. Her eyes were huge, her lips parted. "Geoffrey, are you going riding today?"

He shook his head. "No, love. We're going riding today. I'm spending the entire day with my beautiful wife."

Her face brightened for a moment, then a shadow crossed her features as she nodded solemnly. He arched an eyebrow at her change in demeanor, only more determined to prove his love for her. Slowly. He had to go slowly.

"I'll be downstairs in the breakfast room, Becca."

Becca watched him go, puzzled. She couldn't deny she was thrilled to be spending the day with him. Shaking her head at herself, she rose and readied herself for an outing with her husband.

When she walked into the breakfast room, Geoffrey stood. "I was about to give up on you, Becca."

"I'm sorry I took so long," she answered stiffly.

He gently grasped her elbow and led her to the sideboard. He picked up a plate and asked her what she'd prefer to eat.

She quirked a smile at him. "I can carry my own dish, Geoffrey."

He smiled and kissed her behind her ear. "I know, love. I wish to serve you today."

She blinked at him. With an incline of her head, she allowed it.

After a light breakfast, they were off to Hyde Park. Geoffrey was extremely attentive and she soon found his charm irresistible. By the time they were finished with their ride, she felt more at ease with him.

"Becca," he said as they neared the townhouse. "Would you like to go for a stroll after lunch? We can take tea out today."

She was taken aback. He went on to describe a lovely little tea room not very far from the townhouse.

"Yes, Geoffrey," she said shyly. "It's a lovely day for a stroll."

He smiled winningly at her. He helped her down from her horse and handed the reins to the groom, bowing to her to take the lead. She smiled at his show of gallantry, reminded of their picnic on the Oakham common all those weeks ago. He followed her up the stairs to their chamber. He walked into their dressing room and changed out of his riding clothes. He left her then, telling her he'd collect her a bit later.

Becca sat in front of the vanity, wearing a frown. Geoffrey's actions confused her. He was acting very much like the man she'd met at Raven's and she felt herself falling in love with him all over again. More's the pity, since he didn't love her. Her heart clenched with the familiar ache that the truth caused. It wouldn't take much more to break her heart altogether.

She changed into a pretty walking dress of white muslin, dotted with sprigs of tiny violets and green leaves, just before Geoffrey knocked on the door.

He peered inside. "Are you ready, love?"

Becca stood and turned to him. His bright blue eyes sparkled and she lowered her gaze, suddenly shy around him. He cleared his throat and asked her to accompany him downstairs. She nodded and they went down to luncheon.

Shortly after the meal, Geoffrey asked her if she was ready for their stroll. He crooked his arm and she took it. They went out into the bright afternoon and slowly made their way down the sidewalk.

He leaned his head close to hers. "Have you been enjoying our day together, Becca?"

"Indeed, I have. It's been lovely."

"I'm sorry I haven't been spending much time with you."

"I understand, Geoffrey. This business with your accounts and such."

"That's no reason to leave my wife on her own for much of the day."

She smiled at his resolve. They continued on, nodding at the other people out enjoying the beautiful afternoon.

A while later, they entered the tea room. It was as charming as he'd said. They sat at a little round table and sipped cups of rich and fragrant tea. They shared a plate of biscuits, lemony and crisp and as fine as any she'd ever served at the inn.

Several acquaintances stopped by their table to greet the couple. They chatted amiably for a bit, and even Becca had to take note of how closely Geoffrey was sitting to her. He might not love her, but he felt … something. She wouldn't spoil their day together with the worry that had clouded her last night. She would focus on this one day of happiness and face the harsh reality of her marriage another day.

Chapter 16

When their tea time was over, they left the tea room and turned down the sidewalk, bound for home. Geoffrey thought it was as good a time as any to broach the subject that had been gnawing at him since last night.

He grasped her hand. "I want to talk about what you said last night."

She stiffened. "Geoffrey, I—"

"I have something to tell you, love."

She looked up at him and her lips thinned. No doubt she was bracing for the worst. God, he had been such a fool.

"Becca, when you said that I don't love you, I was shocked. You took me by surprise."

She simply stared up at him as they continued toward the townhouse.

"You made me realize something," he went on. "Something I should have known a long time ago."

He led her across the street. "Becca." He faltered. How to tell her what was in his heart? He turned to face her fully. "Becca, I have to tell you that I—"

"Look out!" a voice screamed from across the street.

"It's a runaway!" came another one.

Geoffrey turned and saw a carriage bearing down on them, the horses wild-eyed and apparently out of control.

Becca seemed riveted to the spot. Geoffrey grabbed her and ran for the sidewalk, losing his footing on the curb. He went sprawling on the walk and landed roughly on his back. The carriage continued on down the street, rounding the corner and racing out of sight.

It took him a moment to catch his breath. He pushed up to a sitting position and shook his head, then looked frantically for

Becca. He spotted her near the wrought-iron gate, less than five feet away from where he sat. She lay on her side, perfectly still. He scrambled over to her and placed his hand on her shoulder, turning her toward him. Her eyes were closed and there were scratches on her face.

"Becca?" She didn't answer. "Becca!"

She didn't open her eyes. The commotion had everyone out of their houses, murmuring and speculating on the event and the victims.

Geoffrey's butler, Miles, opened the front door, shock on his usually dour face. "My lord?"

Geoffrey turned his head sharply. "Go fetch the doctor, Miles," he commanded. "Now!"

The man ran off to do his master's bidding. Geoffrey scooped Becca up in his arms and carried her into the house. She was as limp as a rag doll in his arms. "Oh, God, no," he breathed.

He carried her into the parlor. "Mother!"

Lady Margaret rushed into the room. "Geoffrey, what is it? Oh, my!"

He laid Becca gently on the settee and brushed her hair away from her battered face. "Becca, please wake up." He swallowed thickly. "Please." He knelt beside her and buried his face in her lap. "Don't leave me, Becca." He choked back a sob. "I only just found you."

He stayed that way for several minutes, silently praying that she'd come back to him. Out of the corner of his eye, he could see his mother wringing her hands.

At last, Becca stirred. Her hand brushed over the back of his head. "Geoffrey?" she whispered.

His head shot up, his gaze flying to her face. He grabbed her shoulders. "Becca!"

He rained kisses on her face and stroked her hair. "I thought I lost you, love," he said brokenly.

She favored him with a weak smile.

"I love you, Becca." He closed his eyes for a moment, then opened them. "I've loved you for so very long."

He hugged her to him and she let out a gasp of pain. He

quickly laid her back down. “I’m sorry, love. Are you all right?”

“I … think so.”

“I’ll be the judge of that,” a voice said from the doorway.

Geoffrey turned to find Dr. Morgan standing there. He was an older man, with white hair and merry blue eyes, and Geoffrey had never been so glad to see a person in his life.

“Kane,” the doctor said, taking charge. “Give your wife some air, for heaven’s sake.”

Geoffrey stepped back and allowed him to examine her.

Dr. Morgan smiled down at Becca. “Had yourself a bit of excitement today, Lady Kanewood?”

She nodded. The doctor examined her face, noting the scratches on her cheeks and forehead.

“I’ll get some warm water and cloths to clean those scratches,” announced Lady Margaret as she left the room.

The doctor nodded approvingly. He felt her head and located a sizeable lump on the right side. He probed it gently with his fingers and Becca winced in response.

“Does that hurt?” the doctor asked.

“Just a bit,” she answered.

He looked into her eyes then and after carefully examining them, smiled. “Your eyes are clear.” He turned to Geoffrey, “I want her to have complete rest, Kane. If her head pains her, use a compress. Or try some brandy. I’ll stop by to check on her in the morning.”

Geoffrey nodded at the instructions. “Thank you.”

“Dr. Morgan, would you care to stay for some tea?” Lady Margaret asked as she walked back into the room with water and cloths.

“Yes, thank you.” He smiled. “I’d enjoy a visit.”

Geoffrey took the tray from his mother, “I can do that, Mother—you see to Dr. Morgan’s tea.” She gave her son a reassuring smile that all would be well and squeezed Becca’s hand, then turned and escorted Dr. Morgan down the hall to the library.

Geoffrey carefully cleaned Becca’s cuts and abrasions, a worried frown on his face.

“I’m not going to break, Geoffrey,” Becca said gently. “I’m

going to be all right. You heard Dr. Morgan."

"I could have lost you," he said in a shaky voice. He briefly carressed her face, then gingerly lifted her into his arms to carry her upstairs. He dropped kisses on her hair, and her face, as he carefully laid her on the bed. Mary stood close by, anxiously waiting to see to her mistress's comfort.

Geoffrey permitted Mary to fuss over Becca, taking the time to splash some water on his face and try to collect himself. He'd never been so frightened in his entire life. When he recalled that moment out on the sidewalk, an indescribable pain settled in the pit of his stomach. She'd been so still. He savagely pushed the thought away.

With Becca changed into her nightgown and wrapper, Mary left them. Geoffrey walked over to the bed. She lay propped up by a half-a-dozen pillows, her hair fanned out around her. Her face was pale, red scratches standing out on her forehead and right cheek. She looked vulnerable but so beautiful to him.

He sat next to her. "How are you feeling, love?"

"I'm tired, Geoffrey."

He kissed her and pulled back to stare into her eyes. "I love you, Becca."

Her brow creased. "Do you mean it?" she asked, using the words he had when she'd first made her declaration to him.

He hugged her gently. "Yes," he whispered against her hair. "I've loved you for a long time. I only realized it—"

"Today?" she finished for him.

He shook his head. "No. Last night."

She nodded and her eyes drifted closed. The sweetest smile curved her lips as she drifted off to sleep. How could he not have known that he'd loved her all this time? She was everything to him.

He settled himself in a chair and watched her sleep. *Thank you, God.*

Becca slept for nearly two hours. When she stirred and whispered her husband's name, he came to stand by the bed. "What is it, love?"

She stared up at him, a small smile on her face. "What time is it?"

"Nearly the dinner hour. Are you hungry?"

"I suppose I could eat a bit of something."

"Why don't I have the cook make some soup for you? And maybe some biscuits?"

She nodded.

Geoffrey brought up the supper tray himself. They shared their meal, though Geoffrey had roast beef along with his soup.

By the time Becca's bowl was empty, her eyelids looked heavy. Geoffrey removed the tray and helped her off with her robe. He bent his head to kiss her, brushing her lips very lightly.

She arched an eyebrow at him. "I'm not made of glass."

He straightened and looked down at her. She did look fragile to him then, and that horrible pain in his stomach returned. He sat next to her and hugged her tightly. "I love you."

She glowed, obviously pleased to hear those words again, then turned on her left side to snuggle into her pillow. "You love me," he heard her whisper.

He brushed her hair from her face and kissed her temple, ever-mindful of that angry-looking lump. "Always," he whispered back.

She sighed and drifted off to sleep.

He quietly closed the door and went downstairs to his study. There he poured himself a brandy and took a big swallow of it. He buried his face in his hands and reviewed the horrific events of the afternoon. Something about the runaway carriage nagged at the back of his mind, but when he tried to ponder it further, it danced away from him. Perhaps in the morning, when he was over the shock of nearly losing Becca, he'd be able to figure it out. He finished his drink and climbed the stairs to their chamber.

Somewhere around midnight, Becca sat bolt upright, a soft cry escaping her. Geoffrey came awake immediately and saw her eyes were wide, fear swirling in their depths.

"Becca?" he whispered.

She stared right through him.

He grasped her shoulders. "Becca, love, wake up!"

She blinked then, finally seeing him. "Geoffrey!" She sobbed and clutched at him. "The carriage was … was …."

"Shh, love." He rubbed her back. "It was just a bad dream. You're all right now."

She gave a small nod and sagged against him. Murmuring soft endearments in her ear, he laid back down. She took a long time to fall asleep, hiccuping now and then as her sobs quieted. He stroked her back, puzzling anew over the runaway carriage.

The next morning, he was awakened in the most pleasing fashion. Becca was sprawled on top of him, placing little kisses on his throat, his chest. He stretched and wrapped his arms around her.

She came up to kiss his mouth. "Good morning, husband."

"Mmm," he answered. "Good morning, love."

She shifted to lay against his side, trailing her fingers lightly over his chest. He closed his eyes again, still not fully awake. That changed quickly when he felt her hand grasp him.

"What are you about?"

She ran her lips over his neck, nibbling on his ear. "I want my husband to make love to me."

With a groan, he stilled her hand. "Love, the doctor said that you need rest."

She folded her hands on his chest and placed her chin on them. "But I've rested enough, Geoffrey."

He smiled, wanting her as much as she wanted him. "I'd like nothing more than to spend the morning making love to my beautiful wife." He kissed her lightly. "But until the doctor tells me everything is all right, I won't do anything that might hurt you."

She nodded. "Will you speak to Dr. Morgan today?"

"Yes. But I daresay it won't be an easy thing for me to ask."

She wore a look of worry. "Geoffrey, would you ever tell anyone what we … that is, how we make love?"

He was shocked by her question and shook his head firmly. "What we do in the privacy of our bedroom …." He grinned wickedly and added, "or in the carriage, or out riding, or …."

She swatted his shoulder. "Geoffrey!"

He grabbed her hand and kissed it. "No, love," he finished. "I'd never speak of such matters with anyone."

She smiled then, obviously relieved.

"Becca, why would you think that I—"

A knock at the door interrupted him. It was one of the servants, announcing that Dr. Morgan was calling to check on Lady Kanewood. Becca donned her robe and pulled up the covers, waiting for the doctor's entrance. Geoffrey sat up and swung his legs over the side of the bed. Becca's gasp of shock stilled him.

"Geoffrey, what happened to your back?"

He tried in vain to look over his shoulder. "What is it?"

"Your back." She caressed him lightly. "It's badly bruised."

He nodded then. "It must have happened when I fell yesterday."

She wrapped her arms around him and placed feather-light kisses on his tender flesh. He turned and hugged her to him, kissing her deeply. Reluctantly, he dragged his mouth from hers. With a sigh, he pulled away and stepped into his dressing room. He hastily dressed and went downstairs to fetch the doctor.

Dr. Morgan felt the bump on Becca's head, pleased to announce that it had shrunken quite a bit.

"Did you sleep well, Lady Kanewood?" he asked her.

She nodded. "I did awaken once during the night. I had a bad dream about the accident."

"Such things are to be expected. All looks very well. Please call for me if you have any discomfort."

"Thank you, doctor," she said.

Geoffrey accompanied him to the door and held him back for a moment. He looked at Becca and turned back to the doctor. "May we resume our, um, marital relations?" he asked softly.

"Of course. Just take care."

"Always."

After the doctor left, Geoffrey couldn't help flashing her a huge grin. The answering blush on her cheeks was all the proof he needed that the love of his life was also his perfect match.

Chapter 17

When Geoffrey arrived belowstairs, Miles announced that Lord Chester awaited him in his study. He entered the study to find Chester looking out the window.

"Chester, what brings you out so early in the day?"

"Good morning, Kane." Chester faced him. "I've been known to rise a bit before tea time every once in a while."

"Yes, once in a great while."

Chester's usually jovial expression turned serious. "I heard about the accident. How is Rebecca?"

"She's going to be fine, thank God." He sat behind his desk. "I don't mind telling you I nearly died when I thought I'd lost her."

"Did you get a good look at the carriage, Kane?"

"No. It all happened so fast. It was as if it came out of nowhere."

"That's what I thought."

"What you thought? What are you getting at, Chester?"

Chester frowned as he collected his thoughts, causing a spark of alarm to strike Geoffrey.

"Speak your mind, man."

"When I heard of yesterday's accident, my curiosity was piqued. I took the liberty of looking into it further."

"And what did you find?"

"Not much, I fear. Just up the street no one reported anything out of the ordinary. And if the carriage was as out of control as you say—"

"It was."

Chester held his hand up to still him. "If the carriage was indeed out of control, how was it able to turn the corner so smoothly as it reached the end of the street?"

Geoffrey felt a chill go through him. "What are you saying?"

"I don't think yesterday's accident was precisely an accident."

Geoffrey jumped to his feet. "Rebecca could have been killed!"

"Or you."

Geoffrey blinked at his friend's statement. He slumped back into his chair. "But who would want me dead?"

"I think this is somehow connected to the missing funds."

"Not possible."

"Do think for a moment. Is Rebecca usually with you during the day?"

"No, she's usually here at the house. Why?"

"That would confirm my suspicions that you were the target."

Geoffrey raked his fingers through his hair. "But I still don't understand why."

"Kane, I found out yesterday that someone has indeed been passing notes in your name."

"My solicitors had told me that several notes had reached them over the past few weeks," Geoffrey said. "They were written for small amounts but were numerous. The firm presumed they were from me, unusual though they were. Do we know yet who has been passing them?"

"No."

Geoffrey rubbed his chin, thoughtful. "I think we should bring Roberts in on this."

"I agree. Roberts travels in some pretty unsavory circles when he wishes to."

"He's also lesser known than you or me."

Chester nodded. "Roberts and I will return this afternoon."

Geoffrey shook his hand in thanks and let him show himself out. He settled behind his desk and mulled over all that Chester had suggested. To think that someone had deliberately tried to run him down.

He could have lost Becca forever. He needed to see her right away, to know that she was truly all right. He left the study, bound for their chamber.

He quietly opened the door to the chamber, thinking Becca might be sleeping. He froze at the sight before him. Becca was turned slightly away from him in the bath, her hands in her hair. Geoffrey watched as she worked her fingers through the long strands, her eyes closed. She wore a look of rapture on her face. He felt his pulse quicken. He stepped toward the tub, drinking in the sensuous picture she made. The water lapped around her, barely covering her pink-tipped breasts. He took off his coat and began unbuttoning his shirt.

Becca ducked under the water once more. When she emerged, her hair streamed down her back. She grabbed it and brought it over her shoulder, twisting the mass into a thick rope as she wrung it dry.

She opened her eyes then, surprise in them as she spotted Geoffrey. "Geoffrey!" She gasped. "How long have you been standing there?"

He smiled crookedly at her as he removed his shirt and unbuttoned his breeches. "Long enough."

She arched a brow at him. "What are you about, husband?"

"I thought I'd join my wife in the bath."

The answering heat in her lovely green eyes was all the agreement he needed.

After they'd bathed each other and loved each other in the big bed, she stared up at him. "Tell me, Geoffrey."

He knew what she needed to hear. "I love you, Becca."

"And I love you," she answered.

He rolled onto his back and she snuggled against him.

"You make me quiver."

He smiled down at her. "And you make me lose control."

She turned to look at him. "And is that a good thing?"

"Yes indeed," he said, kissing her lightly. "That's a very good thing."

They roused themselves after a while and readied for lunch. When Geoffrey had dressed, he found Becca sitting at the vanity. She turned to face him, a frown on her face.

"Is something wrong, love?"

"Look at me. My face is hideous."

He laughed softly. "It would take more than a few scratches

to make you hideous."

"You see through the eyes of love, I daresay."

"Indeed." He kissed her cheek. "That doesn't necessarily mean that my vision is clouded."

She caught his smile. "Never mind that. I'll see you downstairs?"

"Certainly. Don't keep me waiting too long."

When she joined him, John was there, as well. Both gentleman stood when she entered.

"How are you, Becca?" John asked.

Geoffrey looked at his brother sharply. *Becca, is it?*

Geoffrey took Becca's hand in his. "My wife is going to be fine, John."

"Yes, John. How can I not be?" she said smiling at Geoffrey. "My husband loves me."

Geoffrey smiled and placed a kiss on her temple. John cleared his throat and turned his attention back to his meal.

When they were finished, Becca and Geoffrey went into the parlor. Geoffrey saw her settled on the settee, getting her assurance that she'd sit still and not tax herself.

She quirked a smile at him. "And what would be more taxing than what transpired upstairs, Geoffrey?"

He growled at her. "Hush, darling. Lest I take you back upstairs and leave our callers disappointed."

As the afternoon wore on, and the salver grew full, he noted that Becca seemed nearly herself. Just before five o'clock, Chester and Roberts arrived. Lady Margaret escorted the other callers to the front door and Geoffrey told the butler that they wouldn't be receiving anyone else that afternoon. He closed the doors and turned to find his friends standing over his wife.

"How are you, Lady Kanewood?" Chester asked.

"I feel much better. Thank you, Lord Chester."

Lord Roberts took Becca's hand in his. "We were very worried about you, Rebecca."

Geoffrey's eyes narrowed at Roberts's use of her first name. He hadn't forgotten their exchange on the balcony the night of the Winslow ball, and didn't much like the charming viscount's fawning over her now.

"That's very nice of you to say, Lord Roberts," she answered, smiling.

Roberts's eyes glittered and Chester cleared his throat.

"Lady Kanewood," Chester began. "We were wondering if you could tell us anything about yesterday's incident."

She turned to him, puzzlement on her face. Geoffrey shook his head at his friend, silently warning him not to tell her of their suspicions.

Chester gave an almost imperceptible nod and re-worded his question. "Did you notice anything unusual about the carriage?"

Roberts gave a short laugh. "He means besides the fact that it was out of control."

Becca laughed at that. All three men smiled in response.

"Well," she began. "The carriage was dark. Black, or dark blue, perhaps."

Chester nodded. "Can you remember anything else about it?"

She shrugged, looking quite helpless, and Geoffrey joined her on the settee. He placed his hand on hers. "Try, Becca."

She closed her eyes for a long moment. "There was a coat of arms on the carriage."

The gentlemen exchanged curious looks.

"Can you picture it, love?" Geoffrey asked.

"Yes," she said, her eyes still closed. "It was of an odd shape, one I haven't seen before."

"What was its shape, Lady Kanewood?" Chester asked.

She held up her finger and traced a shape in the air. "It was slightly elongated, almost diamond-shaped."

"Like a lozenge?" Roberts offered.

"Yes!" she said, her eyes flying open.

Roberts blinked. "Was there anything on the lozenge?"

Her brow furrowed for a moment. Her frown suddenly cleared. "There was a bird on it. At least I think it was a bird."

Geoffrey looked at Chester, who in turn shrugged his shoulders.

"An eagle, or perhaps a hawk?" the blond-haired man asked.

Becca shook her head. "No, much smaller. It was in profile. Sitting, I think." She turned to Geoffrey. "Is this important?"

"It could be, love. We just want to know everything."

"Don't you remember anything, Geoffrey?"

"I'm afraid not. Other than the sight of those horses coming toward us, I draw a complete blank."

"I hate to see you worried." She gently stroked his cheek.

He stood and urged her to her feet. "Why don't you go upstairs and rest, Becca? I'll entertain these two rogues."

Geoffrey escorted her to the door.

"She's enchanting, is she not?" Roberts asked Chester.

"Yes. And very happily married, Roberts."

Roberts turned with a devilish grin. "But does Kane know how to keep her happy?"

Geoffrey stilled as the man's words penetrated his thoughts, then closed the door sealing Becca out of the parlor. He turned back to his friends. "Would you care to clarifty that statement, Roberts?"

The man grinned in answer.

"Don't give a thought to charming her, friend," Chester said. "Kane has a jealous streak as wide as the Thames where Rebecca is concerned."

"As you say, Chester," Roberts agreed.

"Damn right," Geoffrey gritted between his teeth. *She's mine.*

"Easy, Kane," Chester said wryly. "I don't want to watch my two friends duel."

"And whose second would you be, Chester?" Roberts asked.

"The only second I'll take on is a second apple tart that my cook makes," Chester quipped.

The men shared a laugh and Geoffrey put aside Roberts's apparent infatuation with his wife as they set about the business of deciphering what Becca had told them.

Roberts again mentioned the lozenge on the carriage. "It was a lady's carriage, Kane. That much is clear."

"True," Geoffrey said.

"But what of the bird?" Chester asked. "Do either of you recognize it?"

"I don't," Roberts said. "Perhaps there was more on the coat of arms besides the bird."

"That's precisely what I was thinking," Geoffrey added. "But I'm still confused. Why a lady's carriage?"

"Perhaps someone is jealous of your lovely wife."

"The carriage may have been borrowed," Chester offered.

Roberts scratched his chin. "Hmm. Perhaps I'll pay a call on a certain lady whose acquaintance has proven helpful in the past. She's an insufferable gossip, and I'd wager she'd know on whose crest sits a small bird."

The other two knew of whom he spoke. She was a married woman, and quite taken with the very handsome viscount.

"This goes beyond the call of duty, Roberts," Geoffrey jested.

"Yes." The viscount rolled his eyes. "What I won't do for a friend."

"Come, Roberts." Chester grabbed his arm. "I say we leave Geoffrey to the care of his wife."

"Thank you both," Geoffrey said.

"We'll let you know if we learn anything," Chester said.

Geoffrey sat down behind his desk, feeling much better for having brought his two friends into the mess, Roberts's infatuation aside. He only hoped that nothing untoward would happen before they could get to the bottom of it. As long as he was in danger, so was Becca.

He'd die before letting anything ever happen to her again.

Chapter 18

For the next week, Geoffrey held several meetings with Lords Chester and Roberts. The latter had an interesting bit of news to share one afternoon after his visit to the enamored gossip.

It seemed that a certain young widow was in a bad way financially. Lady Joan Balsam, the married woman so fond of Roberts, told him that Priscilla Brooks was in dire straits. Her late husband, the Earl of Brookdale, had amassed gambling debts before his untimely demise. Lady Joan was only too happy to add the fact that Lady Brookdale had practically nothing left except her pretty face.

"Does a bird figure prominently on Brooks's coat?" Geoffrey asked.

"Yes," Roberts answered. "A quail."

"Were you able to learn if Lady Brookdale is involved with anyone?" Chester asked.

"No." Roberts shook his head, a crooked smile on his face. "It seems that Lady Joan was quite jealous of my interest in the lovely widow."

Geoffrey nodded, returning the man's smile. "It's a wonder you got out of their with your virtue intact, Roberts."

"I thought that I'd pay a call on the poor, lonely widow," Roberts volunteered.

"That could prove interesting," Chester added. "Do you think she'd be involved in this?"

Roberts shook his head. "From what I remember of the late earl's wife, she's quiet and shy."

"The earl died only a few months past, I believe?" Chester asked Roberts.

"Seven months, according to Lady Joan. Why?"

Chester stood and paced as the other two men watched

expectantly. After a while, he spoke. "It seems to me that she wouldn't be openly involved with anyone. Could she have let someone use her carriage that day?"

"It's possible." Geoffrey looked at the clock on the desk. "Gentlemen, if you will excuse me, I promised my wife that I'd change and be ready to escort her to dinner this evening."

His friends stood then, crossing to the door.

Chester pulled the door open and turned. "Are you going to any of the parties tonight, Kane?"

"Rebecca and I plan to make the rounds, yes. Though with the possibility of someone wishing me harm, I'm tempted to keep her out of the line of fire."

"You don't know if this was deliberate," Chester said. "It seems your wife isn't the type to let you wrap her in silk and keep her at home."

Geoffrey smiled. "Hardly."

"How is she feeling?" Roberts asked.

"She's feeling just fine, thank you," Becca said from the doorway.

The men turned to her. She was dressed for dinner, wearing a gown of deep violet. She smiled at them in greeting.

"Rebecca." Roberts grinned. "You look marvelous. You must be feeling better."

"It's a pleasure to see you so well," Chester said.

Geoffrey joined his friends at the door. "Hello, love." He took her hand and drew her to his side.

"Geoffrey, it seems I was left to find my own way to dinner."

"Put the blame squarely on us, Lady Kanewood." Chester smiled. "We kept your husband from you."

"Yes." Roberts bowed. "We beg your pardon, Rebecca."

They took their leave and Geoffrey pulled her into his arms.

"I'm sorry, Becca," he said softly. "I've been closed in with those two for too long."

"I forgive you, Geoffrey."

"Come upstairs and help me get dressed for dinner?"

"I daresay were I to assist you, we'd both go hungry."

"Hmm. I see the truth in your statement." He kissed her.

"I'll see you in a few minutes, love."

She nodded and left the room, bound for the parlor. She found John and Patricia within, and froze. After their confrontation in the hallway the other day, she was still very uncomfortable in John's company.

"Good evening, John," she said stiffly. "Hello, Patricia."

"Rebecca," Patricia responded cooly.

John stared "How are you this evening, Bec— Rebecca?"

"Very well, thank you." She took a seat on the settee.

"Good evening, everyone," Lady Margaret said as she joined them. "And where is my eldest son, Rebecca?"

"He was detained by Lords Chester and Roberts, Lady Margaret. He should be down in a few moments."

Geoffrey strode into the parlor just then, barely acknowledging his brother and sister-in-law. He kissed his mother on the cheek and took Becca's hand. "Sorry to keep you waiting, love."

They went in to dinner and, afterward, went upstairs to ready themselves for the round of parties.

* * * *

By the time they reached the third party, Becca was growing tired. It was a large affair, and the rooms were quite crowded and noisy. After greeting their hostess, Geoffrey grasped Becca's elbow and led her to the main ball room. He bent his head to hers. "Would you care to dance?"

"Actually, I'd like to rest for a moment."

"Certainly, love."

He led her over to a row of chairs and sat beside her. They were almost immediately surrounded by Geoffrey's friends.

"Kane!" Viscount Leed exclaimed. "Where have you been all evening?"

"Rebecca and I have been making the rounds, Leed."

"Lady Kanewood, how are you?" Chester asked.

"Very well, thank you. We've been having a splendid time."

"Good evening, Kane," Lord Roberts intoned, shouldering

his way between Chester and Leed. He took Becca's gloved hand in his. "Rebecca."

"Good evening, Lord Roberts," she said.

"Kane," Chester began, his tone light. "Leed and I would like a word with you when you get a chance."

Geoffrey looked uncertain.

"Go on, Kane," Roberts said. "I'll keep Rebecca entertained."

After a brief hesitation, Geoffrey agreed to speak with the other gentlemen.

Becca arched a brow. "Is anything wrong?"

He shook his head. "Don't fret, love. I won't be long."

He kissed her lightly and followed Leed and Chester to the other side of the room.

Roberts took the chair her husband had vacated, his leg brushing lightly against hers. She barely noticed his closeness, her eyes still on Geoffrey. He turned his back to her then, deep in conversation with the other two gentlemen. With a sigh, she turned back to the man seated beside her.

His eyes sparkled as they ran over her. "May I say, Rebecca, that you look splendid this evening. Like a goddess."

She smiled at his choice of words. "It's the gown, I daresay."

Roberts shook his head at her. "No, though it's quite beautiful."

She nodded at his compliment. "Thank you."

Roberts began to amuse her with stories about the other party-goers. Each time one passed by, he'd tell her something of them. Most of the stories were from when they were all young and foolish. She smiled to learn that even members of such high society had their mistakes and foibles.

* * * *

Across the room, Geoffrey listened intently to Leed. The man had worked with them many times over the years, and was very trustworthy in Geoffrey's opinion.

"Kane," Leed began. "I don't know how to tell you this, but

someone has been passing notes in your name."

"We were aware of that, Leed."

Leed's piercing blue eyes bore into Geoffrey's. "No, you don't understand. Someone is pretending to be you."

Geoffrey looked from one man to the other. Chester nodded solemnly.

"But who would do such a thing? I'm surely not the wealthiest peer, not by many standards." Geoffrey sucked in a breath. "Who held these notes, Leed?"

Leed shrugged. "Therein lies our problem. The notes passed through a few hands before ending up on your solicitor's desk for payment."

"I was afraid of that," Geoffrey said. "When they informed me of the notes, I had no notion of their origin. I daresay they poured over the ledgers with a fine-tooth comb to discover any errors, though now we know the notes were forged."

"The notes were paid, then?" Leed asked.

"Of course," Geoffrey said. "They had no way of knowing I hadn't written them myself. Can they be traced, Chester?"

"That's what Roberts is looking into now. He and Leed here will try to find out who held them originally."

Geoffrey nodded and opened his mouth to comment. He heard Becca's laugh then, a sweet sound that carried from across the room. He turned and watched Roberts with his wife. Their dark heads were nearly touching. The viscount was obviously using all of his charm on her. Becca laughed again, placing her hand on Roberts's arm.

Geoffrey's eyes narrowed. "Gentlemen, if you will excuse me. I think my wife needs my attention just now."

He reached Becca's side, drawing Roberts's attention as the man leaned closer to whisper in her ear. "Telling tales, Roberts?"

Becca looked up at him, tears of laughter in her eyes. "Geoffrey." She giggled. "He knows the silliest stories."

Geoffrey nodded, smiling at the delight on her face.

Roberts sat back. "And all of them true, God help us all."

She laughed again. Geoffrey stood over the other man, waiting for his intentions to become clear. Roberts, however, didn't catch his meaning quickly enough.

"If you will excuse us, Roberts," he said, taking Becca's hand. "My wife has promised me a dance."

She stood up and smoothed her dress. She happily let her husband lead her out onto the dance floor.

"Did you enjoy Roberts's stories, love?"

"Yes, very much so. Only he wouldn't tell me any about you."

He arched a brow at that. "What is it you would like to know?"

She shrugged. "Just a bit about you when you were young and mischievous."

"I never got into the slightest bit of trouble, I assure you," he answered in mock-severity.

"I don't believe that for a moment, husband."

He smiled at her, drawing her closer. "Never mind."

"Hmm," she said, a playful look in her eye. "Perhaps I can persuade Lord Roberts to tell me all your secrets."

He stiffened for a moment, not liking the idea of her being alone with the man. He also didn't want her to know about his government work years ago, when he'd been embroiled in heated debates regarding Parliament's insistence that England have no standing army.

He and Roberts, along with others, had worked furiously in the background to bring changes to the system, finding nothing but frustration at every bend. He saw his efforts as a failure, and preferred to keep the matter from Becca's observance.

"Geoffrey, what is it?"

He shook his head and flashed her a smile. "Nothing, love." He lowered his voice. "And we already share the most delicious secrets."

A faint blush covered her cheeks as he brought his lips to her ear and whispered all the intimacies he wanted to share with her that very evening.

* * * *

With the Season nearly at an end, Geoffrey and Becca returned to Kanewood. Geoffrey was eager to get out of London and the danger it presented. Becca and Lady Margaret would be involved with preparations for the ball they would host in just two weeks. Many of the friends they had seen in town would come up to Kanewood for the bash to celebrate their nuptials. Of course, with the estate being so far flung from London, they would all stay for a time. It promised to be a lengthy affair, with the men hunting and the women gossiping for at least a week. A true house party set in one of the loveliest parts of England.

Becca and Lady Margaret wrote out the invitations while still in London, making sure all were delivered. The replies began to arrive at the townhouse the day after the invitations were sent. It seemed that all of the earl's acquaintances were looking forward to celebrating their union, as well as spending a week in the country on the beautiful Kanewood estate.

They stopped at the Raven's Inn on the way back home to invite Thomas to the affair. His chest puffed out with pride to be included in the festivities.

Once back at Kanewood, Lady Margaret began her tutelage. Becca listened intently to the woman, for Kanewood had hosted many an affair when Geoffrey's father was alive. The older woman went over such matters as planning the menu, and selecting what types of flowers with which to dress the ballroom. The men would undoubtedly entertain themselves during the days as the hunting was quite good. And Lady Margaret was looking forward to spending unhurried afternoons in good company and pleasant conversation.

The day before the guests began to arrive, their preparations were long-finished. The staff readied the guest rooms and the kitchen was prepared. That morning after breakfast, Becca took herself up to the nursery to visit with Ann. The little girl squealed happily to see her aunt. Becca told her that she'd missed her very much when they were all in London. She played with the little girl, even sharing her snack of milk and biscuits. Ann seemed to crave the attention and it was a shame that the child's mother didn't show such affection to the girl.

Geoffrey found Becca in the nursery later. Ann seemed shy around him and stayed close to Becca's side.

"Hello, Ann." He smiled down at her. "How are you this fine day?"

"Hello, Uncle Geoffrey," she said softly.

He turned his attention to his wife. "I wished to see you, love. Before I went out."

"Where are you going?" Becca asked him.

"I need to see to those repairs we spoke of."

She nodded and crouched down to the little girl. "I have to go now, Ann. But I'll come back to visit you again."

Ann threw her arms around Becca's neck and placed a noisy kiss on her cheek. The obvious and open affection between Becca and the child touched his heart. There was no doubt in his mind that she would make a wonderful mother should they ever be so blessed. Like he had been, their child would be assured of its parents' love. It was a shame that Ann did not have that certainty.

They left the nursery and went back downstairs.

Geoffrey took Becca's hand as they reached the main floor. "I probably won't return until after tea time."

She placed her hands on his chest and kissed him lightly. "I'll see you then."

After taking lunch, she joined Lady Margaret and Patricia in the parlor. The two women were busily working on their needlework, so Becca set about painting the fire screen she'd been decorating. It wasn't very large, but the design she painted was quite intricate. She wanted to use it in her and Geoffrey's chamber and chose a design of flowers to offset the masculine furnishings.

The three ladies passed the afternoon and when tea time was nearly upon them, Patricia suddenly sighed irritably.

Becca looked at her sister-in-law in surprise. "Is something wrong, Patricia?"

Patricia set her needlework aside and stood. "Yes," she answered, full of pique. "My husband has been out all day and I have need to speak with him."

Becca blinked at her. She looked to Lady Margaret, who simply gave a slight shrug of her shoulders. Becca turned back to Patricia. "I'm certain he'll be back soon."

A smile curved Patricia's lips. "And where is Kane?"

"Geoffrey had to take care of some matters on the estate," she answered easily. "I don't expect him back much before dinner."

Becca's calm response seemed to only make Patricia more irritated. With a swish of her skirt, she left them.

"I wonder what made her so angry?" Becca asked.

"Patricia is used to getting her own way," Lady Margaret answered. "Don't take it personally, dear."

Becca nodded and returned her attention to the fire screen. She would not give Patricia and her prickly behavior another thought. Instead, she focused on how pleasant it was to pass the time without that woman in the room.

She was just filling in a lovely pink tulip on the screen when Geoffrey strode into the room. She was focused on her work, biting her lip in concentration.

"Hello, love," he greeted her from the doorway.

She looked up, startled. A smile slowly curved her lips as she took in his appearance. He'd indeed been working on the estate. He'd removed his jacket at some point and his shirt was open at the collar. It was rumpled and soiled, and his breeches were dusty. His hair was tousled and dirt was smudged on his face. He looked absolutely gorgeous to her, like the plainly-dressed man she'd first met at Raven's. He affected her as he had that very first day, causing her heart to trip and her breath to catch.

"Geoffrey, what have you been about?" Lady Margaret asked.

"Seeing to some repairs, Mother."

"You look a fright."

"Oh, I disagree," Becca intoned. "I think he looks like quite the rogue."

Geoffrey smiled, his eyes twinkling. He crossed to her and kissed her lightly. He pulled back and looked at her, suddenly grinning.

"What is it, husband?"

He reached out a finger and rubbed her nose. "I'm afraid I left my mark on you, wife."

She shooed him out of the room and watched him as he left. She turned to Lady Margaret, noting the laughter in the woman's eyes. She smiled at her mother-in-law and once again bent her head over her work.

Chapter 19

Awaiting dinner in the dining room, John and Patricia discussed the upcoming event. Lady Margaret hadn't yet joined them, so they talked freely.

"Heaven help us, John," Patricia began, rankled. "All of Kane's friends will be here. The place will be overrun."

"I disagree, my dove. I, for one, am looking forward to the hunting. It'll be pleasant to have some spirited competition."

"But what of the ball tomorrow night? Yet another evening devoted to the earl and his 'ravishing' bride."

"Careful, careful," he gently chided. "Do I see the green-eyed monster peeking out from your beautiful blue eyes?"

She sighed irritably. He chuckled then and grasped her hand. "Rebecca is quite stunning. But she can never outshine you in my eyes."

Patricia let his words convince her of his loyalty.

John turned his attention to the doorway just as Geoffrey and Becca entered the room. He stood as they entered. "Kane, where have you been all day? I could have used your company on my outing. The pub was a dreadful bore, I daresay."

"I had work to see to, brother," Geoffrey replied. "Something you are always welcome to help me with."

"Now why ever would I do that, brother?" John shrugged. "You're the earl and therefore the work must be yours to shoulder just as the rewards are yours to reap. I am merely the second son."

"You've had plenty of rewards, John," Geoffrey retorted. "Father left you well taken care of."

John gritted his teeth and then shrugged. "Perhaps." He effectively dismissed his brother by turning to Rebecca, with a charming smile. "Good evening, Rebecca."

"Hello, John," she answered in a small voice, apparently uncomfortable as his gaze raked over her emerald green gown.

She nodded to Patricia and sat down next to her husband's place at the head of the table. Apparently, the good earl hadn't missed John's lustful glare or Becca's blushing response to it. Geoffrey looked from one to the other, a speculative look on his face. Finally, he took his place at the table just as Lady Margaret joined them. John took his gaze off Becca and greeted his mother ambiably.

Dinner was filled with talk of the guests due to arrive on the morrow. "Most should be at Kanewood by tea time, love," Geoffrey said. "That should leave them plenty of time to settle in and ready themselves for the ball tomorrow evening."

Becca nodded.

"When will your father be arriving, Rebecca?" Lady Margaret asked.

"He should be here the same time as the others, I presume."

Lady Margaret looked to her eldest son. "Geoffrey, are you ready for the revelers?"

Geoffrey chuckled at his mother's choice of words. "I suppose so. I trust that your friends' unattached daughters will be coming? Those scoundrels Chester, Leed and Roberts will be here, you know."

Lady Margaret smiled slyly at her son. "Perhaps there will be another wedding or two to celebrate by the time the Season rolls around again."

"I can't see Roberts settling down with one woman, Kane," John said with a grin. "Those matrons had better lock up their daughters if they ever want to see them wed."

Patricia stiffened beside John, obviously once more feeling left out of the conversation. The rest of them finished their meal in pleasant conversation, with Patricia nodding at all the appropriate places.

Shortly after dinner ended, Lady Margaret bade the others good night and retired for the evening. Using his hard work of the day as an excuse, Geoffrey begged off an after-dinner drink with John. He thanked John and led Becca upstairs to their chambers. John watched them go, the image of the delectable

Becca readying herself for bed dancing through his mind. With a sigh, he turned to Patricia who was regarding him closely.

"Is something troubling you, John?" she asked

"Hmm?" he stalled. "No, my dove. Nothing." He crossed over to her and took her hand. "Shall we follow their lead and make it an early evening?"

With a shrug of her shoulders, she acquiesced.

* * * *

After breakfast the next morning, Geoffrey told Becca that he had some matters to attend to in his study. She reluctantly agreed, but only after getting his assurance that he'd join her for lunch. With a tender kiss, he left her in the capable hands of his mother.

Lady Margaret was very excited about the coming guests, and Becca found her enthusiasm catching. The two women went into the kitchens to reiterate some of the instructions the staff had been given. After being assured that all was as they had requested, they adjourned to the library. While Becca absently thumbed through a leather-bound book, Lady Margaret sat at the small desk, pen and paper in hand.

"Rebecca, dear," she began, a thoughtful look on her face. "I was thinking that before the guests arrive, we might think of some possible matches."

"Matches?"

"Yes. Although Geoffrey was merely jesting last evening, I believe we just might marry off some of the lovely young girls set to arrive today."

Becca quirked a smile at her mother-in-law. "Lady Margaret, aren't we getting a bit ahead of ourselves?"

"Perhaps, dear," she conceded. "But we should still consider our guest list, at least for possible dinner partners."

Becca nodded. "Well, we know that Geoffrey's handsome friends will be here. What young ladies will be in attendance?"

Lady Margaret held up her hand for a moment, jotting down a few notes. "First things first, dear," she instructed. "The Earl of Chester will be here, along with Viscounts Leed and Roberts, correct?"

"Yes."

"Let me see, then. I know for certain that Lady Beatrice is bringing her daughter, Constance," she said, adding to her notes.

"What is Constance like, Lady Margaret?"

"When last I saw her, she was a tiny thing, with white-blond curls. I'm sure she's quite lovely now. Oh," Lady Margaret added. "I believe Beatrice mentioned that her niece might come along. Sarah, I think her name is."

"That's two," Becca said with a smile.

Lady Margaret nodded. "Lady Helen will undoubtedly bring her daughter, Michelle. Do you remember meeting her?"

"Hmm, I believe so. Didn't she call after the accident?"

"Yes, she did. She's around your age, I'd imagine."

"And very pretty, with all that shining red hair."

"Very comely, yes," Lady Margaret agreed. "She'll no doubt have them at her feet."

Becca caught Lady Margaret's zeal for matchmaking "Splendid! Any others?"

"Lord Henry will be in attendance. He and the late earl were dear friends."

Becca caught the tone of melancholy in her voice and nodded in sympathy.

Lady Margaret straightened her shoulders and went on. "His daughter, Diane, was nearly betrothed to John."

"Really?" Becca asked in surprise.

"Yes. If only .... Oh, never mind that."

Becca knew that Lady Margaret wouldn't speak of John's and Patricia's betrayal of Geoffrey, and wisely kept her own opinion of her husband's brother to herself. If Lady Margaret knew all that John had been about of late, she'd surely be upset.

"What is Diane like?" Becca asked.

"She's a very sweet girl, with pretty blue eyes and dark blond hair."

Becca's brow furrowed as she pondered the possible matches. "How will we know who to match with whom?"

Lady Margaret wore a sly grin. "When the guests assemble before the ball, we will simply watch the gentlemen for any signs of interest."

"This could prove very fascinating, Lady Margaret. But how will we know so soon?"

"How long did it take you to fall for my son, dear?"

Becca blushed and Lady Margaret nodded sharply, her point made. For the better part of the next hour, the ladies discussed their opinions of which gentleman would prefer which lady.

It was soon lunchtime, so they set aside their discussion and adjourned to the dining room. Geoffrey wasn't in the room, much to Becca's disappointment. She told Lady Margaret that she'd return in a moment and went in search of her husband.

Becca knocked on the door to the study. Getting no answer, she opened the door and peeked inside. Geoffrey stood at the window, staring out over the grounds. She took advantage of the moment, letting her gaze wander over him. He certainly cut a dashing figure. A small sigh escaped her and he turned sharply at the sound. The brooding look on his face gave her pause.

His frown cleared quickly and a smile spread over his features as he crossed to her. "Becca."

They shared a sweet kiss.

"What had you so absorbed, husband?"

He wrapped her in his arms. "Nothing, love."

"Geoffrey, I saw the worry on your face when I came in."

He looked at her closely, then shook his head. "Let us go in to lunch."

"But I want to talk to you—"

"It's nothing. Please don't concern yourself."

She let him lead her out of the room, vowing to herself to get some answers out of him. She wouldn't let him fall back into the habit of keeping his worries from her.

After lunch, they went for a stroll in the gardens. They were quite lovely, divided formally into sections by low hedgerows. Geoffrey led her over to a large stone bench set off in one corner. He sat down, taking her with him. Becca saw the worry cross his face once more.

"Geoffrey, what is it?"

He shook his head again. "I was just thinking about how crowded Kanewood will be with all of our guests here."

She quirked a half-smile at him. "Husband, we could have the entire House of Lords for a visit and Kanewood wouldn't be crowded."

He laughed at her, pulling her close. "I don't want to share you with anyone, Becca. There will be so many people here, I fear I'll get lost in the shuffle."

She brought her hand up to his cheek. "No one could ever take your place, Geoffrey. I love you."

He bent his head to hers. "I love you so much, Becca," he said, his voice husky. "I don't want anything to happen to you."

His sudden intensity confused her. "Nothing will happen to me, husband. Not with you to protect me."

He settled back against the bench, still holding her close. "Are you looking forward to tonight's festivities, love?"

"Oh, yes. I do so love to see my husband dressed in his formal attire."

"And what will you be wearing, wife?"

"That's a surprise."

"Hmm," he said, scratching his chin as if in thought. "Please tell me you're not wearing the pink gown again. I don't want to throw any of the gentlemen off the estate for drooling over my wife."

She gave him a playful nudge. "Oh, really. Well, perhaps I shall wear it just for you. On special occasions."

"Woman, don't tempt me when our guests are about to arrive," he growled in her ear.

She laughed and kissed his cheek. "Very well, I won't tempt you for the rest of today. But I cannot promise about tonight," she quipped.

"Most assuredly, you will be free to tempt me all night long," he whispered in her ear.

She gave a delicious shiver as he tipped up her face and kissed her deeply. Becca loved spending quiet time with Geoffrey. He was always so busy and preoccupied of late that even a stolen moment in the garden was a gift. But even while he kissed her, worry flitted at the back of her mind. She wished he would confide in her and share his burdens. But how could she convince him?

The sound of an approaching carriage pulled them from their interlude. He helped her from the bench and they walked out of the garden and out onto the cobblestone drive in front of the house.

* * * *

The remainder of the afternoon was spent welcoming the guests and getting them settled into their rooms. Becca herself showed Thomas Kingsley to his room. Her father couldn't get over the size and grandeur of the estate, commending her—and himself, by extension—on making such a great match. With Thomas firmly ensconced in his room, Becca went down to tea.

Several of the guests took tea with the ladies in the parlor while the servants brought their belongings up to the guest rooms. Geoffrey's male friends passed the time with him in his study.

John soon joined them. "Gentlemen, I fear the ladies will be watching you all very closely."

Lord Chester arched a brow. "What are you talking about, John?"

"Well, my mother is intent on marrying off some of the young women who will be in attendance."

"Wonderful," Leed intoned dryly.

"What's the matter, Leed?" Geoffrey asked with a grin.

"Kane," Leed began, "just because you found marital bliss doesn't mean it's a desirable state for everyone."

"Ah, but my brother has the lovely Rebecca." John laughed.

"That's right, Leed," Chester added. "If she could change Kane's mind about matrimony, perhaps there is hope for the likes of you and me."

"Never mind," Leed grumbled.

"I fear poor Leed is a bit shy around the ladies," Roberts intoned.

Chester laughed. "Not all of us can be as charming as you, Roberts."

"Yes." Roberts grinned. "The ladies do enjoy my company."

They talked a bit more, making plans to go hunting early in the morning. After a while, Geoffrey showed them to their rooms and left them to ready themselves for the evening. He walked down the hall to the wing where his and Becca's chambers were located and found her in the little study off the hallway, bent over the desk. Sheets of paper littered the top of the desk, and she was busily poring over them.

He leaned against the door jam and watched her for a moment. "What are you about, love?"

"Geoffrey!" She gasped. "How long have you been standing there?"

"Just a short while," he said, crossing to her. "What's all this?"

She covered the papers with her forearms. "Oh, just some notes."

"Becca." He smiled down at her.

She laughed and showed him the papers. "They're just notes about the young ladies Lady Margaret and I discussed this afternoon."

He read over a few of them and turned to her.

"I fear I have gotten caught up in your mother's matchmaking," she admitted.

"Matchmaking? Oh, no. Not you, too?"

She shrugged. "I just want everyone to be as happy as we are, Geoffrey."

"That, love, would be impossible." He pulled her up out of the chair. "Come, wife. Let's ready for the party."

She left her notes on the desk and let him lead her into their chambers.

* * * *

A while later, Becca stood waiting for her husband. Mary had swept her hair up into a mass of glossy curls. The pearls glowed against her skin, matching the satin of her gown. Becca wore the gown she was married in and she could hardly wait for

Geoffrey to see her. When he came for her, his reaction didn't disappoint her.

"Becca," he breathed. "You're even more lovely than when you first wore that dress."

She favored him with a sweet smile, twining her gloved hands up around his neck. His eyes sparkled down at her as he bent his head to hers. Their kiss was gentle, sending shivers through her. He pulled back and sighed. Without another word, he led her out of the room and downstairs to await the guests in the ballroom.

The evening was a smashing success and, except for one awkward moment when John asked to dance with her, Becca enjoyed the ball immensely. Geoffrey didn't leave her side, and the danger they'd left in London had little to do with it. He'd let none of his friends twirl her out onto the dance floor despite their persistence. She was his and his alone. She'd never felt so cared for and protected. There was no doubt in her mind that he loved her.

In the wee hours of the morning, they ascended the grand staircase and retired to their chambers. Geoffrey took his time that night. He slowly unfastened the many hooks in the back of her gown and unlaced her stays trailing tiny kisses down her back. By the time he had her undressed, Becca was trembling with anticipation.

"Geoffrey." She breathed, needing his possession. "Please ...."

He swept her up into his arms and placed her gently in the middle of the big bed. She watched him as he slowly removed his clothes. When they came together at last, it was in an explosion of splendor.

They slept entwined in each other's arms.

Chapter 20

The next morning began the very pleasant routine of a long visit in the country. Geoffrey, John, and the other gentlemen went hunting after breakfast and the ladies spent the morning in the parlor, discussing the affair of the previous night.

Lady Beatrice's daughter, Constance, could barely hold herself still in her chair. "Oh, Rebecca! The ball was everything wonderful. The music, the dancing, the food. Simply marvelous."

"I take it you enjoyed yourself, Constance?" Becca asked her.

"Oh, yes."

"Constance," Lady Margaret intoned, "I believe you spent quite a bit of time with a certain gentleman?"

Constance lowered her gaze, blushing. "Lord Chester and I only danced two dances, Lady Margaret."

"It would seem to me that two dances were enough." Becca laughed.

Constance nodded.

"I daresay we have quite a few eligible young men with us for a visit," Lady Margaret said.

"Yes, indeed." Lady Helen nudged her daughter, Michelle, with her elbow. "Isn't that so, Michelle?"

The pretty red-haired girl sighed and looked heavenward. "Yes, Mother."

"And whom did you prefer last evening, Michelle?" Becca asked, smiling.

Michelle returned her smile, her eyes twinkling with mischief. "Hmm, I don't know," she began, a thoughtful look on her face. "I think I rather liked all of them."

"Michelle!" Lady Helen gasped.

Becca joined Michelle in her laughter while Lady Margaret hid her grin.

Becca schooled her expression. "I believe Viscount Leed was quite taken with you."

Michelle lost her smile then. "He didn't ask me to dance. Not once."

Becca leaned over to whisper in her ear. "But the looks he gave you from across the room …."

Michelle's eyes rounded. "I didn't know that anyone else noticed."

Becca simply nodded and sat back.

Lady Margaret spoke then. "Didn't any of you girls find Lord Roberts attractive?"

"Oh, yes!" came the response from nearly all the young women present.

It was the older ladies' turn to laugh then. The girls ignored the laughter and went on, extolling the viscount's every virtue.

"He danced divinely," gushed Sarah, Constance's cousin.

"His eyes," began Diane, "are most beautiful."

Patricia snorted at the girl's choice of words. "Diane, you act as if you have never seen a handsome man before. Aren't you acquainted with my husband?"

Diane reddened under Patricia's piercing gaze. Becca noticed Diane's discomfort and knew then that Geoffrey hadn't been the only one played false by John and Patricia.

"He wasn't afraid to ask me to dance," Michelle stated.

Becca saw Michelle meant to ease the conversation and Diana's sensibilities. "No," Becca said. "I don't think Lord Roberts would hesitate to ask a pretty girl to dance."

"You didn't dance with him, Rebecca," Constance said.

"My husband was most attentive last evening, Constance." Becca smiled. "I had no room on my dance card for anyone else."

"I daresay my son wouldn't let you out of his sight, Rebecca," Lady Margaret added.

"Oh, Rebecca," Sarah began. "The two of you made a most remarkable pair last evening."

"Thank you, Sarah," Becca returned.

Constance sighed loudly, drawing the others' attention. "If only I could find a love like that," she said dramatically.

"I'm sure you will, Constance," Becca said.

The ladies passed the morning speaking more of the lovely evening they'd shared. After a while, they went into the dining room for lunch. They dined without the gentlemen, who picnicked out in the fields on their hunt.

After lunch, the ladies went their separate ways. Becca went upstairs, stopping in the study to add to her notes. Smiling to herself, she wrote Lord Chester's name next to Constance's and Leed's next to Michelle's. On another line, she wrote down Lord Roberts with a question mark after it. It was obvious that all the young ladies were quite taken with him. Whom would he choose?

Becca shrugged and went into their bedroom. Mary soon joined her and helped her change into a tea gown of moss green. Mary went into Becca's dressing room to ready her clothes for that evening and, leaving Mary to her task, Becca walked to the door and pulled it open. She gasped in surprise.

There in the doorway stood her husband, looking fine and fit. He favored her with a dazzling smile, his eyes twinkling. "Hello, love."

"Hello, darling," she answered, staring up at him.

He kissed her lightly and drew her into his arms. She rubbed her cheek against him, breathing in deeply. He smelled of the outdoors, fresh and masculine.

"I've missed you," she said against his chest.

"Didn't you have a pleasant day, Becca?"

"Yes, of course." She disentangled herself from his arms and crossed to the fireplace.

"What is it, love?"

"I know we must spend time with our guests, but I would also love to spend some time with you."

He walked over to where she stood and grasped her chin gently. He tilted her head up to look her in the eye. "Ah, Becca."

She watched as he brought his mouth to hers. She lowered her lashes as their lips touched, the contact brief. He held her in his arms once more. "I'll try to spend more time with you, Becca."

She nodded, snuggling closer to him. A long moment passed and Geoffrey finally let her go. "Meet our guests for tea, love. I'll follow shortly."

When Becca presented herself for tea at precisely five o'clock, the parlor was already full of lively conversation. The young girls had changed into tea gowns and it seemed as though all the colors of the rainbow were represented.

Constance approached her. "Rebecca, do you think the gentlemen will join us?"

Becca tried to ease the girl's nervousness. "Constance, I know for certain that my husband will be here. I'm sure that his friends will join us, as well."

The girl nodded enthusiastically, her blond ringlets bouncing. As if on cue, the gentlemen strode into the parlor then. Chester greeted Rebecca, quirking a half-smile in Constance's direction. She returned his smile shyly and asked him if he'd care to join her on the settee. He bowed his assent and they sat down, a proper distance between them.

Michelle caught Becca's eye as Leed entered. With a curt nod in the red-haired girl's direction, he crossed to the window. He seemed intent on the view of the grounds, his back ramrod stiff. Becca gave Michelle a small smile of encouragement. She felt a tap on her shoulder and turned, startled to see Lord Roberts directly behind her.

"Good afternoon, Rebecca," he said, smiling winningly at her.

"Good afternoon, Lord Roberts."

He stood close to her, but she gave that little notice. Her mind on matchmaking, she waved at Diane.

The girl crossed to where the two stood, curtsying to Roberts. "Hello, Lord Roberts." Diane breathed, her eyes like saucers.

"Why, what a pleasure it is to see you, Lady Diane," he said smoothly. "I enjoyed our dance last evening."

"As did I," she answered.

Becca left them then and walked over to where Lady

Margaret sat with the older ladies. She motioned for Becca to lean closer, presumably so she could speak quietly and Becca sat down next to her.

"Rebecca," she whispered. "I think we're off to a wonderful start, don't you?"

"It seems that Chester is quite taken with Constance," Becca answered softly.

"Hmm," Lady Margaret intoned. "If only Viscount Leed would notice the beautiful girl right under his nose."

"Give them time, Lady Margaret." Becca laughed. "I don't know whom Lord Roberts will choose. Do you have an opinion on the subject?"

Lady Margaret opened her mouth to respond just as Geoffrey entered the parlor and nodded in Becca's direction. She started to stand and halted her movement as her husband walked right past her to speak with Leed at the window.

After a few minutes, Geoffrey joined her. He leaned down and pecked her cheek. "Becca," he said near her ear. "I need to speak with Chester and Leed in my study. I won't be long."

"Geoffrey," she said, trying to keep the irritation out of her voice. "You said we would spend more time together."

"We will, love."

"What is this about?"

"Don't worry yourself about it, Becca."

With a bow to his mother, Geoffrey left the room with Lords Chester and Leed in his wake. Lady Margaret stood then, telling Becca she wished for the maid to bring out more biscuits.

Roberts walked over to her, settling himself quite close to Becca on the settee. His leg touched hers fleetingly. "What has you so sad, Rebecca?"

"What?" She blinked. "Oh, nothing."

Once more Geoffrey chose to keep her out of his affairs and worries. She heard little of the conversation around her, all but missed the charming smile of the man seated close to her. Her eyes were on the door as she waited impatiently for Geoffrey's return.

Piqued, Becca stood and excused herself. She hurried out

the door and toward the back of the house and could soon hear voices behind the door of the study. She knocked smartly, at which the voices ceased.

Geoffrey pulled the door open. "What is it?" he asked sharply.

"I … I wanted to see if—"

"I'll join you in a short while, Becca."

He closed the door, leaving her to stand alone in the hallway, hurt and angry. With a gasp of frustration, she took herself outside to the gardens. She sat on the stone bench where she and Geoffrey had sat only the day before.

Hugging herself, she let the tears come.

* * * *

In the study, Geoffrey turned back to his friends.

"Kane, you should share this with her," Chester offered.

"No!" He softened his tone. "I won't have her put in danger. Not again."

"But until we get to the bottom of this mess, she is in danger," Leed added. "Perhaps she should know of it."

"Becca will know of nothing, Leed," Geoffrey vowed. "And when I find the son-of-a-bitch who nearly took her from me, I'll kill him with my bare hands."

"I don't like the way this is going, Kane," Leed said, bringing the topic back to the notes. "The path is getting darker and dirtier the further we travel down it."

"What do you mean?" Geoffrey asked him.

"Well," Leed went on, "Roberts and I have already traced the notes to White's, but none of the regulars remember who passed them. No one had any of them on their persons, either. Seems they wanted payment directly, more's the pity. That leaves us with no recourse but to head to the waterfront ourselves."

"You don't think any of that riffraff is involved, do you?"

"It seems more than possible," Chester answered. "And you know how closed-mouthed those scoundrels can be."

Geoffrey nodded slowly. "Dark and dirty, the path may be.

But I'll be damned if this scoundrel gets away with this."

* * * *

Out in the garden, Becca sniffled as her tears dried. She felt a hand grasp hers and looked up.

Roberts smiled down at her, tenderness in his eyes. "Are you all right, Rebecca?"

She pulled her hand out of his gentle grasp and straightened her shoulders. "I'm fine, Lord Roberts."

He sat down next to her, a half-smile on his face. "You agreed to call me 'Roberts', Rebecca."

"Yes, I did," Becca allowed. "You shouldn't be out here with me, Roberts."

"You're upset. I couldn't sit there in the parlor and let you suffer alone."

Becca smoothed her hands over her skirt. "I'm not suffering."

He brought his hand up to her face, cupping it gently. Becca could only stare at him, shocked by his actions.

"I want to see you happy, Rebecca," he said, a serious look on his face. "Your life should be filled with laughter."

"My life, Roberts, is wonderful, thank you."

He shook his head slowly. "Then why are you out here alone and your husband is closed up with his friends, hmm?"

"Geoffrey has some business—"

"Ah, yes," Roberts interrupted. "The notes."

Becca straightened. "What notes?"

"Never mind about that." Roberts stroked her cheek. "You're so beautiful, Rebecca."

"You shouldn't speak to me so."

His eyes darkened as he bent his head to hers. His lips brushed hers, the contact brief. She jerked her head back, stunned.

Roberts seemed to regain himself and sat up straight. "Rebecca, forgive me. I—"

She didn't let him finish his apology. She jumped off the bench and ran back into the house. The bell sounded as she entered, signaling to the guests that it was time to ready themselves for dinner. As they ascended the grand staircase to their rooms, the ladies chatting excitedly, Becca looked toward the study. The door was still closed tight. The matter didn't concern her?

She took herself up to their chamber and changed for dinner.

Mary fixed Becca's hair and helped her into her gown. The dress was sapphire blue, making her eyes look a deep green. Becca thanked the girl and sent her out of the room, taking the opportunity to think about all that had happened.

Geoffrey had her so angry, she could hardly see straight. Her tears of frustration had burned hotly on her cheeks. But she didn't know what to make of Lord Roberts's actions. She felt nothing for the man, only a kind of friendship. When he'd kissed her, she'd been stunned. Should she tell Geoffrey? What would he do? She didn't want to come between friends, not with Lord Roberts helping him with the sticky business of his missing funds.

She'd never told him about John's behavior before her accident. She would put this incident aside, as well. She would, however, make certain that Roberts knew that such actions couldn't be repeated. She loved her husband and desired only him. No other man would ever touch her again.

Geoffrey let himself into the chamber. Becca stood and stared at him.

He crossed over to where she stood. "Becca, about earlier—"

She shook her head at him. "We don't have time for this now."

"I didn't mean to be cross with you. It's just that—"

"Please ready yourself. Our guests will be waiting."

He paused for a moment. Finally, he conceded to her wishes and went into his dressing room to change for dinner. A short while later, he came out and escorted her downstairs.

Chapter 21

Becca knew the guests were assembled in the drawing room awaiting the bell signaling the dinner hour. As they neared the entrance, she saw Lord Roberts precede them and stride into the room.

"Hello, everyone," she heard him say. "Where are our host and hostess this evening?"

"Kane and Rebecca should be down shortly, I'd imagine," Chester offered.

"Indeed, Chester," Geoffrey said from his place at Becca's side. They entered the parlor and their friends waved them over. Grasping Becca's hand firmly, Geoffrey led the way over to where the other young people stood.

"Kane, Rebecca," Chester smiled, "how nice of you to join us."

Constance gasped at Chester's comment from the other side of the room. Chester simply grinned at her.

"It's quite all right, Lady Constance." Geoffrey laughed. "Chester here is such a trial at these social functions."

Constance shared a meaningful glance with Lord Chester, who nodded in her direction. He all but dragged Leed over to where the ladies stood and drew him into some pleasant conversation. Becca hid her smile. *Nicely done, Lord Chester.*

"Good evening, ladies," Chester said with a bright smile.

The girls curtsied as the gentlemen bowed. Michelle looked at Leed expectantly.

The man's blue eyes bore into hers with an intensity that would have made Becca blanch were she the recipient of that gaze. He cleared his throat. "Good evening, Lady Michelle."

"Lord Leed, how nice to see you," she answered softly, though the look in her eyes was almost a challenge.

Chester turned to Constance. "You look breathtaking this evening, Lady Constance."

Constance blushed prettily and Becca caught the girl's eye winking at her. Lord Roberts stared at Becca, unusually quiet. She put her hand on her husband's arm and held tightly to him. Her gaze never wavered as she curtsied to Lords Roberts and Leed. Geoffrey patted her hand with his own, smiling down at her. She returned his smile and he couldn't resist placing a kiss behind her ear.

Constance sighed audibly, drawing Chester's attention. He looked at her questioningly, at which she blushed and turned her attention to brushing her hands over her skirt.

"So, Kane," Leed began. "What do you have planned for us on the morrow?"

Roberts finally found his voice. "I say we go for a long ride," he said brightly. "Perhaps we can convince the ladies to join us?"

"I think that would be splendid, Roberts." Geoffrey turned to Becca. "I missed my wife's presence miserably today."

Becca nodded. "A ride would be just the thing. Don't you think so, ladies?"

Michelle and Constance agreed, adding that they were certain Diane and Sarah would join them.

Geoffrey bent his head low to whisper in Becca's ear. "I daresay it won't be quite as enjoyable as our picnic, however."

Becca blushed at that, her breath coming fast. The memory of the passion they had shared on that afternoon sent a shiver through her. He must have seen the recognition on her face for the grin on his was decidely wicked.

The others looked at him in open curiosity. Thankfully, the dinner bell sounded and Becca was spared any further embarrassment. Everyone headed into the dining room for the sumptuous feast that awaited them.

Much later, in the solitude of their bedroom, Becca sat at her vanity brushing her hair. Geoffrey had been very solicitous all evening, making her nearly forget their earlier disagreement. But she hadn't forgotten it, and vowed once more to get her husband to share his concerns with her.

As if summoning him with her thoughts, Geoffrey emerged from his dressing room, clad only in his breeches. He saw that she still wore her chemise and petticoat. “Why aren’t you ready for bed, love?”

She set down her brush and turned to him. “I wish to speak to you about this afternoon.”

He stared at her for a moment. Finally, he nodded and leaned against the vanity, his arms crossed in front of him.

“I’m sorry I was cross with you. It wasn’t my intention. You happened upon us in the middle of our discussion.”

“Geoffrey,” she began deliberately. “That isn’t what I’m talking about. I’m hurt that once again you’re not sharing your concerns with me.”

He straightened and looked away from her. “Becca,” he said gruffly, “this doesn’t concern you.”

“If that were so, why can’t you tell me of it?”

He let out a breath. “Love, there seems to be more to the matter than just the missing funds.”

“Do you mean the notes?”

He looked at her sharply. “How did you find out about the notes?”

“Lord Roberts told me.”

When had Roberts told her of the notes? Had he been alone with her recently? He looked at her closely and she looked back at him, her eyes clear and guileless.

“Yes,” he went on. “The notes do present a vexing problem.”

She stood then, touching his arm lightly. “What is it? I can see the worry on your face.”

He wanted to tell her all of it, to unburden himself. He’d told her of the missing funds, and had felt better for sharing his concerns. But this business of an impostor, of someone deliberately running them down .... No. He wouldn’t put her in any more danger.

He gave her a small smile. “Please, Becca. Let me worry about this. I don’t want you involved.”

“But I want to be involved,” she said firmly. “I want you to be able to share your problems with me. Perhaps I could even help—"

"No!"

She flinched and he drew her into his arms. "I'm sorry, love," he soothed. "I suppose I'm just a bit tired."

She relaxed against him. "I want you—"

"And I want you," he said, his voice husky. "I want to feel your skin against mine. To taste you on my lips …."

She lifted her head and all worry left his mind as their lips met. Her mouth opened up for him, welcoming his tongue. Rubbing his tongue with hers, she kissed him back with equal ardor. His lips left hers to trail along the soft skin of her neck. She sighed and leaned her head to the side as he nibbled her ear. He slowly removed her chemise, kissing the skin he was revealing. Finally, when she stood trembling before him, he removed his breeches and held her once more.

He carried her over to the bed and sat, cradling her in his arms. She placed her hands behind his neck, urging him to kiss her again. He obliged her, laying down on the bed and holding her on top of him. She moaned in the back of her throat, the little sound driving him on.

"Ah, Becca," he groaned, running his hands over her. "Your skin is so soft."

He moved out from under her. Before she could turn to face him, he began trailing hot kisses down her back. He brushed her hair out of the way, stroking and petting her as he'd done before. His lips caressed the back of her neck, making her shiver.

"Geoffrey," she whispered.

"I love you, Becca." He placed feather-light kisses all along her spine. "I love the way you respond to me."

His hands caressed her bottom and moved between her legs. His fingers caressed the folds of her, making her wet. She moaned as his fingers delved inside and she was soon restless beneath him.

He brought his face to hers, kissing her cheek, her ear. "Are you ready for me, love?"

"Yes." She breathed in answer.

He lifted her hips gently off the bed, her legs drawing up to rest on his knees. He slowly entered her from behind, moaning with the intense pleasure he felt. She sharply drew in a breath as they were completely joined.

"Oh, my!" She gasped in surprise.

"Shh …" he murmured. "Let me love you this way. I promise I'll never hurt you."

He began to move within her. She clutched at the sheets as their pleasure started to build. He brought his hands to hers, entwining their fingers. He held on tightly, starting to lose his control. Her little moans of pleasure drove him mad. His thrusts became harder, deeper. She cried out with her release, shuddering beneath him. With one final thrust, he joined her in fulfillment, shouting her name as his climax took him.

He rained kisses on her hair, her cheek, catching his breath. He turned her then, kissing her full on her lips. She wore a deep red blush over her smooth cheeks.

"Is something wrong?" he asked with a small smile.

"That …" she began in a whisper. "That isn't …."

"We're married," he assured her softly. "Anything we do with each other is perfectly all right."

She nodded, her eyes huge.

"Did you like it, love?" he asked her.

She lowered her eyes and blushed again in answer. He grinned broadly and kissed her once more.

"Ah, Becca. How you please me."

Without any more words, he wrapped his arms around her. He couldn't let her know of the danger, or the dark turn his friends' investigations took. No.

What had Roberts told her? And when?

She sighed as she slumbered and he pushed thoughts of danger, missing funds, and charming rogues out of his mind and joined her in sleep.

* * * *

The next morning after breakfast, they set out for their ride. The party was of a good size, for all the young ladies agreed to come along. Geoffrey and Becca rode side-by-side, leaving the others to fall into their own order. Mostly the men rode together behind the ladies. It was a beautiful morning, with a nip of autumn in the air.

Much to Becca's obvious surprise, Geoffrey led them to their familiar spot by the brook for the nooning meal. He smiled a secret smile at her and whispered that she was just so pretty when she blushed. Apparently unable to help it, she proceeded to accommodate him.

Not much later, the party returned to the main house. As the ladies readied themselves for tea time, the men promised to meet in Geoffrey's study. Becca heard her husband make plans with Lord Chester and arched her brow at him. He caught the action, and shook his head at her slightly. Without another word to him, she took herself up to their chambers.

In Geoffrey's study not fifteen minutes later, Lords Chester, Leed, and Roberts stood waiting patiently for the Earl of Kanewood to snap out of his reverie. He stood at the window, looking out over the grounds.

Roberts was the first to grow weary of the wait. "Kane, will you kindly tell us what is bothering you?"

Geoffrey turned to the viscount, eyeing him closely. "Rebecca knows of the notes, Roberts. Do you care to tell me how that can be?"

"I thought you told her, Kane," he answered, bewildered. "If she were my wife—"

"What did you say?" Geoffrey cut in, his voice menacing.

"Gentlemen," Chester said quickly. "Why don't we review all that we know so far."

Geoffrey shook his head and walked slowly over to where Roberts stood. "Pray continue, Roberts. What if Rebecca was you wife?"

Roberts bristled under Geoffrey's piercing glare and straightened his shoulders. "Kane, you shouldn't keep matters from your wife."

Geoffrey's eyes narrowed. "My wife is my concern, Roberts. You would do well to remember that."

The two men stared at each other for a long moment, the

tension in the room as thick as the evening fog in London.

Leed cleared his throat. "Kane," he said, waiting for Geoffrey to respond. "Kane!" he repeated more forcefully.

"Yes?" Geoffrey answered, finally turning to the man.

"I think Chester is right."

Geoffrey blinked at him, confused for a moment. He turned to Chester then, arching a brow in his direction.

"We need to review what we have learned thus far, Kane," Chester repeated for him.

With a dismissive glance at Roberts, Geoffrey sat behind his desk. Chester and Leed sat in the chairs facing him while Roberts simply leaned against the wall, his arms crossed.

Chester went over what they had learned so far. Someone had been passing notes in Geoffrey's name, pretending to be the earl. The notes went through quite a few hands before ending up on his solicitor's desk, making them very difficult to trace. A few of the gaming houses in London were in possession of them for a short time, but their origin was, as yet, unknown. There had been no reason to look at them with suspicion however, as the handwriting looked quite like Geoffrey's.

"Well, where the hell did they come from?"

Chester looked to Leed to elaborate.

"Kane, we suspect that the notes originated down by the waterfront. Games can always be found there and it stands to reason that someone could easily pass them at some of the more nefarious houses."

Roberts nodded his agreement. "We need to go down there and find out if any of the scum can be bought. I should think a stout bottle of spirits would loosen a few tongues."

Geoffrey rubbed his chin thoughtfully. "What of the carriage, Roberts? Any news there?"

Roberts shook his head. "I was only able to learn that the carriage may have been Lady Brookdale's. When I return to London, I'll call on the widow myself."

"Turn on the charm, Roberts," Chester instructed. "If she did lend the carriage to someone, we need to know."

"Something doesn't seem to add up," Leed cut in, drawing the attention of the others. "What of the botched repairs to the estate? Could they be related to the notes?"

Geoffrey shrugged his shoulders. "They very well could be. I had no dealings with these supposed businesses before this, and the repairs were never completed—which is why I've been running ragged these past few weeks making sure that all those repairs were actually dealt with."

"The repairs were paid for out of the Kanewood accounts, correct?" Leed asked.

"Yes."

"Could they have been paid for as a matter of course?"

"The funds are usually allocated at the time the repairs are ordered, not completed."

Leed looked off for a moment, lost in thought.

"Leed, what are you thinking?" Chester asked.

"I'm not sure what to think right now, Chester." He faced Geoffrey. "Let me ponder it for a while, Kane?"

"Certainly, Leed."

Silence fell over the room, the men each lost in their own thoughts.

"Well, gentlemen." Roberts straightened away from the wall. "If you're quite finished, I'd like to retire to my room."

"Readying yourself for any lady in particular, Roberts?" Chester asked with a grin.

"Who is the lucky girl?" Leed asked.

Roberts grinned wickedly and said nothing. He couldn't, however, seem to take Geoffrey's eyes on him for more than a moment and hurriedly left the room.

Chapter 22

A few days passed. Becca was still hurt that Geoffrey wasn't sharing his concerns, but she put it aside, loath to argue again. The men continued to hunt each morning while the ladies passed the time in pleasant conversation.

One evening after dinner, the gentlemen and ladies separated, as was the custom. In the parlor, Becca tried to follow the ladies' conversations, but she couldn't take her mind off Geoffrey. What was troubling him? She excused herself from the room, thinking to breach custom and interrupt her husband. Keeping quiet on the matter had taken its toll on her. She needed to talk with him. She was being a fool. With a sigh, she turned to return to the parlor.

"Rebecca," Lord Roberts said, startling her.

She gasped in surprise. She quickly regained her composure and stepped back from him. "Good evening, Lord Roberts."

"What are you about if I may inquire?"

"I was just …," she trailed off. "Never mind."

"Just what?" he asked with a smile.

Becca returned his smile and shrugged. "Roberts, what do you know of …? I shouldn't ask you."

"Rebecca, are you wondering about Kane's troubles?"

She stared at him as guilt slashed through her. Finally, she nodded. "Can you tell me about them?"

Without another word, he led her into the library. He closed the door quietly and crossed over to where she stood.

"What can you tell me of Geoffrey's worries?" she asked. "He says it is nothing, but I know something is wrong. I keep finding him closeted with you or Lord Leed or Lord Chester."

He smiled crookedly at her. "You didn't come in here with me to discuss your husband's problems, did you, Rebecca?"

"Yes, of course I did."

"No." He shook his head. "You wish to be alone with me."

"I wish to know how I can help my husband."

"Rebecca," he said in a husky voice, "you have feelings for me, don't you?"

She gasped. "Roberts, I don't have—"

"Don't try to deny it, Rebecca," Roberts said smoothly. "I saw the notes you made in your study."

"Notes?"

"Your list? Ah, you found matches for both Leed and Chester. But why couldn't you find one for my most excellent self?"

She pulled back from him. "That list was a bit of fun, Roberts."

"You couldn't match anyone to me because you have feelings for me yourself."

"Nonsense!" She turned to go, but he grasped her arm.

"I felt it, Rebecca." He brought his face close to hers. "I felt it in the kiss we shared in the garden."

She was frozen, words of denial stuck in her throat. "Lord Roberts, I—"

Roberts brought his lips to her neck. He nuzzled her skin, his hands on her waist now. "Rebecca," he murmured.

She regained her senses and placed her hands on his shoulders to push him away.

"Take your hands off my wife."

Roberts lifted his head and stepped back from her. Becca flicked her gaze toward the doorway, shocked at the fierce scowl on Geoffrey's face.

"Kane," Roberts started. "This isn't—"

"Isn't what, Roberts?" Geoffrey growled. "Pray, enlighten me."

Roberts turned his back to Becca, standing between her and Geoffrey.

Geoffrey's eyes narrowed to slits. "Don't think to protect my wife from me."

"Kane, none of this is her fault."

"Get out. You'll leave Kanewood at first light."

With a worried glance toward Becca, Roberts took his leave. Geoffrey closed his eyes, his lips a thin line.

"Geoffrey, I—" she began.

He held up a hand to silence her and she honored his request.

After a long minute, he opened his eyes. "Tell me, Becca," he said, his voice thick. "Tell me you did nothing to invite this."

Once again, she couldn't find her voice. She'd never seen him so angry. She could only stare at him, dumb. To her horror, he seemed to take her silence as an admission of guilt. He turned away from her, bracing his hands on the writing desk, and hung his head.

"Geoffrey, please."

She reached out to touch his shoulder and he flinched at the slight contact.

"Take yourself upstairs, Becca. I can't bear to look at you now."

Becca felt tears burning in her eyes as she did what he asked. She walked slowly out of the room, bound for their chambers. Geoffrey obviously believed she'd encouraged Lord Roberts's attentions. Had she? No. Any attraction between them was completely in Roberts's mind. She loved her husband and would never want another man to touch her.

But what of Geoffrey's anger? She'd never been so frightened in all of her life. He'd looked at her with disgust, so sure of her betrayal. How could he think so little of her?

Heartbroken, she changed out of her gown and readied herself for bed. After waiting up for her husband for nearly two hours, she climbed into the big, lonely bed. Hugging her pillow, she fell into a fitful sleep.

Some time later, she awoke with a start. Her lids fluttered open, but her eyes were slow to adjust to the gloom in the chamber. The drapes were open, letting in a slice of moonlight. She looked toward the window. There, in silhouette, stood Geoffrey.

She sat up and rubbed her eyes. "Geoffrey?"

He lit a candle, dispelling some of the shadows. Becca took in his appearance. He wore only his breeches, his feet bare. She brought her gaze up to his face. The expression she saw there was unsettling.

"Get out of my bed," he ordered, his words a bit slurred.

She blinked up at him, certain that she'd misunderstood him. "What are you—"

"I said, get out!"

Becca scrambled to do as he asked, tears blurring her vision. She reached for her wrapper to cover herself, but his hands reached out and grabbed her by the shoulders. He ran his gaze over her as his fingers dug into her flesh and she felt a chill to her soul. He looked like a stranger to her.

She cried out, "You're hurting me!"

Geoffrey stared at her for a moment longer. Finally, he let her go. He turned away and raked his hands through his hair, muttering incoherently under his breath. She began to walk past him, but one word stopped her.

"Why?" he asked.

"What?"

"Why did you let him touch you?"

His eyes met hers then, ablaze with anger. Her breath caught as he stepped closer to her. "You're mine, Becca," he growled. "Mine."

He grabbed at her shoulders once more, tugging at her nightgown. The thin fabric gave way with a harsh tearing sound. His gaze ran over her from head to toe. She read the raw desire in their blue depths a split second before he grabbed her roughly and crushed his mouth to hers.

She whimpered and the kiss changed. His tongue swept through her mouth, teasing her. She caught his passion, reaching up to run her fingers through his hair. He held her tightly, grinding himself against her.

He all but threw her on the bed, staring down at her as he unbuttoned his breeches. He came down on top of her, nearly crushing her with his weight. Her eyes fluttered open, her pulse quickening at the hot glare in his. This was so unlike him, this anger mixed with lust. She trembled in his grasp.

"You're mine, Becca," he ground out. "Say it!"

"Don't do this, please." She gasped. "Not like this."

He froze and grasped her chin and tilted her head up. His eyes met hers, his gaze steady. “Mine.”

This was not like the careful attention he’d paid her since declaring his love. No, this was a possessiveness that was frightening. She squeezed her eyes shut and felt hot tears trickle from them. “I’m yours,” she whispered brokenly.

His hold eased and he lifted himself away from her. “Forgive me,” he muttered.

He rolled away from her. Becca’s mind reeled as the chill from his sudden withdrawal bit into her. His passion had stunned her, his quick desertion just as startling. Yet, she needed more from him: a tender word or soft caress to assure her of his love.

His snores told her he’d fallen asleep. She slowly climbed out of bed and picked her nightgown up off of the floor. It was torn beyond repair. With a sigh, she retrieved her wrapper and donned it, tying it tightly around her waist. She curled up against her husband’s back and fell asleep.

Sunlight streamed through the window, rousing Becca. She stretched, feeling a bit sore. Suddenly, the memory of the night before came back to her. She looked over at Geoffrey’s side of the bed, not surprised to find it vacant. He’d been so angry last night, she’d briefly worried about her safety. But he hadn’t hurt her. In the end, he hadn’t hurt her.

Geoffrey strode out of his dressing room just then. He froze when he saw her, finally shrugging into his jacket. She smiled faintly at him in greeting.

“Good morning, Becca,” he said stiffly.

He seemed distant, cold.

“Where are you off to so early?”

He adjusted his cravat in the cheval mirror. “I’m leaving for London after breakfast.”

“London?” She sat upright. “Why do you have to go to London?”

He turned back to her, an indefinable look crossing his features. “I have business to attend to.”

She lowered her gaze, knowing full well that he wouldn’t share this with her.

He crossed to the bed and sat down on the edge. "Becca, about last night …."

She could only stare at him.

He took a breath and continued. "I want you to know that I don't blame you for what happened with Roberts."

She let out a breath she hadn't realized she'd been holding. Her relief was short-lived, however.

"I never should have left your side," he added. "If you hadn't been given the opportunity to stray, this never would have happened."

She gasped. She couldn't believe that the man she loved, the man she thought loved her, had such a low opinion of her.

"Geoffrey, h-how can you …?"

He stood. "I don't know how long I'll be gone."

He placed a chaste kiss on her cheek and turned to leave. He paused at the door, opening his mouth to say something more to her. Instead, he nodded curtly and took his leave. She watched him go, stunned. After a while, she rose and readied herself for the day. Dressed in a gown of somber gray, she went down to breakfast.

Lady Margaret greeted her warmly. "Good morning, Rebecca. I hear my son has taken himself off to London?"

"Yes, Lady Margaret. He has business to attend to."

Patricia caught Becca's eye. The older girl smiled slyly, as if she held a delicious secret.

"Hmm," she started. "It seems that Viscount Roberts has also left our company this morning. I wonder, Rebecca, if that's merely a coincidence?"

Becca flushed, lowering her gaze. Patricia laughed softly to herself.

It seemed that with the earl's taking himself off to London, the guests realized that they were very nearly overstaying their welcome. Lady Margaret and Becca saw them off that afternoon, accepting their thanks graciously.

Thomas bowed to the ladies, taking his daughter's hand. "Girl, I had a splendid time. I only wish I could have thanked Kane myself."

"Perhaps he'll stop at the inn on his return, Father."

Thomas brightened at that. He took his leave then, and Becca and her mother-in-law stood alone in the cavernous entryway.

Lady Margaret looked at Becca closely. “Rebecca, are you feeling all right? You look a bit pale.”

“Yes, of course,” Becca answered. “I’m just tired, I suppose.”

The ladies went into the parlor, picking up on the pastimes they had abandoned with the arrival of the guests nearly a week earlier. Becca was grateful to have the fire screen to work on, concentrating all of her attention on the intricate details of the floral design she painted instead of her distrustful husband currently running as far away from her as possible.

Chapter 23

Geoffrey sat brooding in his carriage, reviewing the events of the past evening in his mind. When he'd found Becca with Roberts in the library, it had taken all of his control not to throw the man out the window. Her hands had been on his shoulders, pulling him closer. Or had she been pushing him away?

He recalled nothing of what happened after he'd sent Becca away from him. Nothing, that was, until he'd gone up to their sleeping chamber. He'd tried to get her out of the room, to spare her from the rage he'd felt so close to the surface. But in the end, he'd had to have her. At the last moment, he'd come to his senses and let her alone. No doubt he'd terrified her nonetheless.

Shame washed over him. He closed his eyes and settled back against the seat as the carriage rolled on to his London townhouse.

The next afternoon, Miles met him at the door with obvious surprise. "My lord!" the butler exclaimed. "We were not expecting you."

"See to my bags, Miles," Geoffrey said in a flat voice.

The butler looked behind his master, at the carriage on the street and turned back to Geoffrey. "Isn't Lady Kanewood with you, my lord?"

He walked toward his study. "She remains at Kanewood."

Geoffrey began to drown his sorrows, and his conscience, in brandy. Miles had insisted that he eat something later that evening and Geoffrey finally relented, choking down some soup and bread. Very late that night, he took himself upstairs to the room he'd so recently shared with Becca. She was safer at Kanewood, from the danger aimed at him and from him. It wasn't only the matter of the missing funds and attempts to do harm that had him worried. He didn't trust himself around her after his behavior two nights past. With a ragged sigh, he crawled into bed and fell into a dreamless sleep.

* * * *

Geoffrey was kept busy over the next few days, accompanying Leed and Chester on their investigations. One afternoon, the gentlemen went to White's, one of the larger gaming houses in town. Several of the notes had come directly from White's to Geoffrey's solicitors. As Leed had stated earlier, no one could say who had passed the notes, only that they weren't usual patrons of the establishment. The afternoon wore into the evening as Geoffrey began drinking again. Leed and Chester joined him for a round at a public house and soon Geoffrey began to unburden himself to his friends.

"I'm the worst kind of fool, my friends," he said.

"Kane," Chester began, "what are you talking about?"

"I learned a long time ago to never trust a woman. And now look where my trust has gotten me."

Chester nodded to Leed who took a breath and spoke. "Kane, what exactly happened at Kanewood?"

Geoffrey's head shot up. "Ah, Leed. I can't speak of it."

"I think you should," Chester insisted.

Geoffrey looked from one man to the other. Finally, he nodded slowly. "She betrayed me."

"What?" Chester asked. "I don't believe that Rebecca would ever cuckhold you."

"No," Geoffrey said. "She merely strayed. I put the blame on myself."

"And none on Roberts?" Leed asked.

Geoffrey looked at him sharply. "You knew?"

The other men nodded.

"We've long suspected Roberts's infatuation with your wife," Chester said gently.

Geoffrey studied the liquor in his glass, silent.

"Kane, tell us what happened."

Geoffrey took a big swallow of his drink. "I found them in

the library." He paused to take another swallow of his drink, letting the liquid burn a path down his throat. "Roberts was touching her," he went on. "His lips on her skin …."

"What was Rebecca doing?" Leed asked softly.

He squeezed his eyes shut. "She was holding him," he whispered hoarsely. "Or pushing him away. I couldn't tell."

"Then perhaps she's innocent in this," Chester offered.

Geoffrey shrugged and looked at Chester. "She shouldn't have been alone with him."

"I think you're forgetting Roberts's remarkable charm with the ladies, Kane," Chester went on. "He can be very persuasive."

"Perhaps he took advantage of Rebecca's trusting nature," Leed added.

Geoffrey raked his fingers through his hair. His friends' words muddled his mind.

He pushed away from the table and stood. "I won't speak of this any longer."

Blessedly, his friends let him have his way for the time being.

"I believe you should forgo accompanying us to the gambling dens," Chester said.

"Why? I'm eager to put this business behind me," Geoffrey countered.

Leed shook his head. "Someone is using your name. Your money. This may be connected to the carriage accident, as well."

"The perpetrator has had an easy time of it, until now. If you show your face, you show our hand. Let us go and see what can be learned in your absence."

Geoffrey was forced to acknowledge the wisdom of their position.

"All right. I daresay I can find enough drink to keep me at the townhouse."

* * * *

Becca was slow to awaken the next morning. After nearly a

week of sleeping alone in the huge four-poster, she still wasn't used to Geoffrey's absence. All the previous night, she'd tossed and turned. But with the sunlight peeking in though the window, she saw no way out of getting up and facing yet another day without her husband. She swung her legs over the side of the bed and stood. She suddenly felt weak, her stomach queasy. Gripping the thick bedpost, she waited for the feeling to pass.

After a minute or two, she felt better. She crossed to the washstand and splashed some water on her face. Surely, the slight attack was due to the fact that she hadn't been sleeping well. In addition, she'd merely picked at her food for the last few mealtimes.

She sat at the vanity, staring at herself in the mirror. Frowning at the pale face staring back at her, she stood and went into her dressing room to don her chemise and petticoat. When she emerged, Mary was there to assist her with her stays.

"Good morning, Mary," Becca greeted the girl with a small smile.

"Good morning, my lady," Mary answered. "What dress would you like to wear this morning?"

"Just pick any one, I suppose."

Mary simply nodded and went to do her bidding. She brought Becca a walking dress of creamy ivory, the smallest green leaves twining over the fabric. After helping her dress, Mary fixed Becca's hair in a simple style and left her.

Finally ready to face the day, Becca went downstairs to the breakfast room. She was relieved to find that John and Patricia had already eaten. She greeted Lady Margaret and walked over to the sideboard. What had first smelled delicious to her when she walked into the room suddenly assailed her senses. Her stomach churned at the heady combination of eggs, ham, and kidneys. Choosing a single bread roll, she took her seat.

Lady Margaret arched a brow at her. "Is that all you're eating this morning, Rebecca?"

"Yes, Lady Margaret. I'm afraid my stomach is a bit sensitive this morning."

"I hope you're not coming down with anything."

"I don't believe so," Becca said, shaking her head.

The ladies discussed the correspondence that awaited them. It seemed that nearly all of the guests had quickly penned their letters of thanks. Now, it was left to Becca and Lady Margaret to respond to their missives.

When they finished their breakfast, they went into the library. Lady Margaret settled herself behind the writing desk, motioning to Becca to take the chair facing her. Becca froze in the doorway. She hadn't been in the room since that awful night when Geoffrey had discovered her with Lord Roberts. It wasn't the memory of the viscount's actions that plagued her, but rather Geoffrey's quick assumption of her guilt. With a sigh of resignation, she entered the room and sat down in front of the desk.

"I had the letters brought in here, Rebecca," Lady Margaret said. "I find this room so pleasant in the mornings."

"Indeed," Becca said softly.

As she turned her attention to the rather sizable pile of letters on the desk, something suddenly occurred to her. She thumbed through the letters, looking for Geoffrey's familiar handwriting. Becca sighed dejectedly, placing the letters back on the desktop.

"I'm sure that Geoffrey is simply too busy to write yet," Lady Margaret offered kindly.

"Am I that transparent?"

The expression of concern on Lady Margaret's face did little to set aside Becca's misery. She'd heard nothing from Geoffrey since the morning of his departure, and couldn't help feeling hurt.

They hardly spoke as they performed their task. After they shared the nooning meal, with Becca once again picking at her food, Lady Margaret sent her upstairs to rest. Truly exhausted, Becca acquiesced. When tea time arrived, she prepared herself. Mary had chosen a lovely tea gown for her in a soft shade of blue. She nodded her thanks to Mary as the girl left her. Becca sat for a while, once again staring at her reflection. Suddenly, she straightened her shoulders. No more hiding. She was a grown woman, not a child. A countess, not an innkeeper's daughter.

Downstairs in the parlor, Patricia sat, regaling her mother-in-law with more gossip about the guests that had so recently departed Kanewood.

"And did you see that silly Diane?" she went on. "Mooning over Lord Roberts like a pup."

Lady Margaret bristled. "She did no such thing, Patricia. She simply found him charming, as I'm sure the other girls did."

"Hmm, yes." Patricia smiled at Becca. "Wouldn't you say so, Rebecca?"

"What is that, Patricia?" Becca asked.

"Oh, just that Viscount Roberts is very charming."

Becca's eyes widened. "I .... Yes, I suppose he is."

"You suppose?" Patricia laughed. "I daresay you found him a bit more than charming."

"Patricia!" Lady Margaret admonished.

Patricia hid her smile, but Becca didn't miss the triumph shining in her eyes.

Lady Margaret turned from her to Becca. "Did you have a nice rest, dear?"

"Yes, thank you," Becca answered softly.

John came into the room just then. "Good afternoon, ladies," he said smoothly.

Becca looked up then. He gave his wife a peck on the cheek, poured himself a cup of tea, and sat beside Patricia. The speculation in his eyes as he gazed at Becca sent an unwelcome shiver down her spine.

"How are you faring, Rebecca?" he asked.

"Hmm?"

"You must be missing my brother terribly." He sipped at his tea. "Exactly what business has him in town?"

"I'm not sure I—"

"It must be quite important, I imagine, to keep him away from his lovely wife."

She looked away from him, shame and disgust warring within her. As she sat there, her attention on her tea cup, Patricia recounted some other stories of the departed guests. John added that the meals the kitchen had prepared were simply extraordinary. He went on, extolling one particular way the staff had prepared the pheasant they dined on one evening.

Suddenly, the room grew too hot for Becca. She stood, her hand over her mouth as her stomach churned. With a mumbled apology, she ran from the room.

* * * *

In their chamber later that evening, as they readied themselves for dinner, Patricia paced back and forth. John watched her closely, a curious look on his face.

"What is it, my dove?" he asked in a soothing voice. "What has you so upset?"

She turned on him, her eyes flashing. "You know damn well what has me upset!"

John blinked, thinking back to his actions of the past few weeks. She couldn't possibly know about his actions in London. He'd thoroughly covered his tracks. True, she knew about the notes. It had been her idea to forge them in the first place, remarkably devious bitch that she was. However, she couldn't know about his other indiscretions. The so-called ladies he'd been involved with were not the sort to pass into their social circle, for the most part.

Patricia sighed in exasperation. "John!"

He turned his attention to her again. "Yes?"

"That bitch will ruin everything."

"How?"

"She's pregnant, you fool! Surely you guessed it. Her flawless skin turned as pale as linen, for God's sake. If she gives Kane a son, you will never inherit."

John scratched his chin thoughtfully. "As long as I have plenty of money to play with, I'm happy to continue on as the second son." *For now.*

"That is not good enough!"

He longed to tell her that he would be earl soon enough, but he saw the desperation in his wife's eyes.

"Patricia," he began softly, "what can we do about it?"

Patricia's beautiful face turned quite ugly as a sly smile spread across it. "We can get rid of it."

"You don't mean …?"

Patricia looked at him sharply. "As much as I hate the little chit, I'd never harm a child."

"Well, what then?"

She walked over to their bed, taking her clothes off as she spoke. "We'll have to get rid of her."

John shed his clothes and took her hands in his. "And just what is it you plan to do, my dove?" he asked, running his lips over her skin.

"I can be very persuasive, John," she said, pushing him down on the bed. "And I always get what I want."

He let his wife win this one.

Chapter 24

Becca took dinner upstairs in her and Geoffrey's chamber, unable to bear the thought of sitting at the table with Patricia and John. As if nearly disgracing herself in their presence wasn't enough, she had no wish to hear their snide comments regarding Lord Roberts. Apparently, John and Patricia were as quick to believe her unfaithful as Geoffrey had been. What must Lady Margaret think of her?

Once she'd eaten all she could of the meal on her tray, she left the chamber, bound for the little study just down the hall. Crossing to the desk, she saw that her notes still sat atop. In a fit of frustration, she grabbed them up and crumpled them in her hands. Who was she to try and bring people together? She couldn't even convince her husband that he was the only man for her!

Throwing the papers down, she dissolved into tears.

* * * *

At the townhouse, Geoffrey sat in his study, pondering all Chester and Leed had discovered down at the waterfront.

Apparently, several drunken men had asked after him, speaking of him like an old friend. Whoever was impersonating him was doing a fine job of it. One of the serving girls apparently thought she knew him very well, and spoke in no vague terms what she had shared with "the earl" the last time he was in town.

Now, as Geoffrey thought about it, it made perfect sense. It had taken months for the notes to pass through so many channels. And it hadn't been in one lump sum, either. The imposter must have spent many a night down at the waterfront, moving through that unseemly world. But again, why use his name? Certainly he was wealthy, his holdings only growing in value since his father's death. But there were many far wealthier than himself.

Once again, Leed and Chester had no notion of the why. They were mainly concerned with the how. He thanked his friends for their dedication and sent them on their way.

With a sigh, he put the matter aside for the night and climbed the stairs to his bedroom. He stripped and climbed into bed. Closing his eyes, he thought only of Becca. He could picture her beautiful face, her exquisite body. He could very nearly feel her silky-smooth skin beneath his fingers. He felt himself start to harden in response. With a ragged sigh, he willed himself to sleep.

Soon after breakfast the next morning, Geoffrey's butler informed him that he had a visitor.

"Who is it, Miles?"

"Viscount Roberts, my lord."

Geoffrey felt rage course through him. "Tell him I won't see him."

"You will see me," Roberts said, striding into the room.

Geoffrey stood, bracing his hands on the desk. He fixed a steely gaze on Roberts. "That will be all, Miles," he said, dismissing the servant.

The butler closed the door on the gentlemen. Geoffrey was the first to speak. "How dare you come here."

"Listen to me, Kane," Roberts began. "You're being a complete fool."

Geoffrey came from behind his desk to face the viscount. "What do know of my behavior, Roberts?"

"You're here and Rebecca is—"

"Don't you dare speak her name!" Geoffrey punched him square in the jaw.

Roberts went down, sprawling on the floor. He sat up and rubbed his jaw, nodding up at Geoffrey. "I deserved that."

"That and more. Get up!"

"Kane, what you saw wasn't as it appeared. She's completely innocent in this."

Geoffrey grabbed Roberts by the lapels of his jacket and pulled him to his feet. "What are you saying, Roberts? Did you force yourself on my wife?"

"I .... That is, everything that happened was entirely my fault. Rebecca did nothing to encourage my attentions."

Geoffrey stared at him for a long while, weighing his words. He finally let go of him, turning away. "I wish I could believe that."

"What?" Roberts asked.

"Never mind." Geoffrey faced him. "Tell me what happened."

Roberts took a deep breath. "I fell in love with her, Kane."

Geoffrey started toward him, but the man's next words stopped him in his tracks.

"She feels nothing for me. She followed me into the library to ask me about the problems you've been having."

Geoffrey stilled. Roberts's words made a kind of sense. She'd been desperate to find out what was troubling him. Innocent of men such as Roberts, she'd have believed he'd tell her what she wanted to know.

"She loves you, Kane," Roberts insisted. "Damn it, man! She didn't welcome my advances."

"What?"

"Ah, I was a fool to think she would. She loves you! She would never betray you."

"God, I want to believe you." He slumped into his chair.

Roberts went on. "I'll never touch her again."

"Damn right, you won't."

"I don't expect you to forgive me." His gray eyes were intense on Geoffrey. "What I did was despicable. But please, don't blame her for my foolishness."

"I must think on this, Roberts." Geoffrey was quiet for a moment. "I'd be within my rights to call you out."

"I know. I'd like to press on with the investigation if I may."

After a brief hesitation, Geoffrey nodded curtly. Roberts walked to the door and pulled it open. He glanced back at him. "Go to her, Kane," he said softly. "She needs you."

The viscount left him then. Geoffrey hung his head. He'd

been wrong. Becca hadn't strayed. She hadn't betrayed him.

He was the worst kind of fool. He'd set out for Kanewood in the morning. He'd make it up to her somehow. He'd get down on his knees and beg her forgiveness if he had to. If he lost her due to his foolish jealousy, he would never be able to forgive himself.

* * * *

Becca was upstairs in the nursery playing with Ann that afternoon. The little girl asked for a story and Becca happily honored her request, glad for the diversion. She sat in the nanny's overstuffed chair with Ann settled on her lap. Her voice soon lulled the child to sleep, her white-blond head resting against Becca's breast. With a small smile, Becca closed the book and rocked the little girl gently. The stillness of the room soon had a drugging effect on Becca, as well. Thinking to close her eyes for only a moment, she soon drifted into a light slumber.

Patricia found them there and cleared her throat, drawing Becca's attention. Her eyes fluttered open, widening as recognition dawned on her. "Patricia," she whispered. "I must have fallen asleep."

"Yes," Patricia sneered. "Ann? Wake up, child."

The little girl stirred, rubbing her eyes. She looked up at her mother in confusion. "Mama?"

Ann hopped down and stared up at her mother. "Aunt Rebecca was reading me the best story, Mama."

"Was she?" Patricia asked, her smile brittle.

It didn't escape Becca's notice that Patricia didn't embrace the child. Her heart broke for Ann. How she longed to push Patricia aside and draw Ann into her arms. Ann was so sweet and loving. Like all children, she needed a mother's love and attention. Something she'd never had herself. Something she yearned to give Ann.

"I need to speak with Aunt Rebecca. Are you quite finished here, Rebecca?"

Becca didn't want to leave the nursery, nor the comfort or

pleasure she felt simply from holding Ann in her arms. "Can this wait, Patricia? We were reading a story."

"There will be time for stories later," Patricia insisted.

Becca nodded reluctantly. "Very well."

As she stood, Ann threw herself at her legs. "Don't go!"

Patricia's eyes narrowed. She visibly stiffened as she waited for Becca to join her at the door.

Becca crouched down and hugged the little girl tightly. "I'll come again very soon, sweetheart," she whispered, stroking her little cheek. "And then we'll finish our story. Would you like that?"

"Oh, yes!" Ann squealed.

Becca kissed the child and stood, walking over to where Patricia waited. With a curt nod in her daughter's direction, Patricia turned and left the room.

Bewildered, Becca followed. "What is it you wish to discuss, Patricia?"

"I'm afraid that certain matters have gone on far too long to be ignored, Rebecca."

"Matters?" Becca wondered aloud. "Of what matters are you speaking?"

They descended the stairs to the floor where their chambers were located.

"I know your secret."

Becca gasped, thinking that surely the woman referred to the terrible rift between Geoffrey and herself. Patricia's next words surprised her.

"You're with child."

Becca opened her mouth to deny it as the truth settled on her. She hadn't had her monthly since first arriving at Kanewood. Her odd illness now made sense: her fatigue and nausea. A smile lifted the corners of her mouth.

"Kane will never let your child inherit," Patricia said bitterly.

"What do you mean?"

"After the shame you brought to this family, how can you ask such a question?"

"But I—"

"And what of Lord Roberts?" she asked. "Did you think we wouldn't learn of your indiscretion?"

Becca brought her hand to her throat, shaking her head. "Nothing happened between—"

"Kane should never have married someone so common. It was only a matter of time before your true nature became evident. Why, Kane couldn't even be sure your child is his issue."

"Patricia, I don't know why you're saying all of this, but I love Geoffrey. And he loves me."

Patricia smiled then, an ugly thing to see. "Then why is he in London, dear, while you remain here?"

Becca couldn't answer. Couldn't speak.

"Has he contacted you or written you since he's been in London?" Patricia asked in a scathing tone.

Becca's face reddened.

"I thought not. If you think you have his heart, think again. He was in love with me once too and then he abandoned me as well. This is what Geoffrey does. I was fortunate that John stepped in to marry me, otherwise I would have ended up just like you. Alone."

Becca gasped at Patricia's bluntness. But it was true. He had cared for Patricia and then left her when he learned she had slept with his brother. Did he jump to the same conclusions about Patricia and John as he had with her and Lord Roberts? Is that why Patricia had become so bitter? It was all too overwhelming.

"I daresay he realizes he's stuck with you, since you are married," Patricia went on. "But he's in London and you're here. He's no doubt finding comfort with a mistress. He'd never want a child of yours, a by-blow, to inherit his title. Let alone Kanewood."

Becca shook her head, trying desperately to deny all the woman was saying.

"Think on it, Rebecca. He doesn't want you. Not you or that child you carry."

With that, she took herself downstairs to lunch. Becca leaned against the wall, taking deep breaths to steady herself.

Her mind reeled. Was what Patricia said true? Would Geoffrey reject this child as he'd rejected her?

Her hand covered her belly protectively. She'd never let her child suffer because of Geoffrey's quick assumption of her betrayal. Stifling a sob, she ran to their chamber.

She sank down into one of the chairs near the fireplace. What was she to do? She couldn't stay at Kanewood, not without her husband. And from the lack of communication from him, he had no plans to return to the estate in the foreseeable future. She couldn't bear the thought of returning to the Raven's Inn. What would her father think?

Suddenly, the kernel of a thought formed in her mind. At the first ball they had attended as husband and wife, that Scotsman, Gilly McClair, had gone on and on about her resemblance to his lord's wife. Could there be a connection between her and this Lady Charlotte? She'd find out. She rang for Mary and instructed the girl to pack her a few belongings. She told her what she was about, but only after getting her word that she wouldn't tell any of the staff where they were going. Remembering that one of the grooms was Scottish, Becca took herself down to the stables. Luckily, Geoffrey's driver, Fields, was in London with his master, leaving her free to ask the groom to drive her into Scotland.

She found the man. He did indeed know of the McClair holding, and would be pleased to take her there. He was uncomfortable with her request of secrecy, but she persuaded him. Satisfied to have a definite plan of action after living in a kind of limbo these past few weeks, she returned to her room to see if Mary needed any help.

Becca was quiet at dinner that night, worried and nervous about her trip on the morrow. It could all prove a mistake, but she took solace in the fact that she'd be away from Patricia and her cruel insinuations. Lady Margaret watched her closely, worry in her gaze. Declining her offer of adjourning to the parlor, Becca bade her good night and climbed the stairs. She would so miss her mother-in-law, who had been nothing but kind to her since her arrival. What would she think of her once she was discovered missing? She knew Patricia would undoubtedly say something about her and Lord Roberts again. Would Lady Margaret believe the lies? Oh, she didn't want that sweet woman thinking ill of her.

She readied herself for bed and slipped under the covers, her hands resting on her still-flat stomach. A baby! She'd love this child with all of her heart. And if she had to care for it alone, so be it. She let out a sigh. She was reminded of Ann. She didn't want to leave her. But how could she stay after everything Patricia had told her. She doubted that Patricia had any maternal feelings for the child. At least Ann would have Lady Margaret to watch over her and shower her with love. Something she would no longer be able to do. She would have to carry yet another burden now. The burden of leaving Ann as well. But she had no choice. She needed to be strong. For the sake of her child.

Closing her eyes, she let sleep take her.

* * * *

Geoffrey couldn't fall asleep. He was eager to get to Kanewood and vowed to leave at first light. Chester and Leed informed him of Roberts's actions earlier that evening, as the viscount wisely kept himself from Geoffrey's presence. It seemed that Roberts was very close to finding out the identity of the driver of the runaway carriage. Geoffrey asked them to continue their search, informing them of his imminent return to Kanewood.

Putting those matters aside, he turned his mind to Becca. He should have trusted her. Should have believed her. But what if she never wanted him to touch her again after his brutal near-attack on her the night before he left?

With a groan of frustration, he pulled on his breeches and went down to the study for a drink. Sleep would need a bit of help to find him that night.

Chapter 25

Well before the others took their breakfast, Becca ate and went upstairs to the nursery. As gently as she could manage, she told Ann that she would be unable to see her for a while.

Tears welled up in the child's big gray eyes. "But where are you going, Aunt Rebecca?"

Becca thought it safe to tell her. "I'm going to Scotland, Ann. For a visit." She smiled. "I hear it's beautiful."

"What's Scotland like?" Ann asked.

"Oh, green rolling hills, fragrant purple heather .... Quite pretty."

"When will you come back?"

Becca's throat tightened. She scooped up the child and carried her to the big chair where she sat, holding her close. "I don't know, sweetheart. I hope to return soon."

Ann reached up to wipe away Becca's tears. "I hope so, too."

Sniffling, Becca gave the child a small smile. She stood, set Ann on her feet, and turned to leave. She got to the door, then ran back to wrap her arms around the little girl one last time, tears streaming down her face. She would miss Ann so much. The poor child only got crumbs of attention from her mother. Well, Becca would never treat her own child that way. She knew what it was like to not have a mother's love. Once again, she was thankful that Lady Margaret was there for Ann. She would need Lady Margaret's care as she got older.

The carriage sat waiting near the stables and Becca climbed inside. With a lurch, the carriage pulled out, bound for Scotland. Becca gazed out the window as Kanewood grew smaller and smaller. Emotionally exhausted, she breathed a deep sigh and laid her head back against the cushion.

* * * *

Geoffrey was up and readying himself for his journey back to Kanewood almost before the sun had risen. He rushed through breakfast, intent on boarding the carriage as soon as possible. He was in his study gathering up his papers when Miles knocked on the open door.

"Lords Chester and Leed to see you, my lord."

"Please send them in, Miles."

The gentlemen entered the room, worry etched on their faces.

Geoffrey arched a brow at them. "What has you two so serious?"

Chester was taken aback. "What's happened, Kane? You look alive again."

Geoffrey laughed at his choice of words. "I have been quite miserable, haven't I?"

"Well?" Leed prodded.

"I'm leaving for Kanewood this morning, Leed. I thought I mentioned that last evening."

"Yes, but you seemed …."

"Resigned?" Geoffrey offered. "Yes," he agreed, a frown creasing his brow. "I'm worried about Becca. I hope to God she'll forgive me." His papers in hand, Geoffrey strode out of the study. The others followed him.

"Kane, we have some information about the carriage," Chester said.

Geoffrey stopped and turned, his brow arched.

"It seems that Lady Brookdale is involved with a man," Leed said.

"But her mourning period isn't over," Geoffrey said.

"They've been meeting in secret. Roberts was able to charm the information out of the lovely widow."

"Who's the man, Leed?"

"Your brother."

Geoffrey stared at him. "There must be a mistake. John can be a bit of a bounder, but—"

"He's been romancing her, Kane," Chester added.

"I refuse to believe that John had anything to do with the accident, Chester."

"We're not certain that he did," Chester allowed. "But we thought you'd wish to know."

"Perhaps it's doubly good you're returning to Kanewood," Leed said.

Geoffrey stiffened. "You don't think Becca could be in any sort of danger there, do you?"

Chester shook his head. "We still believe you were the target."

"But my own brother? No. Patricia is cold enough to chill a man's bits, but I can scarcely believe he would take a mistress—"

"Kane, he betrayed you by sleeping with Patricia," Leed interjected. "What's to prevent him from taking a mistress? Mistresses are as common as walking sticks among the ton."

"You have a point, Leed." Geoffrey nodded resignedly. "But tell me he's not involved with the fraudulent notes."

"We haven't found anything to link him to them."

Geoffrey breathed a sigh of relief. "That is something."

"But that doesn't mean he isn't connected," Leed was quick to add.

"I can't think about this now. I'll watch John carefully and get word to you if he reveals anything to me."

The gentlemen agreed, promising in return to inform him of any further developments.

* * * *

Just past the noon hour, Becca's carriage crossed into Scotland. After stopping for lunch, the driver informed her that they would arrive at Ravenwood in three hours' time. Becca gasped as she heard the name of the McClair holding for the first time. There had to be a connection!

Soon a huge, hulking structure loomed ahead.

"There be Ravenwood, my lady," the driver shouted.

Becca wrinkled her nose at the sight. It looked so dark and

ominous. As they neared the building, however, Becca changed her initial opinion of the holding. Flowers covered the slope leading up to the gray stone walls. Green ivy trailed over the stones, softening the edges of the building. It wasn't so terribly ugly up close.

The carriage rocked to a stop in front of the massive wooden entrance. After giving Mary instructions to stay with the driver, Becca alighted the carriage and slowly walked up to the door. The knocker was cold to the touch. She rapped on the door, sure the sound couldn't possibly carry through the thick wood. Much to her surprise, the door was swiftly pulled open by a liveried servant.

"Yes, may we help you?" he asked with a light brogue.

"I …." Why had she come here? She straightened her shoulders and steeled herself, her resolve strong. "I'd like to see Lady Charlotte if I may."

"May I tell my lady who is calling?"

"Yes," Becca answered. "Lady Kanewood."

With a nod, the servant escorted her into the foyer. Becca stood, excitement mixing with her apprehension. The servant left her to walk down the hall, his footsteps echoing on the stone floor. Becca took in her surroundings. Lady Charlotte had certainly done a fine job of warming the castle. The stone walls were painted creamy white, the color brightening the space. Tapestries in rose and blue added to the warmth.

The servant returned to lead her through opened glass-paned doors and into the parlor. It was huge, even by Kanewood's standards. It had obviously been part of the great hall at one time, cleverly divided now into sitting areas to lend it a cozy feeling. Lady Charlotte's head was bent, her focus intent on the needlework in her lap. The servant cleared his throat and spoke.

"Lady Kanewood," he announced.

Lady Charlotte looked up and met Becca's gaze. Becca forgot to breathe. It was like looking into a mirror, but for the eyes.

Lady Charlotte paled. She stood shakily and walked toward her. "My God. Is it truly you? Rebecca?"

Becca gasped. "M-mother?"

Releasing a loud sob, Lady Charlotte wrapped Becca up in her arms. She pulled back, running her gaze hungrily over her face. "I never thought I'd see you again, Rebecca."

Becca blinked rapidly. "I don't understand."

"Come, dear." Lady Charlotte led her over to the couch. "I'll try to make this clear to you."

The woman took a deep breath and began, visibly losing her tension as the words poured forth. "I was betrothed to Laird McClair, but that hadn't stopped Thomas's pursuit. The three of us … we were friends, of a sort. We were in London for the Season when McClair was called back to Scotland." She began to wring her hands, then stopped the motion. "It seemed that thieves were having their way with the holding, killing the livestock and setting the barn ablaze. With McClair away, Thomas professed his love."

"My father?" Becca asked.

"He was a romantic, then. I told him I loved McClair, but Thomas was insistent. I … admitted to having been intimate with him. Thomas had been shocked, but he seemed resigned to the fact that we could never be more than friends. But word reached London of a terrible accident at the holding and McClair was presumed dead."

Becca could see the echoes of the hurt that revelation must have meant to her and her heart went out to her.

"Heartbroken fool that I was, I accepted Thomas's offer of comfort and his attention. I soon learned I was expecting McClair's child." She smiled at Becca. "You. I believed no other recourse was open to me so I agreed to marry Thomas."

"But," Becca started, "that means my father …."

"Yes, dear," Lady Charlotte said gently. "Thomas Kingsley isn't your father."

Bitterness warred with the compassion she felt for Lady Charlotte. So many lies ….

"I was unable to keep you, Rebecca."

"Why not?" she asked, her voice cracking a bit.

Lady Charlotte looked at her, tenderness in her blue eyes. "You see when you were nearly two years old, we came to

London. While there, we learned that Laird McClair hadn't been killed in Scotland. He'd been gravely injured and only just made his way back to town after recuperating in the country."

"What had happened to him?" Becca asked, caught up in the story.

"His leg. He nearly lost it," she answered. "Now, his limp is barely noticeable."

"But what of me?"

She sighed deeply. "It seemed that another man was killed at the holding. Thomas was in possession of some damning evidence implicating McClair in the man's death. If I didn't stay with him, he .... He said he'd see McClair sent to the gallows."

"No!"

Lady Charlotte took Becca's hands in hers. "I tried to stay at Raven's, Rebecca! I truly did. But I loved McClair. I couldn't bear the thought of living without him."

Becca nodded, knowing how strong such a love could be. That was precisely how she felt about Geoffrey. But to leave her child?

"What of your marriage to my—to Thomas? How could you legally wed Laird McClair?" Becca asked.

"We had the marriage quietly annulled. No one knew about it except for us." Becca nodded encouraging Lady Charlotte to continue with her story.

Lady Charlotte took a breath and continued, "But when it came time for us to leave—that was when Thomas refused to let me take you with me. I left for Scotland, for Ravenwood—alone. Thomas kept you with him. He refused to be left with nothing, he insisted. At the time, I felt as though my hands were tied. He held so much power over us. It was the hardest choice I had ever had to make."

"But you never came back to see me," Becca said, unable to keep the hurt out of her voice.

"I know, dear. And it tore at my heart to be set apart from you," Lady Charlotte said sadly. "But Thomas had added one more nail to the coffin before I left. He said that if I ever returned to see you, he would expose McClair and myself as co-conspirators. He also said that from that point on, I was dead.

To him and to everyone. And most importantly to you. He would tell everyone that I had drowned in an accident while on a visit with distant relatives."

Becca was in shock that Thomas could have been so cruel and vindictive.

"My last memory of you was the day I said good-bye to you," Lady Charlotte added, her voice breaking.

Becca recalled that dusty memory she'd had in the attic. Had her mother told her farewell before leaving for good? "I think I remember when you left," she said softly.

Her mother blinked, then she nodded. "I kissed your sweet face, dear. Stroked your silken hair before taking my leave." She took a breath. "I think that was why Thomas wanted to keep you—he knew that he could hurt me forever because McClair could never cross over into England for fear of prosecution."

Becca listened to her mother, tears in her eyes. All this suffering because of one man's bitterness. But Thomas had loved Lady Charlotte at one time and his actions had stemmed from hurt. Becca wondered again if he had grown to care about her. She recalled how choked up he was at her wedding. Perhaps he did—in spite of himself.

"How I wanted one of the clansmen to kidnap you and bring you back home to us!" her mother continued. "But McClair said we couldn't take that chance. Thomas had that evidence and would not hesitate to use it against us. He told me as much before I left. I have no doubt that if I ever tried to take you that he would have had McClair arrested. I knew he would never harm you. Please tell me he never hurt you."

"He did not," Becca said. "He … was always distant, but he cared about me in his own way, I suppose." She wondered if perhaps in addition to hurting Lady Charlotte, he had needed, in some way to have a part of her there always—and the only way he was able to do that was to keep her child. Maybe one day, she would ask him. A part of her never wanted to see him again, but a part of her wanted to know why.

"I feared he would take his anger out on you. I cannot tell you the anguish I went through, leaving you there. I just prayed that you were all right. You grew up without a mother's love and attention. How I wished I could have taken you with me! And yet—" She paused to smile. "And yet here you are, so beautiful and poised. I can scarcely believe you're here."

Becca sat for a moment, weighing all that her mother had said. Finally, she spoke. "This is a lot to contemplate. I … I think I'm beginning to understand."

"Thank the Lord. I won't push you for more at present." Her mother gave her a watery smile. "But I needed to know about you, honey. We needed to know that you were safe. Well-cared for. Every few months, your father would send someone to Raven's."

"Why?"

"To check on you." She sniffed again. "To let us know a little bit about you."

"I don't remember seeing a Scotsman visiting that often."

Her mother laughed lightly. "Oh, we never sent any clansmen. We didn't dare let it be known among the clan. We didn't want to risk Thomas finding out, either. But I was desperate for news of you, even given so dispassionately by one of your father's investigators."

Becca's eyes stung and she blinked to keep from crying. "You did care about me."

Her mother wrapped her arms around her. "Oh, honey. I love you!"

"Charlotte!" a masculine voice boomed from the back of the house.

Lady Charlotte leaned away and looked expectantly at Becca, a smile on her face. "In the parlor, dear."

"Charlotte, what in the world …?"

A big man strolled through the doorway and froze, his brow wrinkled in confusion. He looked from one woman to the other, obviously stunned. Becca breathed in sharply as her gaze ran over Laird McClair. She saw a flash of red in his brown hair, but it was his eyes that caught her attention. They were the same emerald green as her own.

Laird McClair was the first to find his voice. "Can it be?" he asked in a pleasant brogue. "Is this the child?"

"Yes, dear," Lady Charlotte answered, pulling Becca to her

feet. "This is our Rebecca."

With a loud whoop, he grabbed Becca in a bear hug and twirled her about the room. He set her back on her feet, resting his big hands on her shoulders. "Daughter," he said, a smile on his face.

Lady Charlotte looked on, dabbing the corners of her eyes with a lace handkerchief as Becca sought to process all this new information.

A short while later, Lady Charlotte had Becca settled into her room and Mary sent to the servants' quarters. It was a very pleasant space, decorated in much the same style as the main floor. No stone walls were evident here, however, as the castle was refitted with wood and plaster walls. The room was painted a soft green, the color offsetting the heavy wood-beamed ceiling. The window was mullioned, the thickness of the wall evident in the depth of the window seat.

Lady Charlotte led Becca to the window seat, taking her hands in hers. At her mother's insistence, Becca shared a bit of what her life had been like up until now. She told her mother about her life at Raven's, assuring the woman again that Thomas had been kind to her if not overly affectionate.

"You were no better than a servant!" her mother scoffed. "If I had Thomas before me, I would wring his thick neck."

"I am fine now," Becca assured her. "I never resented taking care of the inn. It is a lovely place."

Her mother wrinkled her nose. "You should have been treated like the noblewoman you are."

"I am now a countess," she said. Though estranged from her husband, that was true. "And … I'm expecting a baby." Somehow, saying it aloud made it all the more real.

Her mother clasped her hands in obvious delight. "Oh, a baby! But what of your husband, Rebecca?" Lady Charlotte asked. "Our last report stated that you had married well and left Raven's. Where is your husband?"

Becca hesitated. She couldn't tell her about their problems, loath to see the pity that would surely be evident in her eyes. "He's in London on business, Mother," she answered, a half-truth.

Lady Charlotte seemed to sense there was more to her story than what Becca was telling, but permitted her to hold her own counsel for the time being. She left Becca then, advising her of the dinner hour.

Becca was grateful for the solitude. She was exhausted after her conversation with her mother. There was so much information to take in, she didn't know whether to laugh or cry or both. Her feelings were a muddle, as well. She was overjoyed to be reuinited with her parents but heartbroken that her father, oh, she could not bear to think of Thomas as such any longer after he had kept her from them for so many years. Did Geoffrey feel that kind of anger about her? Did Geoffrey think that she loved Lord Roberts? How could he ever think that?

She needed to rest, for her baby's sake if not for her own. She would puzzle through it all later.

* * * *

On his return to Kanewood, Geoffrey had much time to think. Chester had stated that John was involved with Lady Brookdale. His brother's infidelity didn't truly shock him. But would he romance a woman of the ton? A widow still in mourning? Geoffrey prayed there was no connection between John's affair and the runaway carriage. He'd vowed to kill the bastard responsible for hurting Becca, and the possibility that it was his brother didn't lessen his conviction.

His thoughts turned to his wife, the urge to take her in his arms so strong it was consuming him. He didn't know what he was going to say to her to convince her of his regret. He'd been so quick to think the worst of her when she'd been nothing but trusting toward him. He would do anything to win back her love. He was resigned to groveling at her feet if need be. She'd been so accepting of him from the beginning, so giving. She had always shown nothing but love to him. Hadn't her declaration filled his heart as nothing had before? How could he have been so stupid as to think she would go to Roberts for anything more than information? Time and again, she'd asked to share in his life and his worries. That was what a husband and wife did, and he would give anything now to pour his foolish heart out to her.

He reviewed the events of that fateful night in his mind. When he thought clearly of the scene he'd witnessed in the library, it occurred to him that Becca had been pushing Roberts away. Why had he refused to believe that? Against his will, he remembered all that had happened afterward in their chamber. Shame washed over him afresh. How could he have used her so roughly? He'd stopped, but it had been a bloody close thing. My God, to think what he'd almost done to her! It was unforgiveable, and yet he prayed she would find forgiveness in her kind and generous heart. He had to make this right.

By the time he arrived at Kanewood the next evening, Geoffrey was ready to jump out of his skin. Before the carriage had even come to a complete stop, he jumped out. He ran up the stone steps and pushed open the door. "Becca!" he called. "Becca?"

Lady Margaret walked out of the parlor. "She isn't here, Geoffrey."

He spun around to face her. "What are you talking about, Mother?"

"She's been gone all day."

"Where is she?"

"I don't know." His mother wrung her hands. "When I didn't see her at breakfast, I assumed she was still feeling ill. But when I went to her room—"

"She's been ill?"

"Mildly, yes," his mother answered.

A parlormaid walked past them, her head down and Geoffrey caught her attention. "Can you please send Mary to me? Lady Kanewood's maid?"

"Nay, my lord." The maid's brow furrowed. "Mary left this morning with Lady Kanewood."

"Damn it!" Geoffrey turned to leave, but his mother's gentle touch on his arm stayed him.

"Geoffrey, where are you off to?"

"She's left me, Mother."

"You left her first, Geoffrey."

Pain stabbed at him. "I know."

Her lips pursed, but she said nothing more of Becca. "Why don't you have something to eat, dear?"

"I have to find her, Mother."

"Geoffrey, you can't go racing about. It will be dark soon. The morning will be soon enough."

He dragged his fingers through his hair in acute frustration. "Yes, yes." He blew out a breath. "You have the right of it."

The cook prepared him a platter and he ate in silence. Thankfully, Patricia and John had already taken themselves off to bed.

Geoffrey finished his meal and climbed the staircase, his steps plodding. Once more, he'd sleep without Becca in his arms. First thing tomorrow, he'd question the staff. He might have set Becca aside, fool that he'd been. But no one would keep her from him now.

Chapter 26

When Geoffrey awoke the next morning, his determination was strong. By lunch time, however, his results weren't. No one on his staff knew where Mary had gone with her mistress, and the stables yielded more bad news. In Fields's absence, one of the grooms had driven her. Apparently, none of the others knew of Lady Kanewood's destination.

"I beg your pardon, my lord," one of the grooms apologized. "We have no notion where the Scot took her."

"Well, isn't there anyone who—" Geoffrey began. "Wait. A Scot?"

"Aye, my lord. McGinty was who took her. His wife is ready to bear him another youngun any day now. He's gone home to see to her."

Geoffrey dismissed the men, his mind working. The groom who'd driven her was Scottish. For some reason, that little piece of information seemed significant. "But why?" He filed it away in his mind to contemplate later.

After choking down his lunch, Geoffrey went into his study. Sitting down behind his desk, he reviewed what he'd already learned. Precious little, really. Becca was gone, and he had no idea where. Could she have gone to Raven's? No. She wasn't emotionally attached to her father, and Geoffrey couldn't imagine she'd want to go there if she was upset. She'd taken Mary with her, so obviously she thought to stay away for a while. That fact cut him to the quick.

He sat up suddenly, an idea flitting through his mind. Her clothes! He'd ascertain what type of clothes she'd taken with her. Perhaps that would help point to her destination. He all but jumped out of the chair, bound for their chamber. He rounded the corner and took the steps two at a time. When he reached their room, he crossed to her vanity.

He'd never really paid much attention to the feminine notions that normally littered the top of it, but not much was there now, just some ribbons and hairpins. To the right of the mirror sat a velvet jeweler's box. Recognition dawned on him as he opened the box. Inside lay the pearls he'd given her the night of the Winslow ball. He fingered them, thinking back to how perfect they'd looked against her flawless skin. She'd left them behind as she'd left him.

He snapped the lid closed and turned from the vanity, walking into her dressing room. While Mary kept the room well-organized, he still had no notion what was missing. He pulled open one of the drawers. Inside were only a few nightgowns, indicating that she'd taken several with her. How long did she plan to stay away? His attention turned to the dresses hanging in the large wardrobe. It appeared, to his untrained eye at least, that several were missing. His gaze fell on her formal gowns, his fingers absently caressing the smooth fabric. Something caught his eye. The provocative blush-pink gown hung in the wardrobe, bringing back memories to him in a rush. The thought of all those young pups drooling over her each moment he left her side now made him smile wryly. His reaction had been almost comical. He thought of the passion they'd shared on the carriage-ride home that evening, his blood warming at that memory. The entire time he'd known her she'd welcomed him and only him. She'd never flirted with the men currying her favor at the bashes, either. No, she'd just been the friendly open girl he'd fallen for at the inn. Her passion she'd kept for him alone. He was even more determined to find her. He had to. He'd finally realized what was missing from his life these past many years. And it was Becca.

As he left the dressing room, something nagging at the back of his mind struck him. A Scot! A Scotsman had monopolized her attention for a bit that night, causing her some distress. The man had told her of a woman, his lord's wife, who greatly resembled Becca. Hadn't Becca told him later that the woman's name was the same as her mother's?

What was the Scotsman's name? Mc-something … McCall

… McClair! Could she have gone to Scotland? He'd return to the stables and question the men once more.

Pleased to have a course of action at last, he fairly ran for the stairs. He nearly crashed into his mother at the top. As he began to rush through an apology, the melancholy on her face struck him.

"What is it, Mother?"

"I was visiting with Ann. The poor little thing misses Rebecca terribly."

"She isn't the only one."

"Rebecca spent many hours with her, Geoffrey," Lady Margaret went on, a small smile on her face. "Mrs. Riley told me that Rebecca had been there yesterday morning."

"Mother, do you think she may have told Ann where she was going?"

"It wouldn't surprise me. She and the child have become quite close. In fact, she was talking about Rebecca just before her nap. Something about heather."

"Heather?" Something niggled at the back of his mind. The groom who had driven her was Scottish. Now Ann talked about heather?

His mother shrugged. "Perhaps—"

Before she'd finished her sentence, Geoffrey left her to run up to the nursery. When he opened the door, Mrs. Riley had just set out Ann's afternoon snack.

She straightened, obviously surprised to see the earl standing in the doorway. "Good afternoon, my lord."

"Hello, Mrs. Riley."

His gaze darted about the room and the nanny regarded him for a moment.

"Is there something you need?" she asked.

"Is Ann about?"

Mrs. Riley nodded. "Yes, my lord. She should be in presently."

Ann skipped into the room, coming to a stop when she saw her uncle there.

Geoffrey saw the child tremble, and crouched down so as not to appear so large to her. "Hello, Ann."

"Hello, Uncle Geoffrey."

Geoffrey looked pointedly at the nanny. Obeying his unspoken request, she left the room. Ann walked over to the little table and sat. She picked up her milk and drank, staring at her uncle over the rim of the glass.

Geoffrey folded himself to sit on one tiny wooden chair. "Ann, did you see Aunt Rebecca yesterday?"

"Oh, yes." Ann nibbled on a biscuit. "She was sad."

Geoffrey's heart lurched at that little declaration. "Do you know what made her sad?"

Ann looked at him as if he were simple. "She was sad about going away. I tried to make her feel better."

"I'm sure you did, sweetheart."

Ann nodded regally. "Auntie likes very much to read to me, Uncle Geoffrey."

"Yes, I know."

She smiled back at him and he let the child eat her snack for a short while.

"Ann," he asked finally, "did Aunt Rebecca tell you when she would return?"

Ann shook her head, sadness in her eyes. "No. Won't you go get her and bring her back?"

"I would, but I don't know where she went."

"She went to Scotland, silly," Ann said absently, turning her attention back to her biscuits.

Geoffrey straightened in his chair, struggling to keep his voice level for the child's sake. He'd suspected as much, but to hear it from Ann was astounding. "How do you know that?"

"She told me." Ann shrugged. "There are lots of green hills there, Uncle Geoffrey. And purple heather growing everywhere."

"Is that right?" He stood then. "I've enjoyed our visit, Ann."

He dropped a kiss on the top of her head and left the nursery. Without any further delay, he went back to the stables to question the men once more.

* * * *

The early part of Becca's day passed in a very pleasant fashion. After breakfast, she'd strolled the courtyard with her father. He was incredibly huge, taller even that Geoffrey. But she'd soon put that fact aside as she accustomed herself to his presence. His brogue was musical to her ears, his booming laugh refreshing.

"Tell me, lass," he said, his expression grave. "Tell me you forgive me?"

She didn't wish to speak of it again, certain the subject caused him as much pain as it did her. The look in his eyes, green and so like her own, showed his intent as well as his regret.

"Lady Charlotte told me about the danger to the both of you. I understand."

"But do you forgive me? 'Tis a far different thing, my girl."

She reached for his hand and squeezed it. "I do."

Upon hearing her words, his big shoulders slumped in relief.

She decided to broach the subject they'd all been avoiding since her arrival. "But you must promise me something."

"Anything, Rebecca," he said.

"We need to clear this matter up—so that you and my mother may come back into England without fear of arrest."

He shook his head. "I don't know if that's possible."

"Father, you did nothing wrong. My—Thomas has held this over your head for almost twenty years."

"Ach, lassie, he loved your mother, too. So much time has passed."

"Precisely. It's time to put all of this in the past. I was never very close with Thomas, but … that is, I believe he does care for me."

"You shouldn't have to speak on my behalf," her father bristled.

"Never mind. I will make this right. Not just for you and Mother. But for my baby."

His eyes teared up and she found herself enveloped in a crushing, loving hug. She didn't know if she had any sway over Thomas, but she would try her best. For all of them.

Now she stood in the guest room she'd been given, readying

herself for tea. Being English, Becca's mother still insisted on tea each afternoon, much to Laird McClair's chagrin. Becca had found her first smile as she listened to them bicker over the ritual, warmth in their voices.

Her dress was of rose-colored silk, one of the first Geoffrey had given her. She regarded herself closely in the cheval glass, seeing both of her parents' features evident in her reflection. She ran her fingers through the curls at her temple, her mind working. Her mother had told her that Thomas had named the inn for her. The ton had bestowed the nickname "Raven" upon her very shortly after her debut, because of her raven-black tresses. When Charlotte had returned to the holding with McClair, he renamed his family home for her, as well.

Becca thought back to how Geoffrey had always professed to love her hair. He'd always called her beautiful. Had his love for her been that shallow? He'd cast her aside so easily, perhaps it had been only her looks that had held his heart. Her stomach clenched at that thought. She ran her hand gently over her abdomen. She would have to be strong for her child. She couldn't afford to fall apart. And she would love it enough for two parents, even if she had to do it alone.

Sighing, she turned away from the mirror and went downstairs to tea.

* * * *

At Kanewood that evening, Geoffrey paid little attention to his dinner, his mind on the morrow. Fields had promised him he'd learn where the McClair holding was and Geoffrey trusted the man at his word. He noticed then that John never appeared for the meal.

"Where's my brother, Patricia?"

"It seems he had some appointments to keep in London, Kane." She sipped at her wine. "It's a shame you came back so soon. You could have kept an eye on my husband for me."

Geoffrey started at her choice of words. He'd told Chester and Leed that he'd do just that and now John wasn't at Kanewood.

"Don't you usually accompany him on these trips?" Lady Margaret asked.

Patricia bristled. "He shall not be gone long, Lady Margaret," she responded sharply.

His mother arched her brow at the woman's reaction, but held her tongue.

"Which is it then, Patricia? Will he be gone a while or back shortly?" Geoffrey asked. "What, precisely, keeps John in London?"

She pursed her lips. "He will be back when he returns. I trust my spouse, Kane."

The dig missed its intended mark but still stung. He should have trusted Becca. That was the truth of it. The remainder of the meal passed in uncomfortable silence, though he still found it preferrable to Patricia's venom.

Much later, Geoffrey stood at the window in his study on the main floor, looking out at the dark landscape. His upcoming trip distracted him, preventing the hope of getting to sleep tonight. He poured himself a brandy and swirled the liquid in his glass, trying to puzzle through all that muddled his mind.

A knock sounded at the door. Geoffrey went to it, thinking it could be Fields with information for him. He pulled the door open and blinked in surprise. Patricia stood there in her wrapper, the collar closed tightly under her chin.

"Patricia, what are you doing here?"

"I couldn't sleep." She strolled into the room. "I knocked on your chamber door, but there was no answer."

"You went to my chamber?"

"Yes." She turned slightly to gaze at him over her shoulder. "I needed someone to talk to."

He closed the door and leaned against it, his arms crossed. "What did you wish to discuss?"

"I was lonely, Kane." She crossed over to stand very close, nearly touching him. "You must be lonely without Rebecca."

Geoffrey straightened, putting some distance between them, but she promptly bridged the tiny space he'd made and loosened the collar of her wrapper, showing him quite a bit of her bosom.

"Kane." She pressed herself against him. "I can make you forget all about her."

"I don't want to forget about her."

"You cast her aside." She caressed him through his breeches. Her gown was open to him now, showing him she wore nothing beneath. She nibbled on his ear. "I have acquired many talents since our engagement, Kane. More than Rebecca, I daresay. Let me show you."

She knelt down to unbutton his breeches. He grabbed her fingers then, nearly crushing them.

"Get up," he barked.

She blinked up at him and stood, placing her hands behind his neck.

He grabbed her roughly and pushed her away. "What do you think you're doing? You're my brother's wife!"

She simply shrugged, closing her wrapper with an imperious toss of her head. "I thought we could make each other feel better, that's all. But I can see you're as passionless as you were all those years ago."

His eyes narrowed. "I only have passion for my wife. A whore like you would never entice me."

"Whore!" She ran at him, her hands in fists as she pummeled his chest.

He easily stopped her assault, holding her away from him. "Don't think to try this again, Patricia."

She looked into his eyes and must have finally grasped his anger. He opened the door and watched as she walked out. She stopped in the doorway, turning in a last show of defiance. "Your bed will be cold and lonely, Kane," she warned. "And then you will come to me."

With that she left, presumably for her and John's chamber. What kind of marriage did those two share? He shuddered in disgust at her attempted seduction. He couldn't believe he had almost married that bitch. Judging from what he had found out about his brother—they deserved each other.

If Becca had come upon the two of them tonight, a scene far more suspect than hers with Roberts, would she have believed his protestations of innocence? In his heart, he knew that she would. Guilt sliced into him once more. He had been so quick to think the worst of the most loving woman he'd ever known. Well, he might not deserve her forgiveness, but he was damn well going to beg for it. He needed her. The prospect of living his life without her in it was something he would not contemplate unless that horrid future presented itself.

After that, nothing else mattered.

Chapter 27

On the waterfront in London, Leed, Chester and Roberts were at last making progress in their investigations. They went once more to the pub where the serving girl had asked after Geoffrey and the three of them sat at a table in the corner, observing the crowd. Loose women circulated among the gamblers and drinkers. Drunken men lolled about, spewing lewd suggestions as they guzzled their cheap liquor. The stench of ale and unwashed bodies assailed them.

"What disgusting rabble," Leed muttered.

Chester nodded his agreement. He flagged down the serving girl, recognizing her as the one who had propositioned Geoffrey. They questioned her, with Roberts using all of his charm on the wench.

"Aye, but you're a handsome one," she purred, sliding closer to him.

Chester cleared his throat to gain her attention. "Miss, do you recall the gentleman you asked after on our last visit?"

"Yea." She tore her gaze from Roberts, an absent smile on her face. "Pretty one, that. Quite the treat between the sheets, too."

"From where do you know him, may I ask?"

"From here, where do ya think?" she stated. "He couldn't get enough of me."

"I can see why," Roberts interjected, oozing charm.

The girl turned back to him. "I made Lord Kanewood very happy, I can tell ya."

The men exchanged a look then.

"He has gray eyes, too," The girl went on, stroking Roberts' cheek. "I like gray eyes."

Chester sat bolt upright, turning his head sharply to Leed.

"What is it, man?" Leed asked in a whisper.

"Gray eyes," Chester hissed.

Leed's mouth gaped open as realization hit him. "John," they said together.

Roberts managed to disentangle himself from the serving girl and the three of them stepped out into the relatively fresh air.

"I didn't think you'd come out of there alive," Leed told him.

"I promised her I'd ask for her on my next visit." Roberts snorted. "Safe bet, as I plan to never cross that threshold again."

"What is our next step?" Chester asked.

"We can't go to Kane without proof, Chester," Leed insisted.

The others were inclined to agree with him. They climbed into the rented hack and returned to Chester's townhouse.

Once in the carriage, Roberts turned to his friends. "The solicitors still have the false notes in their possession."

"That's it!" Leed said.

"Pray share with us, friend," Chester said.

Leed quirked a smile. "Altough the writing looks close enough to Kane's to arouse no suspicions, there must be something in the notes to give away John's hand. The solicitors are certain to have several samples of John's handwriting."

"And that should be the last piece of evidence we need to force John to admit his misdeeds," Roberts finished for him.

Chester nodded. "Sound notion. What will we do if we get such a confession from him?"

Leed shook his head. "That will be for Kane to decide, I imagine."

"Confronting one's own brother on such a matter?" Roberts said. "I'm pleased I'm an only child."

* * * *

At first light, Geoffrey was up and out of bed. He instructed his valet to pack his belongings and hurried down the staircase.

Fields was waiting for him at the bottom. "Beggin' your

pardon, my lord, but I thought you would want to know right away."

Geoffrey looked at him expectantly. "What is it, Fields?"

"Seems that the gamekeeper has a cousin who lives in Scotland, not far from the McClair holding. He gave me the directions."

Geoffrey let loose a whoop of joy, grabbing the driver by the arms. "Fields, I could kiss you."

The driver's eyes rounded. "Please don't, my lord."

Geoffrey laughed and slapped him on the back. "Ready the carriage, man. I wish to leave within the hour."

"Certainly, my lord."

Geoffrey strode into the breakfast room with a big grin on his face. Lady Margaret, already seated at the table, looked at him in obvious confusion.

"What happened, Geoffrey?" she asked.

"I think I've found her." He served himself from the sideboard. "I leave for Scotland within the hour."

"Scotland? What on earth is Rebecca doing in Scotland?"

Geoffrey shook his head at her as he took his seat. "It's complicated, Mother, and a bit of a long shot. I promise to tell you everything."

His mother furrowed her brow, then gave a short nod. Geoffrey devoured his breakfast, truly hungry for the first time in weeks. Patricia entered the room and looked at him pointedly.

He threw her a dismissive glance and stood up. "Well." He drained the last of his tea. "I'm off."

"Good luck, Geoffrey," Lady Margaret said.

He placed a kiss on his mother's cheek and nodded.

"Good luck?" Patricia arched a brow. "And where are you off to with such haste?"

"I'm going to fetch my wife," he answered.

Patricia's scowl was as ugly as her behavior last night, and Geoffrey was eager to leave it behind.

* * * *

In London, Viscounts Roberts and Leed met at the Earl of

Chester's townhouse. The butler ushered them into the breakfast room.

Chester stood as they entered. "Capital! I had hoped our late night wouldn't delay you two."

Leed groaned in answer, rubbing his eyes.

Roberts grinned at his friend's discomfort as he fixed himself a plate. "It appears Leed had a bit too much ale last evening."

"Never mind the ale," Leed grumbled. "The brandy he poured down me was what did it."

Roberts shrugged as he sat and began his meal. "We were celebrating. We've finally unveiled the son-of-a-bitch who has been passing those false notes."

"We don't know for certain, Roberts," Chester cautioned, sipping his tea.

"Do you think there is any chance the handwriting won't match, Chester?" Roberts asked, arching a brow.

Chester waited a beat. "No."

Leed joined them at the table, a roll on his plate. Chester eyed him with humor and Leed scowled at him.

"When are we to pay our call on the solicitors?" Roberts asked.

"I sent a note this morning," Chester said. "They responded and are expecting us shortly."

Roberts let out a breath. "I can hardly believe John would stoop to such dastardly measures."

"Normally, I'd be inclined to agree," Chester allowed. "But with his appetite for the gaming tables, he was bound to work his way through his monthly stipend."

"But to risk Kane's and Rebecca's lives?"

"I don't believe he meant to hurt Rebecca," Chester said. "Unfortunately, she got in the way."

"Do you think he meant to hurt Kane, or to simply distract him?" Leed asked.

Chester set his cup down. "That, gentleman, is the crux of the matter."

They finished their meal and set out to meet with Geoffrey's solicitors.

The solicitors, two gentlemen of extreme discretion, led them into a private office and closed the door. Without a word, the older of the two, a Mr. Hall, handed Lord Chester three pieces of paper. One was a false note bearing Geoffrey's signature, another one with a proven signature of his. The third was a note penned by John, a lengthy missive requesting an advance on his stipend. As Leed and Roberts looked on, Chester felt the blood drain from his face. Though the difference was miniscule it was irrefutable: John had penned the false notes. The implication was far darker than the stolen funds, however.

"That's it, then," Chester said.

"How are we going to tell Kane?" Leed asked.

Roberts suddenly stiffened. "My God! If John was the one responsible for the carriage accident, Kane and Rebecca could still be in danger."

"A note won't do, gentlemen," Chester said. "We must go directly to Kanewood."

Leed nodded and headed for the door, but Roberts's hand on his arm stilled him. Leed looked at him in question.

"I can't go to Kanewood," Roberts stated. "I'm the last person Kane would want to see."

Leed clapped him on the shoulder. "I'll make certain Kane knows of your part in this, Roberts."

Leed and Chester dropped Roberts at his home. As he climbed the steps to his front door, Chester called out, drawing his attention. Roberts looked at him expectantly.

"You're a good man, Roberts."

With a curt nod to his friend, he let himself inside and closed the door.

Chester and Leed retrieved what they would need from their respective homes and were soon off to Kanewood.

* * * *

Becca sat with Lady Charlotte in the parlor at Ravenwood. While her mother was busily working on her tapestry, Becca embroidered tiny flowers on a square of linen. The handkerchief would be quite lovely when it was completed, and Becca tried to focus on the pretty design.

The butler suddenly appeared at the doors leading off the entryway and Lady Charlotte looked up expectantly.

"A visitor for Lady Kanewood, my lady," he stated.

Becca looked up and gasped in surprise. There, behind the servant, stood Geoffrey.

"Hello, Becca," he said, his gaze holding hers.

Becca stood then, her needlework falling to the floor. She held herself ramrod stiff, afraid to move lest he vanish from her sight. Slowly, she walked over to where he stood until she couldn't help but fly into his arms.

"Oh, Geoffrey!" she sobbed.

Geoffrey stroked her hair and hugged her as if he'd never let her go. Becca pulled back to gaze up at him, tears spilling over her lashes as he smiled down at her tenderly.

Lady Charlotte broke through their reverie. "I take it, Rebecca, that this is your husband?"

"W-what?" Becca stammered. "Yes, this is he."

Geoffrey draped his arm around her shoulders and turned to the woman seated on the couch. His eyes widened as he looked from her to his wife and back again. "And I take it, Becca, that this is your mother?"

The older woman smiled, rising up off the couch to clasp her hand with his. "A pleasure to meet you, Lord Kanewood," she said, curtsying.

Geoffrey bowed to her. "And it's very nice to meet you, Lady Charlotte."

Lady Charlotte informed them that she had to see about dinner, an obvious excuse to which neither Becca nor Geoffrey objected. She pulled the glass doors closed, affording them privacy.

When they were alone, Geoffrey took Becca's hand in his and led her to the couch her mother had just vacated.

Becca looked up at him expectantly. "How did you find me?"

Geoffrey quirked a half-smile at her. "It wasn't an easy feat, love. But well worth the trouble."

She nodded, smiling back at him.

"I had to see you, Becca," he began. "And when I arrived at Kanewood to find you gone—"

"You were at Kanewood?"

"Yes, love. Why wouldn't I be?"

Becca looked down at her hands. She could only hope that he wasn't at Kanewood long enough for Patricia to tell him her secret. She didn't know how she would tell him herself.

"I've missed you, Becca." He hugged her to him. "I've been such a fool." He held her away from him, running his gaze over her face. "I should have trusted you. I know that now. I'm so sorry for everything."

Becca saw a strand of hope and sought to grasp it. "Do you mean it?"

"Yes." His expression turned serious. "I saw you with Roberts and, innocent though the circumstances were, I leapt to a horrid conclusion."

"You seemed so certain, so ready to think I would ever …." She couldn't put into words what he'd thought she'd done with Lord Roberts. "You believed I would be unfaithful."

"I know. You have never given me any cause to think such a thing, Becca. I should never have measured you by any other woman's actions."

"Patricia's," she guessed.

He nodded. "I know that you are your own woman, one who is passionate and faithful and more than I deserve." A small smile teased his lips. "I should have known you would never betray me."

She felt her own lips twitch in response to his expression. "How would you know that?" she had to know.

"Because you love me."

She let out a small laugh, her first in what seemed like forever. "I do love you, Geoffrey!" she said happily, wrapping her arms around his neck.

"I love you too, Becca," he said softly in her ear.

She pulled back to gaze at him once more. With a low moan, he brought his mouth to hers, rubbing gently. She opened her mouth to him, needing very badly for him to deepen the kiss. He did, slanting his mouth over hers. He broke the contact and, with a loud sigh, leaned back against the couch, taking her with him.

When Lady Charlotte returned, she found them sitting as closely as possible, Geoffrey stroking Becca's cheek as she stared up at him. Becca was the first to notice her mother's return and turned with a smile.

"I trust all is well?" Lady Charlotte asked.

"Yes, very well thank you, Mother," Becca answered.

Geoffrey straightened, turning his attention to Lady Charlotte. "I can scarcely believe Rebecca found you, Lady Charlotte."

"My daughter is a very bright girl, Lord Kanewood. And very forgiving."

Geoffrey saw the double meaning in the woman's words. He glanced over at his wife. "I'm aware of that, rest assured. How did all of this happen?"

She took a seat across from them. "I'll let Rebecca tell you the tale, Lord Kanewood."

"Please. Call me Geoffrey."

Lady Charlotte smiled and inclined her head. "Geoffrey, then."

Becca thought to tell him of her real father. "My mother isn't the only discovery I made here, Geoffrey."

Geoffrey arched a brow.

"Hello!" McClair filled the space, wearing a big grin. "And who is this lad?" he asked, looking at Geoffrey.

Becca stood and Geoffrey followed suit.

"Laird McClair," she began, "may I present my husband, Geoffrey Kane, the Earl of Kanewood."

Geoffrey extended his hand. McClair took it, pulling him into his arms for a strong embrace. "Kane, my boy! High time you came for my daughter."

Geoffrey's eyes widened. "Your daughter?"

The big man released his hold on Geoffrey, who looked at him closely. No doubt he saw the resemblance Becca had seen that first day.

"I'm very pleased to meet you, Laird McClair," Geoffrey said with a bow.

"Nonsense, boy." McClair slapped Geoffrey on the back. "Call me McClair."

Becca smiled at his obvious bemusement.

"McClair," Geoffrey said.

"Geoffrey," Lady Charlotte said, "I've seen to your belongings. You'll find them in Rebecca's guest chamber."

"Thank you, Lady Charlotte."

"Now, why don't we go ready ourselves for tea?" Lady Charlotte suggested.

"Tea." McClair snorted. "Ridiculous ritual, ridiculous drink."

Geoffrey started to laugh, turning to Becca. She shook her head at him.

"Now, McClair," Lady Charlotte started, leading him from the room. "You know how I treasure this time."

"Stuff of nonsense," McClair boomed.

Their voices trailed off as the couple climbed the stairs. Becca let Geoffrey see her smile then. He looked at her quizzically.

"They have that same argument every afternoon," she said.

He laughed at that and took her hand. "Will you show me to our room, Becca?"

"Certainly, husband."

They walked toward the massive stone stairs, Geoffrey looking about. "This place is incredible, wife. And the grounds. We simply must go riding while we're here."

"Oh, no. I can't go riding."

He stopped then. "Whyever not, love?"

Becca froze, unsure of what to say. She wanted to tell him about the baby later, when the house was asleep and he held her in his arms. "Um … I didn't bring my riding habit."

His brow furrowed at her excuse. He must have sensed her nervousness, for he let the matter drop. He followed her to their chamber where they readied themselves for tea.

Chapter 28

As the Earl of Chester's carriage pulled up in front of Kanewood, Leed looked at Chester worriedly.

"How are we going to tell him?" Leed asked.

Chester alighted from the carriage. "We'll simply tell him what we know, Leed."

Leed nodded and followed him to the front door. Chester knocked and the servant let them in, closing the door behind them.

"What can we do for you, gentlemen?" the butler asked.

"We need to see Lord Kanewood," Chester stated.

The man's eyebrows shot up in surprise. "But the earl isn't at Kanewood at present, my lord."

"What?" Leed asked. "Where is he?"

"Perhaps my lady can assist you, my lord," he offered.

He led them into the parlor, where Lady Margaret sat. She looked up in surprise. "Lord Chester." She stood. "Lord Leed. What on earth are you doing here?"

The gentlemen bowed to her in greeting.

"We're here to see Lord Kanewood," Chester answered.

"He isn't here."

"Where is he?" Leed asked.

Lady Margaret blinked in surprise. "He's in Scotland, I believe."

"Scotland?" Leed asked. "Whatever for?"

"He believes Rebecca may be there."

"Rebecca is also gone from Kanewood?" Chester asked.

"What is troubling you two?" she asked.

He and Leed exchanged a look, silently agreeing to discuss this alone.

"Nothing of import, Lady Margaret," Leed said. "We

simply wished to ask Kane's advice about the business dealings of a mutual acquaintence."

"It seems that will have to wait," Chester added with a smile.

"Well." She tilted her head to one side. "At least join me for tea."

They acquiesced as the butler saw to their personal effects into guest rooms abovestairs. As soon as they could manage, they finished their discourse with Lady Margaret and went upstairs to the room set aside for Lord Chester's use.

Leed closed the door and faced Chester. "With both Kane and Rebecca gone, we don't have to worry about John at present."

Chester paced the room. "We could use this time to work on Kane's brother."

Leed nodded. "Let's ready for dinner."

They were surprised to later learn from Patricia that John was in London. The four of them sat in the dining room as Lady Margaret informed them of Becca's flight and Geoffrey's pursuit.

"None of this would have happened, of course," she went on, "if my son hadn't deemed it necessary to leave for London without his wife."

Patricia smiled slyly, an action that Chester didn't miss. He arched a brow at her. "Did you wish to say something, Patricia?"

"Oh," she began with a small smile, "nothing, I assure you. I was simply wondering why Viscount Roberts isn't with you gentlemen."

Chester knew full well what she was intimating.

Leed cleared his throat. "Lord Roberts was detained in London."

With a slight shrug of her shoulders, she turned her attention to her meal.

Later, once more in Chester's room, the men discussed their predicament. Patricia's behavior rankled.

"How did John get involved with such a cold-hearted witch?" Leed asked.

"Kane should thank God each day that he never married her," Chester said. "I wonder if Kane located Rebecca."

"And when they'll return to Kanewood," Leed added. "I hope that John is truly in London and not prowling the countryside."

"I don't like not knowing where that son-of-a bitch is, Leed. He could be up to more mischief."

Leed gave a nod of worried agreement.

* * * *

At the McClair holding, Geoffrey and Becca had just finished dinner. It had been a lively affair, filled with stimulating talk and much laughter. After bidding her parents good night, they climbed the stone steps to their room. She'd no sooner closed the door when Geoffrey pulled her to him.

"I've missed you so much, Becca."

"I've missed you, too."

His lips touched hers, the contact gentle. She opened her mouth for him as if begging him to deepen the kiss. He obliged her, sweeping his tongue into her mouth. She clung to his shoulders as his pulse pounded in his ears. If he didn't slow down, he'd take her there on the stone floor.

He sat down on the huge bed, taking her with him to hold her close. He couldn't put off the inevitable any longer.

"Becca, I'm so sorry," he said, his voice low.

She leaned up to look at him. "You've already apologized, husband."

He shook his head at her. "No, love. Not about doubting you. About that last night, in our chamber."

"Geoffrey, you don't—"

"I was out of control. I never should have treated you that way."

She was so quiet, her hesitation cutting him to the bone. What was she thinking? Would she send him away now that he finally had her back in his arms?

"God, love," he said, drawing her close. Tears stung his eyes, choked his throat. "Instead of cherishing you as I ought …

Ah, I almost did the unforgivable. Even touching you in any way that wasn't sweet and gentle …."

He found it hard to continue, the truth of his behavior heavy on his soul.

"You didn't hurt me, not physically." She took a breath. "What hurt me most was that you didn't believe me."

"I know."

"You left me. You shut me out of your life."

"Becca, you are my life."

His heart stilled, its every beat dependent on what happened next.

She smiled at last and his heart began to beat again. "Then I forgive you. For all of it."

He let out a sigh of relief and hugged her to him once more. She felt perfect to him, curving sweetly into his body as she rested her head on his shoulder. "We'll leave for Kanewood on the morrow if that suits."

"Oh, yes," she said. "I cannot wait to see Ann!"

"She commanded me to bring you home, love." He dropped a kiss on her brow. "I shall not disappoint her."

The affection on Becca's face told him how much she cared for the little girl. It was a pity Becca wasn't Ann's mother. She was warm and loving and everything a child could want.

"We're going to have a baby," she said softly.

"Hmm. If matters continue the way they have been, love, we will have more than one."

She let out a soft laugh. "No, husband, you misunderstand me. I'm carrying your child."

His eyes widened as the truth settled on him. He cupped her face with his hands. "I love you, Becca!"

They talked then, about their plans and hopes and dreams. They readied for bed, and Geoffrey was as gentle as he should have been that last night. It was passion, but it was more than that. It was a promise of forever with every kiss and caress and it was unbelievably satisfying.

* * * *

The next morning, after Becca shared a tearful farewell with her newfound parents and a promise to visit again before too much timed passed, she and Geoffrey returned to Kanewood. She'd also repeated her promise to speak to Thomas, despite her mother's obvious worry. No matter. She would see to the matter of her father's innocence. She wanted her baby to have the opportunity to know its grandparents, and if they weren't permitted to visit England that would be most difficult.

Geoffrey opened the front door that evening, surprising the butler.

"My lord!" he exclaimed. "My lady, welcome home."

Geoffrey nodded at the servant and led Becca to the parlor. "My mother will be so pleased I found you, love."

They entered the parlor, finding Lady Margaret there as anticipated.

She came to her feet when she saw them in the doorway. "Geoffrey!"

Geoffrey grinned. "I found her, Mother."

Lady Margaret hurried over to where they stood and embraced Becca warmly. "Rebecca, my dear. It's so good to have you home."

"It's wonderful to be home, Lady Margaret. How is Ann? I've missed her so."

"She's very well, dear. And missing her Aunt Rebecca, as well." She glanced at the clock on the mantel. "She'll be napping right now." The older woman pulled Becca toward the settee and sat beside her. "In the meanwhile, tell me all about your adventure."

Geoffrey watched for a moment, a smile on his face. Suddenly, Lady Margaret looked up at him.

"Geoffrey, Lords Chester and Leed came for you yesterday."

"They're here?" he asked.

"Kane," Chester drawled from the doorway. "High time you showed up."

Geoffrey turned to face his friend. "What is this about?"

"We need to speak with you, Kane," Leed added.

Geoffrey looked from one man to the other. He glanced at

Becca then, seeing the confusion on her face.

He crossed to her, leaning down to grasp her hand. "I'll tell you everything later, love. I promise."

She nodded. "I know you will."

He kissed her and strode from the room, bound for his study. His friends followed him in, Chester closing the door.

"What is it?" Geoffrey asked without preamble. "Only an urgent matter would bring you both here to Kanewood in such haste."

"Kane, we know for certain who has been passing the notes in your stead," Chester said.

"Who?"

"He was pretending to be you, Kane." Leed paused a beat. "And doing a fine job of it."

Geoffrey blinked in confusion.

"He looks very much like you, save for the gray eyes," Chester said.

The awful truth settled on Geoffrey. He closed his eyes and slumped against the desk. "God, no," he breathed.

"It checks out, Kane," Leed went on. "We compared the notes with John's handwriting, and—"

"I'll kill the bastard," Geoffrey said.

His friends let him vent his spleen. Geoffrey paced the room and muttered expletives under his breath, calling John every vile name he'd ever heard. When he'd finally calmed, Leed informed him about the latest development.

"John has left Kanewood," he said. "Supposedly headed for London."

"Yes." Geoffrey scratched his chin. "Patricia mentioned it before I left for Scotland."

"I don't like not knowing where he is," Leed went on.

Geoffrey nodded, finally taking a seat behind his desk. He raked his fingers through his hair, a low groan escaping him. "My own brother." He shook his head. "I can hardly believe it."

"We believe he was involved in the carriage accident," Chester added.

"But why? Could money be that important to him? My God, he nearly killed Rebecca!"

Chester had no ready answer for his friend. "We need to question Patricia."

"Patricia," Geoffrey said with a sneer. "That, that …."

"Careful, friend," Leed said.

"Leed, she tried to seduce me."

"What?" Chester asked.

Geoffrey nodded. "It's true. The night before I left for Scotland. I nearly strangled her with my bare hands."

Leed let out a whistle. "We still need to speak to her."

"I know," Geoffrey said.

* * * *

"Rebecca, I was very worried about you," Geoffrey heard his mother say from inside the parlor. "When you disappeared that day, I didn't know what to think."

"I'm so sorry about that, Lady Margaret," Becca said. "I was very upset and not thinking clearly."

"What had you so upset, dear?"

Becca opened her mouth to answer, but Geoffrey entered the parlor. He pulled her to her feet and kissed her, effectively silencing her. He placed his lips near her ear and whispered to her.

"Why don't we share our news at dinner, love?" He pulled back and winked.

"Geoffrey, what's going on?" Lady Margaret asked.

"Later, Mother," he said with a big grin. "We'll tell you at dinner."

She snorted at that, prompting a laugh from her son. He took Becca upstairs to ready themselves for tea. When they were alone in their chamber, Geoffrey told her of Leed and Chester's discoveries.

"How could John do such terrible deeds?" she asked.

"I don't know."

"Geoffrey, I have to tell you about John's behavior in London." She went on about his actions, his hateful words, and Geoffrey's disgust toward his brother grew tenfold.

"He told me you didn't love me."

"I love you, Becca. I have for so very long." He hugged her tightly to him. "I wonder if I ever even knew my brother."

Later on, in the parlor over tea, Becca told all present about the McClair holding and the discovery she made there. Lords Chester and Leed were fascinated with Becca's tale.

"Your mother, Rebecca?" Chester asked, incredulous.

"Yes, Lord Chester." She nodded. "I could hardly believe it myself, but there was no denying it."

"That's right," Geoffrey intoned. "Lady Charlotte looks very much like my beautiful wife," he added, placing a kiss on her temple.

Becca blushed slightly, lowering her lashes. Patricia sighed irritably and Geoffrey turned to favor her with a scathing look.

She placed her empty cup aside and stood. "I have matters to attend to," she said haughtily. "If you will all excuse me."

Leed came to his feet. "Patricia, we would like a word with you."

She looked at the viscount in surprise. "With me? Whatever for?"

"Indulge us," Chester said.

Patricia looked from one to the other, finally nodding. The gentlemen led her into the study. Leaving his wife in his mother's hands, Geoffrey left to join them. He'd find out everything that the miserable harpy knew.

Patricia walked into the room, her head held high. She sat in the chair facing Geoffrey's desk and folded her hands in her lap. "I can't imagine what this is about, Lord Leed."

When Leed didn't provide a speedy answer to her statement, she turned to Chester. "Lord Chester?"

"I'll ask the questions, Patricia," Geoffrey said.

Patricia stiffened, turning toward Geoffrey. She watched him warily as he crossed the room and sat behind the desk.

"Where's John?" Geoffrey asked.

"I told you, Kane. He went to London on business."

"What business would that be?" Leed cut in.

"I—" she stammered. "I don't know."

"Let me understand this." Geoffrey tented his fingers beneath his chin. "John has no business that I'm aware of. He's never worked a day in his life. Are you saying you don't know what your husband is about?"

Patricia's eyes narrowed. "Does Rebecca know every step you take, Kane?"

"She does now," he said.

"Are you certain John's in London?" Chester asked.

Patricia turned to the gentleman sitting so close to her and looked him directly in the eye. "Lord Chester, I don't know what you're insinuating, but John told me he was bound for London. I believe him."

Chester studied her for a moment then sat back. "I believe you." He looked to Leed who nodded almost imperceptibly.

"Patricia," Leed began deliberately. "When you were in London last, did John do a bit of gambling?"

She blinked. "He went to White's a few times. Why?"

Geoffrey took a breath and entered the exchange. "What do you know about the notes?"

She looked away. "Notes?"

"We know about the notes, Patricia," Leed said. "We would like to know the extent of your involvement."

Patricia's cool facade slipped. "I told the fool that he'd get caught."

Geoffrey stood. "You've known about this all along?"

She'd slipped right into their trap and realized her error too late. She looked down in her lap, running her fingers over the pleats of her tea gown. "Your brother has a fondness for the gaming tables, Kane. I thought you knew that."

"But why pass notes in my name?"

"Who else's?" she asked with a shrug. "The money your father left him as a stipend was meager at best."

"My father provided amply for John, Patricia," Geoffrey insisted. "How can you say such a thing?"

"It isn't enough!" she cried.

Geoffrey felt his control slipping. "Enough for what?"

She pursed her lips in answer. Tamping down his ire, he looked to Chester to continue.

"What do you know of the carriage accident?" Chester asked.

She began to wring her hands, her gaze darting about the room.

Leed fixed a steely gaze on her, pinning her to the spot. "What do you know, Patricia?" he said in a low voice.

Geoffrey watched her closely.

"The wheel wasn't meant to keep you from London for long," she said. "Just long enough that John and I could have use of your townhouse." She waved a hand. "To entertain."

"The wheel?" Leed looked at Geoffrey in confusion.

Realization dawned on Geoffrey, however. "But I made it to London. The accident happened on my way back to Kanewood."

"I know that," she snapped.

Geoffrey placed his hands on the desk to lean closer to his sister-in-law. "Patricia, you tampered with my carriage?"

"Yes," she said sharply. "But if I knew you would make it to London anyway and spoil our fun, I wouldn't have bothered making the arrangements. Or that you would meet that trollop on your trip home—"

"Don't speak of Rebecca that way, you grasping bitch," Geoffrey bit out.

Patricia flinched, sinking back into the chair.

"Patricia, what of the other accident?" Chester asked.

She blinked at him, true befuddlement on her face. "What other accident?"

"Rebecca and I were nearly run down, Patricia," Geoffrey said, his voice rumbling deep in his throat. "What do you know of it?"

"I know nothing of it, Kane," she insisted.

Geoffrey stared at her for a long minute. He realized she was telling the truth—if John was romancing Lady Brookdale in secret, he surely wouldn't have told Patricia whose carriage was involved. Perhaps she didn't know anything of the runaway carriage. Another decision struck him, one from which he wouldn't be swayed.

"You're no longer welcome at Kanewood," Geoffrey stated. "You're to make other arrangements."

"You can't do that to me!" She came to her feet. "I could

have been Lady Kanewood if that bitch hadn't come back. And now that she carries your heir—"

"That's enough!"

Patricia turned on her heel and ran from the room.

Geoffrey cursed softly. "Will this never be over?"

"Kane," Chester said softly, "she didn't mean to hurt Rebecca. We know that now."

Geoffrey stared at his friend, weighing his words. Finally, he nodded curtly. Leed gave a short laugh.

"What can you possibly find funny, Leed?" Geoffrey asked.

"If it wasn't for Patricia, you never would have met Rebecca," Leed said.

Slowly, Geoffrey smiled.

"Did I hear Patricia correctly, Kane?" Chester asked. "Rebecca's expecting?"

Geoffrey nodded, straightening his shoulders. His friends slapped him soundly on the back, offering their congratulations.

* * * *

That evening, Becca and Geoffrey told Lady Margaret their wonderful news. She was delighted, and told them as much. Lords Leed and Chester offered Becca their heartfelt congratulations, which she accepted with a shy smile. Geoffrey wasn't the only one pleased to notice that Patricia took her meal in her room, leaving the conversation quite easy and pleasant.

Declining an after-dinner drink with his friends, Geoffrey accompanied his wife upstairs to their chamber. The moment the door was closed, Geoffrey assisted her out of her dress and into her nightgown. He stripped and stretched out on the bed, pulling her down beside him. He gently pushed her head down on his shoulder. She began to sit up, but her husband was having none of it.

"Go to sleep, Becca."

"I'm not sleepy."

"You need your rest, wife," he said in mock-severity.

She leaned up and looked at him through her lashes. "I need you, husband."

He sharply drew in a breath, pleased with her statement. He proceeded to show her just how pleased he could make her.

Afterward, she cuddled up against his side. "Did Patricia know of the notes?"

He hesitated. "Yes."

"And of the carriage?" she asked, her eyes wide.

"No, love." He stroked her back. "I don't believe so."

She yawned, making him nearly regret keeping her awake. He kissed the top of her head. "Go to sleep," he said again.

"I'm not sleepy," she mumbled just before drifting off to sleep.

Geoffrey smiled to himself. He held her close as he let his mind work. Where was John? Was he truly in London? He'd talk with Chester and Leed in the morning. They'd find the scoundrel.

And Geoffrey would make him pay.

Chapter 29

Directly after breakfast, the gentlemen adjourned once more to Geoffrey's study.

Lady Margaret watched them leave, puzzlement on her face. "Rebecca, dear, what is it that has them so busy?"

Rebecca didn't wish to worry the woman, so she chose her words carefully. "Geoffrey has been having a bit of trouble of late, and his friends are helping him."

"Dear, you know more of this than you're telling."

Becca hesitated for a moment, finally giving a nod. "Yes, Lady Margaret. But it isn't my place to discuss this. Perhaps Geoffrey will tell you in time."

The older woman looked thoughtful for a long minute. She nodded her acceptance of Becca's word on the subject. Becca could only pray that when the truth did finally come out, Lady Margaret could accept the news that her second son had such vile plans for her first.

* * * *

"I'll track down that son-of-a-bitch if it's the last thing I do," Geoffrey vowed. "And when I do …."

Leed and Chester nodded solemnly, well able to guess what would happen to John when the Earl of Kanewood caught up with him.

"So it's settled, then," Chester said. "We leave for London directly."

"What of Rebecca?" Leed asked.

"What about her, Leed?" Geoffrey asked. "She'll stay here with my mother."

Leed shook his head. "I believe you should keep her close,

Kane. What if John isn't in London? What then?"

Geoffrey was torn. He wouldn't allow even the slightest chance that John once more find her alone. "You're right. I won't have anything happen to her. And if that means bringing her with us to London, that's what we shall do."

He went in search of his wife to tell her to ready for the long ride to London.

Within the hour, Becca was settled in the carriage with the three gentlemen. There was hardly any room for her, what with Geoffrey nearly taking up the seat she sat upon and Lords Leed and Chester sprawled across the seat opposite. She tried to carve out some space for herself, to no avail. Her skirt was getting quite rumpled. She tried to smooth it, but there simply wasn't enough room.

"Geoffrey," she whispered finally. "Please give me a bit of space?"

He smiled sheepishly and moved over a bit. She let out a small sigh, which he heard. He quickly grasped her hand and brought it to his lips.

"Is something wrong, love?" he teased.

"It seems that I'm surrounded by giants," she offered. "Perhaps I was a bit hasty in agreeing to accompany you."

He grinned at her, his mood lightened considerably. He turned back to find his friends trying in vain to hide their smiles. He turned the topic to more mundane matters, happy to put John out of his mind for at least a short while.

They arrived at Geoffrey's townhouse in time to share a late supper the next day. When the meal was finished, Becca bade the gentlemen good night and retired for the evening. Geoffrey and the others adjourned to his study, sipping brandy and discussing their plans for the next day.

"How should we go about tracking the bastard down, Kane?" Leed asked.

Geoffrey set his glass down and shrugged. "Perhaps someone at White's has seen him recently."

Chester shook his head. "Doubtful. John hasn't many friends left at the more respectable establishments in town. We should send a note to Roberts."

Geoffrey stiffened at the mention of the man's name. "I don't know if I want him involved."

"Kane," Leed began, "Roberts was instrumental in determining that John was the blackguard at the center of this mess."

That fact surprised Geoffrey. "How so, Leed?"

Leed told him about Roberts's dealings with Lady Brookdale, about his using his charms to find out with whom she was involved. He also told of their many trips down to the waterfront, including the one in which he got answers out of the serving wench.

"My God, Kane," Chester finished. "It was Roberts's eyes that finally drew out the truth. They're gray, like John's."

"I didn't realize he would go to such lengths. If he wishes to be of assistance, I can't turn his offer down." Geoffrey folded his hands on the table. "The man had best keep his word to me regarding my wife."

"I'm certain that he shall," Leed insisted. "He feels quite guilty over what he did."

"I trust you to pen the note, Chester." Geoffrey pushed away from the table. "Good night, gentlemen."

When he entered the chamber, Becca was sleeping soundly. Without rousing her, he stripped out of his clothes and stretched out beside her. He watched her sleep, a nagging worry at the back of his mind. Was she truly in danger from John? Or was his brother's sole motivation greed?

He let out a sigh and closed his eyes, drawing her close to him before joining her in slumber.

* * * *

Early the next morning, Lord Roberts called at the townhouse. The butler led him into the breakfast room where Geoffrey and Becca sat. Roberts stiffened as she fixed her gaze on him, a question in her eyes.

He turned from her. "Good morning, Kane," he said. "Good morning, Lady Rebecca."

"Roberts," Geoffrey said in greeting.

Geoffrey had informed Becca of Roberts's previous visit to the townhouse, and of his sincere apologies. Becca looked from her husband to the viscount and back again. Geoffrey kept his expression cool and Becca obviously took that to mean she may greet the viscount. She nodded.

"Come in, Lord Roberts," she said. "Please help yourself to some breakfast."

"Thank you, I shall," he answered.

He took his plate and sat at the other end of the table, facing Geoffrey. The earl regarded the man closely, pleased to see his very proper behavior toward Becca.

Geoffrey set his napkin aside and pushed his plate away. "Roberts, Leed informed me of your assistance. I wish to thank you."

Roberts shrugged. "I was happy to do what I could, Kane. Will Leed and Chester be joining us?"

Geoffrey opened his mouth to answer just as Miles announced the gentlemen, who followed on his heels.

"Good morning." Chester smiled. "I trust you slept well, Lady Rebecca?"

"Very well thank you, Lord Chester."

"How are you, um, feeling these days?" Leed asked, a flush on his face.

"Fine and fit," she answered, hiding her smile.

She stood, Geoffrey and Roberts following suit. "I'll be in the parlor, husband."

He nodded and watched her go. When she turned down the hall out of his sight, he brought his attention back to his friends. Leed and Chester had taken plates for themselves and sat at the table.

"What is our first move this morning, gentlemen?" he asked, once more taking his place at the table.

Leed let out a sigh of irritation. "We simply must head down to the waterfront once more, although the atmosphere is dreary at best."

"But that would be our best course right now, Leed," Roberts said.

Leed nodded his acceptance.

The men were finishing their tea when the butler appeared at the doorway of the breakfast room. "My lord, Mr. Hall to see you."

Geoffrey looked up in surprise.

"Your solicitor, Kane?" Chester asked.

"Bring him into the study, Miles," Geoffrey instructed.

"What could he want?" Leed asked.

Geoffrey stood then. "Let us find out, gentlemen."

The four of them filed into the study.

A look of relief crossed Mr. Hall's distinguished features as he spotted Geoffrey. "Kane," he began in a rush, "I was glad to learn that you had returned to town."

"What is it, Hall?" Geoffrey asked pointedly.

"Your brother, Kane," he answered. "He stopped by the offices this morning and—"

"John came to see you?" Chester asked.

"Yes," the man answered. "He wanted an advance on his stipend."

"Son-of-a-bitch," Roberts whispered.

"Did you give it to him?" Geoffrey asked.

"We consulted and agreed to honor his wish."

"Good," Geoffrey said.

"What do you mean, Kane?" Leed asked.

"We don't want him getting suspicious, Leed," he answered.

"Ah." Leed nodded. "And this way we give him a bit of breathing room."

"Or perhaps enough rope to hang himself," Roberts offered.

"Exactly," Geoffrey said. "Hall, did he seem out-of-sorts to you?"

"Not particularly," Hall answered. "He seemed quite relieved when we gave him the funds. However …." The man suddenly stiffened, his eyes growing wide.

"What is it, man?" Chester asked him.

"John mentioned something just before he left our offices," Hall said. "I believe it was to the effect of 'wish me luck' or something like that."

The gentlemen exchanged a knowing look.

"To the waterfront, gentlemen," Geoffrey said.

* * * *

Becca sat in the parlor, attempting to read a book. She placed the book down with a sigh of frustration and went to stare out the window, her arms crossed in front of her.

"What is it, Becca?" Geoffrey asked with a smile.

She spun around to face him. "I so wished to know what you were discussing, Geoffrey. I hope you don't think ill of me."

He shook his head at her and crossed the room, taking her hand in his. "I'm resigned to the fact that I have a curious wife."

"Ah, you forget so quickly," she said. "Keeping secrets was what got you into trouble."

"I remember very well." He kissed her cheek. "We're leaving for the waterfront, love. Please call for Miles if you need anything."

"Certainly. Be careful."

"Of course." He kissed her again and strode to the door. "And Becca?"

"Yes?"

"Please stay inside, love?" he finished. "I don't want you to leave the townhouse."

His intent was clear and she thought she might love this serious, concerned Geoffrey even more than the playful, romantic one. "You have my word."

Chapter 30

Becca managed to eat her lunch, hunger outweighing her apprehension about Geoffrey's errand. Afterward, she sat once more in the parlor. The parlor doors were open, and she heard footsteps in the foyer. Geoffrey! As the sound neared the room, she turned toward the doorway, a smile on her face.

Shock stunned her. "John?"

John crossed his arms and leaned against the doorjamb. "Hello, sister," he said, smiling crookedly.

Becca recovered herself, holding her hands tightly in her lap to keep them from shaking. "So," she began, "what brings you by to visit?"

"Oh, I needed to pick up a few items," he said with a secret smile.

Before she could fully ponder what it was he meant by that, he closed the parlor door. He slowly advanced on her, taking in her appearance in a leisurely fashion. Her hair was plaited in a single braid coiled at the back of her head, as Mary had been left behind at Kanewood. Her gown was simple in design, the front dipping modestly. No matter, though. The way John was looking at her, she might as well have been naked.

She straightened her shoulders, trying to keep the indignation she was feeling in check. After learning all that he'd been about of late, she had no wish to provoke his ire.

"How have you been?" she asked in a pleasant voice. "You were missed at Kanewood."

Her words had the desired effect. The lascivious intent left his eyes as a smooth smile settled on his face. "Did you miss me, Becca?" he asked, deliberately using Geoffrey's name for her.

"Well, I …."

He stood directly in front of her, causing her to crane her neck to meet his gaze. He seemed to enjoy his show of power over her, finally taking a seat very close to her on the settee.

"And where is my brother, Becca?" he asked, studying her closely.

"He had business. Perhaps if you stop by later—"

"No," he cut in. "I'd rather visit with you."

Becca had no response to that. She could only sit there as he ran his gaze over her form.

"You must be feeling well, sister," he offered. "You look positively radiant."

"Th-thank you."

He took her hand in his, applying pressure. She winced, at which he smiled broadly at her.

"I've missed you, Becca," he said in a low voice. "I remember how you trembled beneath my touch when we were last in London."

He sat closer to her, bringing his face to hers. "I could teach you so much, sister." His gray eyes bore into hers. "So very much."

As his mouth nearly touched hers, a knock was heard on the other side of the door. John's head jerked back, turning toward the sound.

"My lady?" Miles asked.

Before Becca could answer, John brought his lips to her ear. "Don't give me away, Becca," he hissed. "If you do, I'll make our union quite difficult for you."

She shivered at his words. He brought her to her feet and pushed her toward the door. She glanced at him then, chilled by the glare in his eyes.

"What is it, Miles?" she asked in a shaky voice.

"I wondered if you needed anything just now, my lady."

"No thank you, Miles," she answered, her face close to the door. "But I'll need the carriage later."

"But—"

Becca spoke quickly before the butler could give her away. "Lord Kanewood wishes me to go to the haberdashery today, Miles. He specifically told me to go out this afternoon."

She knew Geoffrey had told Miles she was to stay in until he returned. *Please understand, Miles*, she prayed. *Please go get Geoffrey.*

Miles was quiet for a long moment. "Ah," he said at last. "Very well, my lady."

As his footsteps faded away from the door Becca stifled a sigh of relief. She turned back to find John grinning at her.

He rose to his feet. "Very good, sister."

He strode to the credenza and fingered one of the tiny crystal figurines adorning the top. Becca watched him warily. What was he about? When he picked up the piece and slipped it into his pocket, she couldn't contain her surprise.

John heard her gasp and faced her once more. "These trinkets are as much mine as Kane's, Becca." He shrugged. "And if I choose to place them on a wager, where is the harm?"

Becca blinked at him, not sure of how to proceed. She watched incredulously as he picked up another of the little figures, this one a swan. He held it up to the light, admiring its fine craftsmanship and flawlessness. He pocketed it as well and turned his full attention back to Becca.

Her heart pounded at the lustful glare in his eyes. It was clear he was no longer thinking about baubles or wagers. She pressed herself against the door, willing the wooden panel to disappear behind her and allow her escape.

John walked slowly toward her, his eyes dark. "Becca, I'll give you such pleasure."

"John, please. You must stop this at once!"

He pressed himself against her, letting her feel the strength of his arousal. "Can you feel how much I want you?"

Becca couldn't answer him, bile rising to choke her as she imagined what he'd do to her.

"Yes." He reached out and caressed her cheek. "Such pleasure that I'll have to place my hand over your mouth to keep your screams from alerting the staff."

He did just that, covering her mouth with his hand. Suddenly, anger replaced her fear. She bit down hard on the fleshy part of his palm.

He let out a grunt of pain. "You bitch!" he hissed, raising a hand to strike her. He caught his movement, a sly smile on his face. "I knew there was fire underneath all that shyness. It'll be my intense pleasure to bring it forth."

With that, he grabbed her wrist and pulled her away from the door. He opened it and pulled her behind him, taking purposeful strides toward the stairs.

"John, please, don't do this. Think of your brother!"

"Ah, Becca." He smiled down at her as they reached the foyer. "I am thinking of him. In fact, I'll be thinking of him as we make use of his bed. I've always wanted to try the esteemed earl's magnificent four-poster at Kanewood but we'll have to make do, won't we?"

Becca grabbed onto the newel post as they rounded the steps, clinging for dear life. John looked back and clicked his tongue at her. He gave a sharp jerk and her fingers slipped off the polished wood. He took the steps two at a time, dragging Becca behind him.

They were halfway up the stairs when the front door burst open.

"Let go of her!" Geoffrey shouted.

Becca's heart leapt at the sound of his voice, first with joy and then fear for whatever John had planned for her husband.

John turned. His eyes rounded in surprise, then narrowed with anger. "Ah, the Right Honourable Earl of Kanewood." He sneered. "And his cohorts, Leed and Chester. Good afternoon, gentlemen."

"I said, let her go," Geoffrey said through clenched teeth.

He took a step toward the staircase, but John held up a hand to still him. "Oh, I shall. Eventually. Once I'm safely away from here." He smiled slyly. "And once I tire of her."

"You son-of-a-bitch," Geoffrey growled. "Take her and I'll kill you."

"But where is the fourth to your little quartet?" John mused aloud as if Geoffrey hadn't spoken. "Ah, Lord Roberts fell prey to Rebecca's obvious charms and was banished from your sacred circle, is that it, Kane?"

"I know everything, John," Geoffrey said.

John hugged Becca tightly to him. "Everything, brother?"

"The notes," Geoffrey went on. "The carriage accident."

"Ah, you found out about that, did you?" John smiled wickedly. "Poor, lonely Lady Brookdale. She was merely passable. Nothing like dear Becca here."

"Were the notes not enough?" Geoffrey asked.

"No! I'd practiced your signature and those foolish solicitors had no suspicions, until you and your friends started sniffing around. I knew that particular trickle of funds would soon dry."

Geoffrey gaped at his brother. "So you thought to kill me?"

John shrugged. "Had you been hit by that carriage, we wouldn't be having this conversation. I would have the title and your lovely wife." He grinned. "And your child, it appears. Fitting, for you almost raised mine as your own."

Becca covered her belly in a protective motion. John would never touch this child.

John rubbed his lips over Becca's cheek, his gaze pinned to Geoffrey's reaction. She cringed at the contact.

"You've taught her well, Kane," John said. "We had quite the time after you left Kanewood for London."

Becca knew how jealous Geoffrey could be. Would he believe John's lies? One look in her husband's eyes told her all she needed to know. They held no anger toward her. He knew she had never betrayed him, would never betray him.

"Yes," John continued. "She's quite good. It's a shame I can't take the time to enjoy her charms just now."

John withdrew a large knife from his pocket, wrapped one arm around Becca and pressed her back against him. Her breath froze in her lungs.

He let out a small laugh, turning the knife in the air. "Quite a wicked-looking instrument, don't you think, fellows? If you know 'everything,' as you say, then you know just how unsavory the circles are in which I have been traveling." He sighed dramatically. "Such items are a necessary evil."

"Why, John?" Geoffrey asked. "Why did you do this?"

"Why?" John mocked. "I told you. I simply want what you have, Kane. The title, the estate, the money. I abhor crawling to your solicitors for funds to supplement the meager stipend father left for me."

"You had every advantage growing up as I did. Father provided well for you."

"No, Father provided well for you! You got everything! The estate, the money, and Becca. And I—I get merely a pittance!

"Apparently, he knew more about your character than I."

"Don't goad me, Kane," John said. "We wouldn't want Becca's silken skin to wear an ugly scar, now would we?"

He held the tip of the blade against her neck, applying only enough pressure to make her aware of the weapon's placement. Geoffrey made another move toward the stairs.

"Don't come any closer," John warned.

A slight movement at the top of the stairs caught Becca's eye. Without turning her head, she glanced up and saw Roberts poised there. He gave her a small nod of reassurance, holding up one finger. He then held up two, showing her he was counting off. When three fingers were in the air, Becca pushed John away from her with all of her might. At that precise moment, Roberts lunged at John, knocking him into the wall.

Becca stumbled, grabbing on to the railing to stop her fall. She clutched the railing as Roberts and John grappled on the stairs close to her, their feet fighting for purchase. John slipped, sending both of them crashing down to land hard on the marble floor. They were still then, Roberts sprawled on top of John.

Geoffrey bounded up the stairs, wrapping Becca in his arms. "Are you all right, love?" he rasped against her hair.

She took a mental inventory, and other than feeling jostled and bruised and frightened out of her mind, she felt fine. "I … I think so. Did Miles come for you?"

"Yes." He hugged her gently. "I'm surrounded by loyal friends and staff, if not family."

They looked down at the pair on the floor. A large pool of blood was spreading on the black and white marble. Two of Geoffrey's loyal friends were jarred out of their stupor. Chester reached Roberts and John first, rolling Roberts onto his back. The blood seeped from a deep gash in his side. Chester removed his jacket and folded it. He held it tightly to the man's side to stem the flow.

"Is it bad?" Geoffrey asked.

"I'm not sure," Chester answered.

Roberts lifted his head and looked around, a crooked smile on his face. "Sorry about the mess," he mumbled just before he passed out.

They turned their attention to Leed, who was crouched over John's still form. Even from her vantage point, Becca could see that his head lay at an odd angle.

"Leed?" Geoffrey asked.

Leed pressed his fingers against John's neck, searching for a pulse. He looked up at Geoffrey and Becca then, the unmistakable truth in his blue eyes.

Becca gasped and buried her head in Geoffrey's chest. He rocked her gently. "I know he did horrible things, but—" he said, his voice thick. "God, he was still my brother."

"I'm so sorry," she said softly.

Geoffrey nodded as he stroked her hair. "As am I."

Miles came upon the scene just then. "My lord, is everything …? Oh!"

"The doctor, Miles," Geoffrey ordered. "And tell him to hurry."

Dr. Morgan arrived and attended Lord Roberts. He saw him safely ensconced in one of Geoffrey's guest rooms after heavily bandaging his side. Leed stayed at his friend's bedside while Chester waited downstairs for the constable.

After seeing to his most critical patient, the doctor went down the hall to the earl's chamber to look in on Becca. Geoffrey had removed her dress and insisted she climb into bed, tucking the covers tightly up under her chin.

"Geoffrey," she began, "I tell you I'm fine."

"Good afternoon, Lady Kanewood," Dr. Morgan said, approaching the bed. "Life is certainly never dull when you're in town."

She smiled at the man, coming up to a sitting position and Geoffrey gently pushed her back down.

"Really, husband."

"You must rest, Becca," Geoffrey said. "Let Morgan have a look at you."

The doctor nudged Geoffrey out of the way and stood by the bed. “How are you feeling?” he asked. “Any pain at all?”

She shook her head.

“Will her fall hurt the baby, Morgan?” Geoffrey asked.

“I didn’t fall, ” she insisted.

The doctor placed his hands on the covers, spanning her abdomen. He gently probed her belly, watching her closely. “Does that hurt?”

“No,” she answered.

“Any bleeding?”

“No.”

“Rest for a while.” He stood. “Everything seems fine to me. But please let me know if you have any discomfort.”

She smiled her thanks and watched Geoffrey accompany him to the door.

“I’ll check on her when I see to Lord Roberts tomorrow,” the doctor told him.

Geoffrey nodded and closed the door behind him. He crossed back to the bed to sit beside her, taking her hand and bringing it to his lips. “I told you all would be fine, Becca.”

She clicked her tongue at him.

* * * *

Geoffrey had a tray brought up to his chamber and took his meal with Becca, pleased to see that her appetite had returned. He tried to keep her mind off what had happened earlier that day, but Becca wasn’t to be put off. With her meal nearly finished, she once more questioned her husband.

“What did the constable say?” she asked.

“Chester took care of it for now.” He set the tray aside and chose his words carefully. “But the authorities will be by to speak with you tomorrow.”

“With me?”

“Yes, love. Chester told them what happened, but they need to know of John’s behavior toward you.”

“Geoffrey,” she said in a small voice. “I don’t know if I can tell them. Some of the things he said ….”

"It'll be all right," he soothed. "I'll be with you."

"You will, won't you?"

"Always."

She threw her arms around his neck and squeezed with all of her might. "I love you."

"Becca," he began, his throat tight. "When John held that knife to you—"

"Don't speak of it."

He nodded and stroked her back.

She pulled back to favor him with a small smile. "Hold me, Geoffrey," she requested, her voice husky.

He lowered her to the bed and wrapped her in his arms. "I'll never let you go."

Chapter 31

The next morning, Lords Leed and Chester arrived in time for breakfast and found Geoffrey alone in the breakfast room.

"Where is Rebecca, Kane?" Chester asked.

"She's all right, I hope," Leed added.

"Yes, she's fine," Geoffrey answered. "I wanted her to rest."

"Oh, I'll wager she wasn't pleased with that request." Chester laughed.

"You know my wife well, Chester," Geoffrey said with a smile. "I daresay by this afternoon, she'll be ready to throttle me."

"And what of Roberts?" Leed asked.

"Morgan is with him now," Geoffrey told him.

Leaving his friends to their breakfast, he took himself upstairs to check on Becca's hero. Dr. Morgan met him in the hall outside the guest room door.

"How is Roberts faring, Morgan?" Geoffrey asked.

"He seems to be doing quite well." He smiled. "It appears Lord Roberts is as stubborn as you are, Kane."

Geoffrey simply nodded.

"I thought to check on Lady Kanewood if I may."

"Yes, please do," Geoffrey said, letting the man by before knocking on the guest room door.

"Come in," Roberts said from within.

Geoffrey opened the door and took in Roberts's appearance. Except for a slight lack of color in his face, the viscount seemed his old self.

"How are you feeling, Roberts?"

"Hale and hearty!" His grin faltered at Geoffrey's raised eyebrow. "A bit weak, I'm afraid."

Geoffrey nodded and crossed to the bed. He pulled a chair over and sat. "Roberts, I haven't thanked you for what you did yesterday," he began awkwardly.

"Kane, I only did what anyone would have."

"No. I know that you took the risk because of your regard for Rebecca. I daresay I never imagined I'd be grateful for those feelings."

"I'd have done it regardless of my feelings." Roberts looked him straight in the eye. "I'd have done it for you."

Geoffrey weighed the man's words carefully. He extended his hand to his friend. Roberts grinned broadly and took the forgiveness offered.

They were sharing a bit of laughter when Leed and Chester strode into the room.

Chester looked at them and smiled. "Well, you seem on the mend, Roberts."

"Quite." He smiled back.

Leed threw a glance down the hall, then arched a brow at Geoffrey. "I see you chose the guest room farthest from your chamber, Kane. Coincidence?"

"Never mind," Geoffrey answered.

"Perhaps we'll duck down the hall and visit with Rebecca," Chester said.

"Not without me, you won't." Geoffrey laughed.

He bade farewell to Roberts and left his friends to their visit. Becca was dressed and ready when Geoffrey entered the room. She turned to him and his breath caught. She wore a beautiful dress of indigo blue, her eyes appearing a deep green. Her hair curled about her face. Her beauty still amazed him after all this time. He remembered himself finally, and the instructions he'd left her.

"Why are you out of bed?"

"Before Dr. Morgan left, he proclaimed me perfectly fit."

Geoffrey crossed to her. "He got the 'perfect' part correct."

He kissed her gently, running his hands over her back. He sighed and rested his chin on the top of her head.

"When will they be here?" she asked.

He knew that she spoke of the authorities and thought to put her fears to rest. "They should be here shortly, love. It'll be a good thing to get it over with."

"Indeed."

The constable came by soon after, and Geoffrey and Becca met with him in the parlor. He listened carefully to her story and nodded his satisfaction.

Afterward, Geoffrey escorted the man to the foyer. "Please keep the matter quiet. I don't want my mother upset more than she needs to be."

The man nodded his assent and took his leave.

They ate lunch, Leed and Chester joining them. Afterward, the gentlemen took their leave. Geoffrey brought Becca into the parlor, getting her promise to rest a bit. With a dramatic sigh, she acquiesced.

He went into his study to write out a few instructions for his solicitors. He'd arranged to send John's body back to Kanewood, but only after posting a note to his mother. It was the most difficult letter he'd ever written. He left out the horrible deeds John had committed, merely calling his death an unfortunate accident. He prayed she wouldn't request any further explanation.

He'd made arrangements for his niece's care, as well. Ann would be provided for, but Patricia would receive nothing of the estate. He regretted that the little girl would remain in the cold woman's care, but his hands were tied in the matter. Geoffrey would make certain his money would pay for excellent nurses for the child.

Becca found him there, evidently having grown tired of her endless resting. He looked up as she entered, setting aside the day's tasks.

"Is anything wrong, husband?" she asked, closing the door.

"I'm afraid Ann will be leaving Kanewood, darling."

"Oh, Geoffrey!" Becca cried, her hand coming to rest over her heart. "Is there nothing we can do?"

He stood and came around the desk to her. "I'm afraid not."

Becca looked thoughtful for a moment. "Why can we not keep her with us?"

"Patricia would never allow it." He thought for a moment. "She will need funds."

Realization dawned on Becca's face. "Would she give her up for money?"

"I don't know. She's a spiteful bitch, love." He smiled sadly. "We should be grateful that she has so little to do with her daughter."

Becca frowned. "What kind of mother has such disregard for her child?"

"Shh," he said, rubbing her shoulders. "I'll see what I can do. Ann should stay at Kanewood. I know someone who will be a wonderful mother."

She looked up at him, her frown clearing. Geoffrey placed his hand on her still-flat belly, patting gently. "To Ann and to our child."

She held his hand there, closing her eyes. "That's your papa holding you," she whispered.

He laughed. She opened her eyes and gave him a look of consternation.

"You're talking to our child?" he asked.

"He hears me," she teased. "Or at least I like to think he does."

"He?"

She simply shrugged her shoulders. He shook his head with a small smile. He ran his gaze over her. She looked beautiful as ever in her blue dress, a sweet expression on her face. She'd been through so much these past few weeks. He wished he could undo all of the pain she had endured.

"Ah, Becca," he said wistfully.

She placed her hand on his cheek. "What is it?"

"I've put you through so much, love. If only—"

"You've given me your trust and your love. That makes up for everything."

"At long last, fool that I was. Becca, I am so grateful to you because you have given me your trust and your love. And that means more to me than even the passion we share." He looked deeply into her eyes, seeing the change coming over them as they darkened to deep green. His gaze fell on her lips. She placed her hands on his shoulders and stood on tiptoe as he bent his head to hers.

"Becca," he whispered as his lips brushed hers. "I love you so much."

His kiss was gentle at first, but when she opened her mouth to him, he felt the familiar desire flare. He placed his hands on her waist and lifted her, sitting her on the desk. He proceeded to devour her, nibbling on her lips and tasting all she had to give. She kissed him back just as fiercely, moaning as she did so.

He managed to unfasten a few of the hooks in the back of her dress, but his fingers began to fumble. With a soft growl, he tugged the bodice down, running his hands over her.

She arched in response, filling his hands with her breasts. "I want you so much …."

His response was a sensual growl in her ear. He gently pushed her down on the desk, one hand reaching under her skirts to caress her. He removed her drawers and placed his mouth on her. She writhed beneath his tender assault, sending papers to the floor. She was close to her release, teetering on the edge as he kept up the sweet torture.

"Oh, please!" she said breathlessly.

He undid his breeches and came into her then. She cried out, but it wasn't over. He thrust deeper still, bringing her to orgasm again even as he sought his own. Afterward, he held himself above her on the desk, his breath slowing.

She smiled lazily up at him. "I didn't expect this when I came looking for you."

"Disappointed?" he grinned.

"Never."

She licked her lips and brought his head down to hers. She kissed him deeply, darting her tongue in and out of his mouth. He groaned and kissed her back. He moved within her then, pleased to feel himself wanting her once more. She gasped and looked at him.

"Again, husband?" she asked, truly amazed.

"Apparently so," he answered with a wicked grin.

* * * *

A few days later, they left London for Kanewood. Lord Roberts had since taken himself back to his own home, well on the mend. At Geoffrey and Becca's insistence, he agreed to come for a long visit in the country sometime soon.

Geoffrey saw to John's funeral, speaking not a word to Patricia as he made the arrangements. He'd had his solicitors draw up two sets of papers. One left her nothing of the estate. The other offered her a small stipend, should she bow to Geoffrey's demands regarding little Ann.

Blessedly, Ann was kept away from the event. It broke Becca's heart each time she thought of the little girl's leaving, and she prayed that Geoffrey would find a way to keep her with them.

Lady Margaret cried softly at John's service, holding tightly to Geoffrey's arm. He and Becca agreed to tell his mother the truth, but not just then. The hurt was too fresh for all of them.

The day after the funeral, Geoffrey called Patricia into his office.

"What is this about?" she snapped. "I am in the middle of preparations, Kane. It will be no easy journey, traveling with a child and her nurse for God's sake. Ann will surely be a handful."

"Ann is the reason I called you here."

Patricia blinked, then narrowed her eyes. "She wants her, doesn't she? It's not enough that she carries the Kane heir, she wants my child, too?"

"Patricia—"

"No! I have nothing left of John. And no money."

Geoffrey leaned back in his chair. "Have you looked at the papers I sent to your room?"

She shrugged. "I glanced at them. They confirm what you told me. I get nothing!"

"Here." He took the folder holding the second set of papers and slid them across the desk to her. "Take a look at these."

Clicking her tongue, she grabbed the folder. Geoffrey watched as she perused the first page, then hurriedly flipped through the few remaining ones.

She lifted her head to stare at him, her mouth agape. "You'll give me ten thousand pounds? And a stipend?"

"If you relinquish any claim on Ann." He held up his hand. "Now legally, you remain her mother. But you must agree to have no contact with the child."

She frowned, then a slow smile slid across her lips. "I shall miss her terribly."

"Do not try to get more money out of me, Patricia. Ann will want for nothing, but my generosity does not extend to you."

He watched as her slick mind worked, and suppressed his disgust when he caught the moment she made up her mind to accept.

"It will pain me, but I do want what's best for Ann."

"Of course you do," Geoffrey said evenly.

"These papers seem to be in order, Kane. I trust your man of business."

"Sign them." He handed her a pen. "Sign them and you can be on your way."

She did so, then stood. "I suppose we shall see each other in London now and again?"

"Not if I see you first," he said.

She pursed her lips, then turned on her heel. "I am off to town, then. Tell the child …. Oh, tell her what you wish."

With that, she took her leave. Geoffrey gathered the papers and set them to the side.

"Geoffrey?" Becca called softly from the doorway.

He gave her a smile. "She is ours, Becca."

She let out a shout and clasped her hands. "Oh, may I …?"

"Go upstairs, love. Patricia won't be saying her goodbyes and I'm afraid Ann may be confused."

Becca nodded and hurried up to the nursery.

* * * *

Becca found Ann sitting on her bed, her little hands folded in her lap. She was such a sweet little thing, and now that she was to be hers and Geoffrey's, Becca could shower her with all the love she needed.

"Ann?"

Her face brightened when she saw Becca. "Auntie, I'm off to London."

Becca turned to the faithful Mrs. Riley, standing near an open trunk. Tiny clothes and such were tucked within. "Mrs. Riley, may I have a moment alone with Ann?"

The nurse opened her mouth, no doubt to make the obvious question, then nodded and left the room.

When she was alone with Ann, Becca crossed over to the bed and settled beside her.

"Ann, I'm afraid you're not going to London."

"But Mama told me we have to leave Kanewood." Her face screwed up as she fought back tears. "I don't want to leave, but Mama says I have no place here."

Becca stroked her cheek. "You will always have a place here, Ann."

Ann's frown cleared. "Is Mama off to London?"

"Yes." She worriedly watched the child for any unease. "Does that trouble you?"

Ann shrugged. "She is always in town."

Becca took a breath and forged ahead with her news. "Your mama won't be coming back."

Ann blinked her big gray eyes. "Ever?"

Becca shook her head. "I'm sorry, sweetheart."

Ann chewed her lower lip, tears threatening again. "Mama doesn't want me."

"We want you, Ann." She gathered the child in her arms. "Your Uncle Geoffrey and I will keep you with us. Here at Kanewood."

Ann sniffed, pulling back to gaze up at Becca. "Truly?"

"Yes. Your mama will always be your mama, but you will be our little girl, too."

Ann grinned. "Oh, that is lovely!"

Becca hugged her again, giving a silent prayer for the wonderful man who made this remarkable gift possible. So much had changed since she'd met Geoffrey, and she had somehow managed to grow into this new life with great hope for the future. She'd gone from her simple life at Raven's to become a countess. She'd gained a wonderful mother in Lady Margaret, and received the chance to know the mother she'd thought she'd lost. And now? Now she was to be a mother herself, to the babe in her belly and to this sweet child in her arms. She felt more than up for the challenge. She was not the young, naïve girl she was a few months ago. No, loving Geoffrey had helped her find her strength. Perhaps she'd had it all along. But being with Geoffrey had helped her to see it. If she needed another reason to love her husband beyond reason, this was it. She smiled against Ann's silky hair.

And she surely didn't need another reason to love Geoffrey.

Epilogue

April, 1823

Lady Margaret watched her son, her lips curved in a small smile. Geoffrey paced the floor of the parlor, nervously tugging on his cravat.

"What is taking so long, Mother?" he asked her, not for the first time.

"Geoffrey," she soothed, "these matters take time."

He frowned at her, unhappy with the answer. They had returned to London the previous month, leaving Ann in the care of Mrs. Riley. Though Becca hadn't wanted to leave her, Geoffrey had insisted on Becca's being attended by Dr. Morgan when her time came. The last thing he wanted was to be stuck up in the country if something were to go wrong, he'd told her.

He'd ventured into their chamber two hours earlier, only to be sent away by Mary.

"Her ladyship needs privacy, my lord," she'd insisted. "The doctor and I will look after her."

He'd grudgingly agreed and turned to go, only to hear Becca's scream from within the room. He pushed the door open, frantic. "Becca!" he shouted, striding into the room.

Dr. Morgan waylaid him in the sitting area. "Kane, you must have patience. I assure you Rebecca is doing fine."

Geoffrey had finally gone back downstairs, his fists clenched.

"Look at you," his mother said with a smile. "Your hair is tousled, your clothes rumpled. The perfect expectant father, I daresay."

Geoffrey stopped his pacing for a moment and let out a breath. "Thank you," he grumbled.

"Have you thought of a name, Geoffrey?"

"We haven't quite decided."

He resumed his pacing.

"Rebecca is in perfect health. I'm sure if there was any problem—"

"Kane," Dr. Morgan called from the doorway.

Geoffrey stiffened. His mother urged him to go see what the man wanted and he left the room to follow the doctor up the stairs.

"Is she all right, Morgan?" he asked.

"Just fine, my boy." He smiled, letting Geoffrey into the chamber.

Mary was in the sitting area, her smile bright. Geoffrey was suddenly nervous. Morgan nudged him toward the sleeping chamber.

Geoffrey opened the door slowly, peeking his head into the room. Becca sat in the middle of the big bed, her hair fanned out on the fluffy white pillows behind her head.

She looked fatigued but wore a beautiful smile. "Geoffrey."

He crossed the room to stand by the bed. He noticed the small bundle in her arms then. All that was visible was a tuft of honey-colored hair.

Becca loosened the blanket swaddling the infant to show him the perfect little face. "Your son," she said simply.

Geoffrey looked from the baby to his wife and back again. He reached out his finger to gently stroke the soft little cheek. "So tiny," he said in awe.

"He didn't feel so when he was trying to come out," she said with a small laugh.

Geoffrey smiled at that. The baby stirred, drawing his attention back. The second-most beautiful green eyes he'd ever seen stared back at him.

"Becca," he breathed, "he's …."

"Incredible?"

"Yes. And so tiny. Wait until your father sees him."

Becca smiled. "Hopefully, that will be soon, my father and my mother both."

She'd been able to convince Thomas to refute his testimony

regarding Becca's father's supposed crimes and now her parents could come freely into England. Geoffrey guessed her own relationship with Thomas would take more than words to mend, however. He'd kept her mother from her, had lied to her the whole of her life. Hell, he'd nearly sold her in marriage. But that was a matter for another day.

"The big and burly Laird McClair will surely crumble when he sees his tiny grandson," Geoffrey said.

He sat down on the bed, hugging her gently. He kissed her tenderly, so full of love he thought he'd burst. He'd nearly lost her more than once, this girl with emerald-green eyes and hair as black as a raven's wing. He'd never let anything happen to her or to their children.

And Geoffrey Michael Kane, the seventh Earl of Kanewood, kept his word.

Author's Biography

JoMarie DeGioia has been making up stories for as long as she can remember and has spent years giving voice to the characters in her head. She's known Mickey Mouse from the "inside," has been a copyeditor for her town's newspaper, and currently works as a bookseller. She writes Historical Romances with a touch of mystery and Contemporary Romances with a touch of home. She divides her time between Central Florida and New England, and you may contact her at JoMarie@JoMarieDeGioia.com